JAPANESE
D[...] AIN

To Oscar
Cheers!

[signature]

Also by Dave Weaver
Jacey's Kingdom

JAPANESE DAISY CHAIN

DAVE WEAVER

機織り

Elsewhen Press

Japanese Daisy Chain
First published in Great Britain by Elsewhen Press, 2014
An imprint of Alnpete Limited

Copyright © Dave Weaver, 2014. All rights reserved
The right of Dave Weaver to be identified as the author of this work has been asserted in accordance with sections 77 and 78 of the Copyright, Designs and Patents Act 1988. No part of this publication may be reproduced, stored in a retrieval system or transmitted in any form, or by any means (electronic, mechanical, telepathic, magical, or otherwise) without the prior written permission of the copyright owner. 'Finding Uncle' first appeared in Hertfordshire University's 'Vision' anthology; 'Keeper of Lost Things' first appeared in Kinglake Publishing's 'Ten Modern Short Stories 2010'.

Elsewhen Press, PO Box 757, Dartford, Kent DA2 7TQ
www.elsewhen.co.uk

British Library Cataloguing in Publication Data.
A catalogue record for this book is available from the British Library.

ISBN 978-1-908168-40-5 Print edition
ISBN 978-1-908168-50-4 eBook edition

Condition of Sale
This book is sold subject to the condition that it shall not, by way of trade or otherwise, be lent, re-sold, hired out or otherwise circulated in any form of binding or cover other than that in which it is published and without a similar condition including this condition being imposed on the subsequent purchaser.

This book is copyright under the Berne Convention.
Elsewhen Press & Planet-Clock Design are trademarks of Alnpete Limited

Printed and bound by CPI Group (UK) Ltd, Croydon, CR0 4YY

This book is a work of fiction. All names, characters, places, ghosts and events are either a product of the author's fertile imagination or are used fictitiously. Any resemblance to actual events, spirits, places or people (living, dead or ethereal) is purely coincidental.

Coke and Diet Coke are trademarks of The Coca-Cola Company; Google is a trademark of Google Inc.; Hello Kitty is a trademark of Sanrio Company, Ltd.; Honda is a trademark of Honda Motor Co., Ltd.; iPhone is a trademark of Apple Inc.; Mitsukoshi is a trademark of Kabushiki Kaisha Mitsukoshi; Nissan is a trademark of Nissan Jidosha Kabushiki Kaisha; Pocari Sweat is a trademark of Otsuka Pharmaceutical Co., Ltd.; Seven-Eleven is a trademark of 7-Eleven, Inc.; Sony is a trademark of Sony Corporation; Suzuki is a trademark of Suzuki Motor Corporation. Use of trademarks has not been authorised, sponsored, or otherwise approved by the trademark owners.

Contents

The Old Man on the Mountain 11
Finding Uncle 25
Idol 37
Clutter 45
Train Man 53
The Cat 61
A Boy Called Simon 67
Keeper of Lost Things 75
Unlucky 83
Aftershock 93
Tap – Tap 99
Shrine 105
Seconds 113
The Last Protester 123
The Girl Downstairs 137
The Cop and the Monk 147
Whispers 159
Empty Seat 171
The Fox in the Park 179
The Investigator 187
Getting Rid of Aki 195
The Glass Wall 205
Non-Sleeper 213
The Room 221

For Takami

The Old Man on the Mountain

Arata Kawabata climbed off the bus, waiting patiently behind the others until his sandalled feet touched the hot tarmac. He pulled on his baseball cap, slung the canvas holdall bag across his back and stared over at the restaurant, shielding his eyes from the noon sun. Then he looked up at the broken-topped mountain. A thin plume of smoke curled around its crater, almost indistinguishable from the clouds that skimmed the volcano's peak. Stretched up its sides like thin strands of hair against an old man's face, he could just see the cable-cars that would take him to the summit. Even down here, heavy sulphurous air was stifling.

He'd arrived over an hour previously in Aso town's dusty main street, kicking his heels in the few shops open while he waited for the bus. Eventually it appeared, stuffed full of tourists, and they'd begun the short haul up the winding road to the foot of the mountain.

Arata felt some of them had stared at him, possibly because he was on his own. He didn't care.

Inside the restaurant Arata bought a small bento lunchbox and, dumping his bag on the floor, sat down at a window seat overlooking the valley they'd just traversed. The plastic bench felt sticky next to his skin as the thin material of his shorts bunched up his legs. Yellow-smocked schoolchildren gave him odd glances as they scuttled after their teacher like day-old chicks.

Arata continued to look out of the window for a while at the impressive view. Now he'd finally got to the volcano he felt a relaxed mood replacing his former edginess. This might be his only holiday for a while, now he had graduated; he should relax and enjoy it. He had the rest of the day to see the sights, after all, the last cable car down was seven-thirty that evening.

For a moment he caught himself wondering how he knew this, then remembered; he'd been here before with his parents during the holiday they'd spent at Beppu. He remembered with fondness their visit to the spa town on the eastern coast of the island with its hot springs and ancient bathhouses. How could he have forgotten the beautiful arcs of vermillion and ocean-blue geysers as they shot out of their boreholes, above the delighted shrieks of the crowd?

How old had he been then – eight or nine?

Arata played absently with the sushi in the little plastic box. He wasn't actually that hungry. Although he'd skipped breakfast he still felt a certain dullness of appetite, as if his stomach was already full of an indefinable something else. He pushed the food away.

He took out his wallet and looked at the photograph again. He'd found it earlier that morning on the train while searching for his ticket. Vaguely aware of the inspector's impatient tapping of his puncher, Arata had stared at the torn image of himself; half a picture, the jagged white edge amputating a bare arm that rested on his shoulder. Whose arm, he wondered? It looked female, but he failed to identify a time or place.

He was wearing the same t-shirt he had on today, the same denim baseball cap. He picked the cap up. It looked shabby and smelt musty. In the picture it looked brand new, like the t-shirt.

Arata looked up at a polite cough. An old man was attempting to slide into the seat opposite him, at the same time making enquiring gestures with the hand not holding a precariously balanced tray of tea and biscuits. Arata motioned for him to continue, afraid for a moment that he'd tip the whole lot on top of him. He returned to his study of the picture noting the background; a noodle stand with a bright Pocari Sweat sign above it. He had a polystyrene dish held up to his mouth as if he were about to eat.

The old man said something to him in a muffled tone.

"I'm sorry?"

"Sorry – I was just saying it's a fine day to visit the crater. The weather I mean…"

"Yes, I suppose it is."

Arata put the picture face down on the tabletop and looked across at the stranger; an anonymous old man in uncomfortable-looking grey suit, neck buttons undone and tie loosened. He vaguely recollected seeing him on the bus. The face was square, its squat features reddened with the heat. The man stared back at Arata, a hand rising uncertainly to dab the sweat away from his forehead with a saturated handkerchief.

"Here on holiday?" the old chap tried again, as if taking Arata's attention as a sign to continue.

Arata smiled. "I might be, why?"

"Just...you know, making conversation. I'm sorry if I..."

"No, let me apologise," Arata told him. "My answer was rude. I'm taking a short break after my finals. I've come all the way along the coast. Tomorrow..." He wasn't quite sure what he'd be doing tomorrow.

"Going home?"

"Pardon me?"

"Tomorrow, I was just saying you'd be going home, maybe. Where would that be, if you don't mind me asking?"

Arata did rather mind.

"Osaka. I've been studying law at Osaka University. It's got one of the best departments in Japan," he told him.

"Yes, I've heard that said. Do you know your results yet?"

"I've graduated with honours." Arata told him proudly.

"I see, most impressive." The old man unexpectedly pointed to the photograph. "Who's that then, girlfriend?"

This was none of his business but Arata would humour the guy. He turned the picture over. "Looks like it doesn't it?" His reply sounded oddly flippant. He hastily corrected it. "I'm not sure who it is actually. It's an old photo I've just found that's all."

"A mystery...! Perhaps you have a double?" The old guy smiled strangely at him, watery eyes almost twinkling with imagined intrigue.

"What the hell do you mean by that?"

"It's just a saying..."

Arata immediately felt he'd been rude again. He tried to regain some breeziness.

"Have you been here before?"

His fellow diner's eyes slid passed him to the view behind. There was a slight pause. "Yes, I've been here before. Not recently though." There was another pause. "It doesn't seem to have changed much, apart from all that touch screen stuff in the centre of course; very clever. Well, I suppose I'd better be going. See you later perhaps?"

He squirmed out of the seat and stood up, bowing slightly, and then headed for the exit. The biscuits lay untouched in their cellophane wrapper.

Arata felt the swing of the cable car's floor beneath his feet. The thing was packed tight, a mid-afternoon crowd of late-comers willing the carriage to go faster in their eagerness to make up for lost time.

He'd waited around too long in the restaurant, as if somehow hesitant to complete the last section of his journey. Cups of coffee and random trips to the toilet had meant it was nearly three o'clock when he finally took his seat. In a thin gap through a forest of legs he saw the man from the restaurant standing at the far side of the car. He seemed to be staring directly at him, the sun's rays forming around the silhouette of his balding head like a crown. Arata looked away without acknowledgement. When he turned back the old guy was gone.

At the top a concrete slope took them up from the tin-roofed cable car shed to the main concourse, a wide asphalt pathway leading to the rim of the crater itself. He allowed the crowd to pull him forward, occasionally glancing over his shoulder for signs of a bald head bobbing in the queue behind him. Why was the old guy following him? It wasn't coincidence; he'd left Arata at the restaurant at lunch time but had waited to catch exactly the same car. That was a strange thing to do, surely? Perhaps he'd been waiting in the centre? No, he said he'd already done that.

At the rim, the crowd spread itself out along a narrow concrete walkway following the contours of the great crater's lip. The unavoidable rotten egg smell of sulphur prickled Arata's nose. A short wooden fence stood between him and the drop itself, so that he could easily look over and down the steep bolder-strewn slopes.

With a metallic 'ting' the public address system whined into life, its words echoing around the inside of the giant volcano's mouth:

"Due to recent renewed volcanic activity this is the first

day for two months that Mount Aso has been open to the general public. The situation is still being constantly monitored. Please be aware of the warning sirens situated at stages along the walkway. If you hear them, quickly make your way to the nearest cable car station and wait there to be collected – Thank-you."

He wasn't aware that the mountain had been closed off to the public for so long. It seemed extraordinarily lucky then that he should choose today for his visit.

Arata lent over the fence again and peered down at the bubbling pools of black soot-coated lava, an occasional fiery slash of red tearing the rubbery surface. Feeling a sudden push in his back, he gripped the fence in a momentary panic. He turned to see a swaggering group of young men wearing designer t-shirts and expensive-looking trainers. One wore a little gold chain around his neck. He gave Arata a slight lift of the head as if challenging him to remonstrate.

"Something the matter?" the boy asked him easily. He looked very confident of himself, as if used to getting his own way. The others smirked indulgently as if they'd seen it all before.

The boy took a few steps towards Arata. "What the fuck are you wearing grand-dad?" He pointed at Arata's t-shirt and cap. "You look a proper wanker in that get-up, how old are you anyway?"

"Leave the poor sod alone, Junichi!" Another jeered, and they all laughed.

'Junichi' gave him a mocking bow. "Respect grand-dad!" He turned, pleased with himself, and high-fived his mates.

A security guard stepped between Arata and the little group. Turning his back on him he shouted at the boys to move on, gesturing as if directing sightseers away from an accident.

"Sorry about that sir. You know kids."

"That's alright, officer."

The man looked at him strangely, nodded and walked away. Arata found he was shaking.

"Looked like a bunch of spoilt brats from the city after a fight. You were right not to get involved." The old man addressed him from a concrete bench on the side of the walkway. He gestured for Arata to come closer. "Sit with me for a minute to gather your composure. You look a bit upset."

Arata stared at him for a moment as he felt the anger rising inside him. He bunched his fists and strode across the walkway. "That's none of your business! Are you following me or something?" He looked at the retreating back of the security guard. He'd look ridiculous if he called him back again for nothing, but this was annoying!

The old man patted the bench beside him. "Sit down for a minute."

"I asked if you were following me!"

There was no reply. Arata stared down at him for a moment longer then took the proffered seat.

"Do I know you? Because I'm damn sure you don't know me!"

"Why do you think they picked on you? They didn't like your clothes, was that it?" the old man asked.

Arata glared at him. "I don't understand what that's…"

"Because," he continued, "I'd say they have a point, personally. I'm no judge of teenage fashion but I'd say you're a bit old for that get-up."

"I'm twenty-four." Arata replied swiftly. "I'm just a few years older than them."

"You don't look twenty-four to me."

He took something silvery out of his jacket pocket and held it up in front of Arata. The sun caught the surface and made it sparkle. Arata held up a hand to shield his eyes and found he was looking into a mirror.

He pushed the old man's hand away. "Don't do that!" he told him.

"What did you see, more like a mature student maybe?"

"I don't want to talk to you anymore!"

Arata sprang up and stormed off down the concrete pathway. A slap-slap noise behind told him the old man was attempting to keep up, but he willed himself not to look round.

By now they were on the far side of the crater. A small wooden bridge took him over a ridge and onto a wooden-planked path across the basin of blackened ash. It was flat like a desert, with just the path stretching across it to the

crags of the volcano's edge a few hundred yards away.
Arata kept up a stilted walk which was not quite a run until the slats eventually ran out. He saw a dusty track with a guide rope vanishing into the rocks and started towards it. He found that he was panting the thin air clutching at his chest. He hadn't felt this bad in years. The image in the mirror came back into his head. He could banish it while he was walking, as if every stride left it further behind, but when he stopped it was there again.
Arata stopped.
He didn't want to go any further. Everything around him had grown still. There was no breeze, no sound of any kind except for a distant drone of cicadas in the valley below. Turning slowly, he saw a motionless silhouette in the distance patiently waiting for him. Arata knew now that the old man would stay there all evening, even into the night, long after the last cable car had jerked its passengers back down the mountainside.
Bent over with hands on haunches, he took a few deep breaths then began to trudge back.

They were sitting on a bench inside one of cylindrical concrete pill boxes that dotted the rim. Ostensibly for emergency cover in the case of an overactive belch of sulphurous ash from the crater, these doubled as a cool dining area for tourists. There was no litter of course, other than the odd Coke can left there by a gaigin.
"Do you know why you're here Mr Kawabata?" The old man asked.
"You know my name." Arata wheezed. "Are you the police? Have I done something wrong?"
"Don't you know?"
Arata said nothing. The expression on the stranger's face was unreadable.
"We've met before Arata, just yesterday actually. I came to your room to check on you like I do every day. That was at lunchtime but something happened later that evening, something very regrettable."
"I don't know you, I haven't seen you before." But the bald statement sounded false even as he said it.

"Sorry, I'm getting ahead of myself. My name is Dr. Hiro Takamura. You've been staying at the care home I run for quite some time now. I know you don't believe that to be the case but please humour me for a few minutes more while I explain what's happened."

The old man looked Arata directly in the eyes as if to emphasise the truth of what he was about to say. He was no longer smiling.

"Quite a few years ago now you had a very serious accident, a fall, which resulted in you receiving severe head injuries. You were twenty-four at the time. This fall caused severe brain damage to both your long and short-term memory. You can no longer retain any factual information about people or events for more than twenty-four hours before your mind flushes everything away. Your motor skills and basic low-level functions are still intact – the names of objects and places for instance, or the ability to eat and dress yourself. Anything new however doesn't stick. You won't remember this conversation tomorrow, or where you've been, or who I am. You won't even remember your own name."

"I know my own name, doctor." Arata told him.

"Yes, Arata Kawabata is the name you signed yourself out of the care home with, but it's not your name. You made it up. Arata is the first name of a law student who graduated with top honours from Osaka University last week. It was in the paper, along with an article about Mount Aso re-opening today. Unfortunately a cleaner stupidly left a copy in your room yesterday. We try to keep you insulated from the outside world to avoid confusing you. If you see things continually changing all around you it destroys our efforts at maintaining a calming environment. Kawabata is the name of a long dead writer whose book is on your bedside table. We gave it to you because his stories are only a few pages long. You read the first six or seven over and over again."

"Why are you making this up? What do you want?"

"I'm not making it up. I want you to come back with me now, while you can still retain the information I've just given you."

"When did this 'accident' happen to me?" Arata asked.

The old man looked away from him. "It was in the summer

of 1986."

Arata saw the glimpsed image in the doctor's mirror again; his face had been deep-lined and jowly, cheeks and jaw unshaven with streaks of grey in the uncombed hair. The eyes had been full of confusion, dull and slightly sunken. Not a young man's eyes. He raised a hand and felt the stubbly skin beneath his fingers, tracing the deep lines as if trying to decode their meaning. He let the hand fall.

"I'm afraid there's more, if you're ready..." Takamura told him.

Arata nodded, not trusting himself to speak.

"You were on holiday with your young wife and daughter when the accident occurred. The marriage had been under some strain since the birth. You'd been staying at Beppu but had decided to stop off at Aso on your return journey, to see the volcano. You had a job as a teacher in your home town of Kumamoto where Yuriko was also training to be a nurse. She'd arrived there from Tokyo a few years before."

"How do you know all this?" Arata asked. "And I haven't got a kid."

"It's all in the police report on the incident. Apparently you had some kind of argument in the cable car, that carried on when you got to the rim of the crater. Witnesses remember the two of you shouting at each other. Then Yuriko rushed off in tears and you ran after her. You were so angry you knocked a child over.

"Yuriko's body was found sometime later that afternoon by security officers, half wedged under a bolder on the eastern slope. Her neck was broken. They found you unconscious a little higher up with a broken leg and your head covered in blood. You couldn't tell the police what had happened, when you came round in hospital, or about your last moments together. They tried to build a case against you but there were no witnesses and by then you couldn't ever remember being on the mountain. You couldn't remember who Yuriko was or that you had a daughter. You didn't even know your name. There were terrible nightmares every night but in the morning your mind had blanked everything out again. They sent you to a top specialist in Nagasaki who used hypnotherapy to stop the dreams, then to the care home in

Kumamoto. You've been there ever since."

Arata took a long look at Takamura then shook his head. "That all sounds tragic doc, but you're talking about another guy. You've made a mistake. I'm Arata Kawabata, not what's-his-name..."

"Toshiro Masayuki." the doctor told him.

"Whatever. I'm not him. I admit I'm dressed a little silly and I'm not as young as I was, who is? I'm a little hazy on some other things as well, it's hot up here... but I've never killed anyone."

"No-one said anything about killing, Toshirio. It was just a terrible accident that happened a long time ago. But I want you to believe that you need my help now!"

Takamura stood up abruptly, as if suddenly impatient with himself. He reached down to take Arata's elbow.

"Come with me now. I'll show you exactly where it happened. If I can do that will you at least try to believe me? Come back to the care home with me tonight. If you still think you're Arata Kawabata the Osaka law student in the morning then you can leave with my blessing!" He let Arata go and walked quickly out of the shelter. Arata hesitated for a moment then followed.

On the rickety little bridge Arata saw Takamura look back to see if he was still there. He did it again as they crossed the sea of black ash, their lone footsteps echoing on the rocks. The doctor had reached the roped path now. He must have noticed Arata's hesitation for he waved him on.

"There's nothing to fear Toshiro – Arata... trust me, it can't hurt you anymore. Whatever happened you're free from it now. But I must prove to you that I'm right."

Arata swallowed hard then followed. He found himself in a dark little gully. The ground began to fall sharply away as he pulled on the rope to steady himself, slapping it against the rock. As he wormed his way along he saw the other's feet suddenly stop. He looked up.

The doctor was framed against the sky at the path's end in a cleft half-blocked by two crossed and rotting boards. He held something in his hand. As Arata approached he saw it was one half of a torn photograph. A petite pretty girl in a light summer frock was standing in front of a noodle stand; her left arm resting on some invisible presence cut off by the picture's jagged white edge. To her right he saw a wooden board with 'Cable Car Timetable' printed on it in red letters. "You don't remember my daughter Yuriko, do you Mr Masayuki? But then again, you don't remember anything. Your temper, your ridiculous jealousy; they're all things of the past."

He backed to one side to show Arata the drop below. "This is where you pushed her over. Then you threw yourself down the mountainside in remorse for your crime. I'm sure you meant it at the time and wanted to die, but you didn't did you? You gave yourself a perfect alibi instead, wiped the slate clean and, every day since, you've wiped it again and again so you'll never have to remember what you did. When I became Director at the care home six months ago I couldn't believe my luck. I checked the files but it was definitely you. I was just an ordinary doctor in Tokyo when the 'accident' happened but now many years later, here I was in charge of the man who'd destroyed my life."

A small gun with a silencer attached appeared in Takamura's other hand. "I couldn't bring myself to kill you when I found out about your condition, but you damn well deserved to die! I decided to leave the newspaper in your room hoping it would trigger some kind of mental response, that you'd finally remember your act of violence and do the job yourself." Raising the gun Takamura pointed it at Arata's head, his finger tightening on the trigger. "I didn't expect this to happen but now I see the perfect synchronicity of it all. I'm the only one who knows you're here, Toshiro! Now it's me who's committing the perfect crime..." The old man was crying. He thrust the torn picture at Arata. "Remember her now, Masayuki? She was so beautiful, my beautiful little girl..."

A siren blared somewhere and Arata instinctively lunged forward. The gun rattled against the rocks as the old man fell backwards across the boards. There was the sound of snapping wood then Takamura was gone, tumbling away from him down the dusty slope. As the body gathered momentum, it cart-wheeled against the boulders, span limply into the air like a rag doll and disappeared in the heat haze.

Arata stared after it in shock.

There was a drumming in his head that made it difficult to think; to set the last few moments into any kind of context. What had just happened, why had the old man suddenly threatened him? Who was he, and how did he know Arata? There was a fog of uncertainty in his mind. He knew where he was but not why. Why had he come here today, to this desolate place all on his own?

At least, he'd thought himself alone, just a young man having a break from his studies. That's right, he'd just graduated; this trip was a celebration. And then some lunatic spoils everything... He should tell someone about the old man; but then they'd blame him, accuse him. Arata didn't want that, he needed to get away from here.

A metallic voice crackled in the air around him. *"Sumimasen; evacuate crater area as soon as possible. Mount Aso is being closed for the rest of the day due to sulphurous gas cloud emissions. Make your way quickly to the cable car station. Arigato!"*

He should do like they said; go now, quickly, before anyone noticed that he was missing... Arata turned back along the narrow gully path.

Ten minutes later he was pushing his way through the small crowd awaiting the last cable car down the mountain. There was a general atmosphere of peeved annoyance, especially amongst those late-comers who had only just gained access to the summit. The stench of sulphur had grown noticeably more powerful even in that short time. A pungent mist had fallen across the plateau, making some of them cough as they politely queued for departure.

"How long will they close it for this time?" one asked a security guard as he hustled them swiftly inside the car.

"Could be a few days, could be months," came the laconic reply.

There was a bus waiting to take them to Aso town railway station where, after a short wait, Arata caught the train to Beppu. He didn't look back at the volcano as they crossed the green fields of the caldera, nor indeed at anything outside the carriage until the approaching lights of the small coastal city awoke him at dusk.

He groggily got to his feet and pulled the bag strap over his shoulder, catching his reflection in the train window as he did so. He had an awful t-shirt on, quite inappropriate. Arata made a mental note to throw it away and change into a proper one as soon as he found a good hotel. He noticed that someone had left an old denim cap behind on the seat opposite and shrugged to himself. People could be so careless.

At the hotel he waited to sign the register behind a young couple who, judging by the girl's giggles, were on their first holiday together. Arata smiled indulgently. He was faintly annoyed with himself for sleeping all the way from Kumamoto. He'd wanted to break his journey to visit the volcano at Aso, and now he'd just seen on the evening news in the lobby that they'd closed the place down again. The whole day had been a bit of a waste really. He still felt very tired and was already looking forward to his bed.

The couple moved off to the lifts and the desk clerk looked up as Arata stepped forward.

"A single en-suite room for the night please."

"Just the one night, sir...?"

Arata thought about that for a moment. He'd only made plans for tomorrow. He was going to take a tour of the town's hot springs then maybe relax in one of its bath-houses. He'd never been here before but had heard they were most impressive.

"One night should do." He told the clerk.

"Thank-you sir, if you wouldn't mind signing the book."

Arata picked up the pen and scribbled his name. The clerk glanced down as he gave him the room key. "Thank-you, Mr Takamura. Breakfast will be between seven-thirty and nine o'clock."

"That'll be fine." Arata told him.

Finding Uncle

The museum was dark and empty. Now it was just him and old man Oharu until the cleaners arrived the next morning and, after them, the daytime staff. As they briskly took up their positions around the fading sixties concrete building, Junichi Kamada would be on his way home.

He would be snoring loudly when the large glass entrance doors were being unlocked to allow the public past the pretty girls with their pert grey uniforms, polite smiles and guidebooks.

He'd been working there as night watchman for the last three weeks. His father, a successful businessman in Hiroshima's financial district, profoundly approved of his son's vacation job; in fact it had been his idea. Unwilling to pander a moment longer to his only son's various scrapes with his Suzuki GTX he'd arranged a means for the boy to pay for them himself. His old school chum, now General Manager of the Peace Memorial Museum, would help him out, especially now with the new exhibit. The item was in all the media:

"*New Excavations Find Blast Shadow Wall Intact.*"

His son needed to learn some humility and respect, Kamada mused.

So five nights a week, instead of his usual tour of the city's more fashionable clubs and bars with his wealthy young friends, Junichi headed grumpily along the concrete pathways and finely manicured lawns of the Peace Park. He vaguely remembered it from the junior school outings they'd all had to go on; the international peace statue festooned with paper cranes in the summertime, the eternal flame under its U-shaped dome, and the museum, now somehow slightly smaller and more weather-worn than he remembered it.

As usual, he gave a small sigh of bored resignation as he pulled open the staff entrance door.

This night was like all the others. Oharu-san, the old duffer who shared his watch, was stomping around loudly somewhere in the upstairs galleries checking the windows, despite the computerised alarm.

Oharu-san didn't trust computers. 'Silly old fool', thought Junichi.

The noise took him unaware at first. It seemed to drift along the downstairs corridor towards him as if a distant echo had lost its way amongst the various display cases gleaming in the moonlight. Then, when it finally broke the stillness of the night, he still wasn't quite sure it was actually there. The same thing had happened the previous evening, to the extent that he'd actually got up from his chair to investigate.

He'd found nothing of course.

Now it seemed louder though, more distinct. It sounded human; the high-pitched note trapped inside it maybe that of a small child crying. More likely the wind, he told himself, irritated, but that meant a window was open somewhere on the ground floor, despite the lack of anything blinking on the bank of monitor screens he lounged in front of.

He searched them one by one for the source but saw nothing moving other than old man, Oharu-san, upstairs unnecessarily fiddling with one of the door locks.

'Shit!' he thought. He'd just rolled a nice fat joint, already his third of the night. As usual, it was making him feel slow and drowsy.

Should he call Oharu-san on his two-way to take a look? He knew the guy hated his guts the first time they'd spoken; thought him a pampered little shit, taking somebody else's job just for pocket money. He didn't care about that; they'd never speak to each other outside this place. No sense in antagonising him though; he would need to bribe the old guy to cover for him while he slipped out to meet Hiro and the others at Club Metro that weekend.

He'd just have to go and look himself.

Halfway along the ground floor corridor it came again, and this time it seemed to make a beeline for him. Piercing his ear it shot through his head.

He cried out in pain and there was immediate silence. Junichi's eyes watered as he staggered against the nearest wall. Standing in the darkness, flashlight flickering across shadowy images of death and destruction, he knew sudden fear.

Then it was gone.

Almost gently this time, it crept up on him again; a distant unwavering note of childlike despair that began to float in his head like a gas, permeating his senses until he could think of nothing else. Whatever it was, he had to find and turn it off. Without knowing quite how, Junichi found himself in the Special Exhibits room.

And there in front of him was the wall.

Feeling across for the light switch he remembered they'd all been turned off at the mains. He threw the powerful torch beam around the room in an agitated motion, keen to be out again. It lit up pictures of the wall's excavation, then a tall glass display case half full of various dusty objects found on the site nearby, before finally settling on the wall itself.

Junichi had seen the wall before, when Oharu-san had given him a bad-tempered tour of the building on his first night. It was just a cracked slab of rotting grey cement smelling of soot and decay. Some pieces had been forced back together by small metal bars and rivets, in other areas loose chunks had been placed carefully on top of each other to build up the rest. It had been meticulously done with a thin glass screen placed in front of the whole tottery edifice to make sure it remained in place.

There were markings on the front of the wall; two different sized human shadows etched strangely into the rough surface by the bomb's light flash. The smaller one looked like it might be a child's. It was hunched down and kneeling as if in hiding.

The wailing in his head rose as Junichi slowly approached the wall. Now the child-shaped shadow was swimming in the torch's beam. It seemed almost alive, as if it belonged to a real person hunched down on the floor in front of him.

Before he realised what he was doing, Junichi reached out a hand.

He felt the cool of the glass for an instant before a rougher texture prickled his skin. It was coarse, flaky cement against it now, and it was hot. He let out a little stammer of surprise and trained the torchlight on his hand. It was resting flat on top of the glass, fingers splayed outwards, but the tips of them still felt like they were burning. He tried to pull them away but couldn't. They felt glued to the glass. The heat grew less. Now the crying had stopped as well.

"It must be cramp," he reasoned. "Or maybe I'm just more stoned than I realised..."

"Who's there?"

It was a small, tremulous voice. Had he really heard it? He glanced over his shoulder waving the torch at the empty room. His hand was still stuck to the glass. "Is that you, Oharu-san?" he called out, under his breath murmuring "stupid old sod..." If this were one of the old man's tricks he'd kill him!

"It's me..."

The answer formed itself in his mind and he knew instantly that it was not Oharu-san. It was a child's voice, whispered in his ear.

He flung himself backwards sprawling on the parquet floor, the wall above shuddering behind the glass as if it would fall on him. He felt cold sweat, shirt sticking icily to his back. The torch rolled in the darkness picking out snapshots of light, throwing the elongated shadows of the display case's contents across the ceiling.

Junichi got up and grabbed it, then slowly walked back. Crouching down on his haunches again, after a moment's hesitation he put out a hand. Somehow it never occurred to him just to leave the room.

Again there came the sucking connection, then...

"Is that you, Uncle?"

He was going mad.

"Who...what...?" Junichi's tongue froze in his mouth. He gave a dry gulp and tried again. "Where...are you? What do you want?"

No-one would believe this because it wasn't happening.

"Uncle, I'm stuck under the stones. My skin hurts..." the voice sounded small and pathetic but not as scared as Junichi had first believed.

"I'm not your uncle."

What was he saying? Who was he talking to, himself? But he'd felt a connection inside his mind. It was like the crying again, only this time gentler, softer; a sudden two-way flow of emotion that made his skin tingle, his breath catch in his

throat. Something cut there had found him, chosen him.
"Uncle Kazuo?"
"I'm not him. Who are you?"
"I'm Taro. Where's Uncle Kazuo? He was in the cellar with me before the bang."
"What bang, kid?"
"The big bang just now, and the light. Are you a spirit?"
Junichi ripped his hand away so fast it felt like he'd left a layer of flesh behind. Why was he doing this? It's not real, he told himself. If he weren't so stoned right now he'd be running through the building screaming at the top of his lungs. But he was just sitting there, talking to a wall. To a kid who didn't exist.
"Where have you gone...?" The edge of despair caught him off-guard. It sliced through a nerve inside him. Whatever it was he couldn't leave it now. His fingers touched the glass again.
"I'm here, kid. Tell me what happened to you."
"Are you a family spirit?" The voice had momentarily lost its fear, replaced by a child's sense of wonder.
"Am I a what?"
"A ghost. Uncle Kazuo says our family spirits live in the cellar. That's where they go to when they die."
"OK then, I'm... Uncle Junichi."
"Are you a ghost, Uncle?"
"Look kid, where's your Uncle Kazuo now?" He glanced up at the taller adult shadow on the wall above. "What happened to him...Taro?"
"I think the wall fell on him. He was looking for me. He wanted to take me to school, but they bully me everyday, the big boys, so I was hiding from him. When the big bang came the wall fell down. I can't hear him anymore." The kid was crying again. Small and muted, the sound grated like a rusty gate swinging in the wind. He had to stop that sound.
"How old are you, kid?"
"Six." Stifled sobs.
"Where's your mum?"
"She's working at her office in the city."
"And your dad...?"
A pause, then, "He's away, fighting."

"Fighting?"

"Fighting the Americans."

Did it, he, mean fighting with the Americans, in Afghanistan perhaps? He'd said a bang, a big bang. Maybe he meant a gas explosion? Or a terrorist bomb, like those crazies in the Tokyo subway a few years ago? But that had been gas, hadn't it? And the kid had said a bang, a really big bang, almost like... like... 'Shit!' Junichi thought.

"Uncle...?"

"Taro, have you done dates at school yet? Can you tell Uncle what today's date is? Try and tell me."

"That's easy, Uncle. It's August the sixth."

"What year, Taro? What's the year?"

"What do you mean, Uncle? Don't you have years where you are?"

"Just tell me, kid!"

"Its 1945 Uncle."

Junichi realised two things at the exactly same time. He was sweating again – icy droplets sliding down his back – and his arm ached, held up at its unnatural angle. He suddenly found it difficult to remember a time when he wasn't crouched down on the floor with his fingers spread on the glass partition. His body convulsed in a shiver he hardly noticed. His mind raced. The real world, his world, had receded to a small pinprick of light somewhere out on the horizon. He was no longer part of it.

He was in a collapsed cellar with a hurt and scared little boy who was going to die horribly. Unless he got him out.

"Taro, tell me if you can move. Can you move the stuff around you out of the way?"

"I can move my legs a bit, and my hands. There are stones on my tummy, though." The voice sounded weaker now.

'He's getting tired now,' Junichi thought, 'and the radiation... There can't be much time left.'

"Try to move your hands to lift them off, but do it gently. Don't move anything else until I say."

Junichi tried to remember the Internet article about the wall. It had been discovered on the west side of the city, nearly three miles from the hypocentre over the ruined A-bomb dome. He still had a chance.

A long pause, then, *"I got them off Uncle."*

"Good boy. Now try to slowly turn around onto your stomach. When you've done that try to dig out the stuff above your head; do it slowly, try to use something hard nearby to push the stones away."

"I've got my toy fire engine with me, Uncle. Shall I use that?"

"Yeah, kid. Use it to dig, but be careful. We don't want any more rocks falling on you."

Junichi felt his limbs begin to ache as if he was pushing the stones away himself. A claustrophobic vision of the caved-in cellar invaded his mind and he was there; flint edges stinging his hands, tearing his fingernails, ripping open the naked flesh on his arms. Phantom dust caught in the back of his throat as he began to gulp for air, lung's empty of everything but the smothering soot and ash. Then suddenly, when it was almost too late, he felt a draft of cooling air hit his face and flow smoothly down inside him.

The boy must have broken out. He was nearly free, nearly away from him. "Taro – you still there? Listen kid, when you get out the world's gonna look a different place. There's bad stuff in the air you shouldn't breathe. Get some cloth, anything you can find; get it wet and put it over your head. Keep going out of the city; don't go back looking for your mum. She'll come and get you later. Just keep walking until you get to the fields outside and someone there'll help you find her."

For a few moments he thought that the boy had gone then the small voice came again. *"Uncle, I'm nearly out but I can't see anything..."* It was thin and distant now, moving away from Junichi as if into another land where he couldn't follow.

"Taro?"

Then just a faint whisper, falling though the air; *"It's gone Uncle; the city's all gone..."*

The sudden slab of white light across Junichi's eyes made him cringe in shock, snapping his head back. As he ripped his hand away from the glass to cover them an electric jolt coursed through him. He lost control of his bladder then, feeling the warmth on the inside of his thighs.

Through shaking fingers he saw the figure of old man Oharu-san peering down at him, and behind, the Museum's General Manager. He looked tired and befuddled, as if he'd just been pulled out of his bed. The white room was fully lit now but its tiny square windows told him it was still night outside.

He felt Oharu-san grab the lapels of his uniform and jerk him to his feet.

"Where the hell have you been?"

"Wha…?"

"Where have you been? We've been looking for you for hours!"

He couldn't think straight, couldn't form the words. "I…I've been here…"

"You weren't here half an hour ago when we searched the place!"

"Oharu-san, would you come over here a minute please. Would you care to explain this?" Oharu-san joined the General Manager at the display cabinet and they both looked down at something Junichi couldn't see. Then they both turned to look at him.

"I have to warn you, Mr Kamada. Stealing from the museum is a serious offence and will be prosecuted."

Junichi walked shakily across the room to them and looked through the glass door to where his boss was pointing. Just visible in the light dust was a rectangular shape left by a missing object. The General Manager stared at him and Junichi could see now that he was angry. But his voice was still ominously quiet. "Where is it, Mr Kamada?" he asked him simply, "What have you done with the toy?"

The hesitant knock on the front door was almost missed by Junichi's father as he finished his coffee. A thin old man stood in front of him in a smart blue blazer, wisps of white hair half-covering a balding head. His face was lined in wrinkles, especially around the eyes, but those eyes were as bright as shiny grapes and the wrinkles were arranged in a benign grin. His right hand was tightly clasped around a bulky object in a plastic bag.

"Ah, I'm sorry to trouble you, but does Junichi Kamada

live here?"

Kamada senior groaned. They'd had nothing but trouble since the story appeared in the paper last week. Why did the boy have to blurt out his ridiculous story to his old friend, the museum General Manager, within earshot of that Oharu-san character? The press must have picked it up from him. He hoped the guy had got a good price for it. It had made Kamada a laughing stock in the city and ruined his son's immediate career prospects; whatever those had been.

And of course he'd lost his job at the museum.

"Why can't you leave the boy alone?" He asked the old guy.

"Oh, I see what you think. No, I'm not from the media. I've been looking for your son for years, or someone like him," the old man added strangely, "and after I read his story in the newspapers I knew that I'd finally found him. I have something for him, you see."

'Another madman,' Kamada thought to himself tiredly. The boy didn't deserve this. He'd changed considerably since the incident, hadn't been out clubbing once and barely left his room for the last week. Whatever kind of breakdown he'd had in that place had affected him so badly his mother had even considered psychiatric counselling. Kamada thought that might only make matters worse, but he hadn't said so.

"My son is not in a proper frame of mind to see anyone at the moment."

"I see..." The old man stared off into space for a moment or so as Kamada shuffled his feet impatiently. "Yes, of course he is. Then I won't take up anymore of your time. But please give him this."

He opened the plastic bag and pulled out a rusty and very old-looking child's toy. Kamada thought it looked like a fire engine. He made no move to take it but the old man looked up at him from the step below with a sadly beseeching smile.

"Please..."

The harsh morning sunshine was on his face now, and Kamada could plainly see more than just wrinkles in the parchment-like skin. The mottled scars picked him out as one of the old city's survivors. 'There can't be many left of them now,' he thought. He took the toy from the old man's outstretched hands.

"And please tell your son thank-you."

"Who shall I say…?"

"Tell him Taro-chan says thank-you. Thank-you Uncle."

Kamada turned to put the toy down. When he looked up again the old man was already walking quickly away down the street. For a moment the sun lit up his white hair like a halo then he'd reached the main road and turned the corner.

Kamada stared after him then slowly shut the door.

"Who was that?" His wife called from upstairs.

"No-one…" he replied. A little while later he went out again to put the toy fire engine in the rubbish bin.

Idol

Sato Oharu thought his wife must be completely mad. This was nothing new however; he'd been thinking it for some time. Take what was happening to him right now, for instance. They were at the Hiroshima Carps soccer game but they hadn't come to see the match. Oharu couldn't stand the sport; too frenetic by far. He'd loved baseball as a kid, long ago before the J League brought soccer to Japan. He didn't have time for it these days though, what was the point now? He wouldn't go on his own anyway, couldn't.

The tickets for today had cost him a bomb but they had to be the most expensive ones to get anywhere near the makeshift stage in front of the main stand where Miki Kuroda would be singing his new hit song to the delirious delight of his pre-pubescent girl fans before kicking signed plastic footballs into the packed crowd.

And he was there with Etsuko to witness this momentous event. Surely life didn't get any better than this; paying half his wages to watch a spoilt brat hit a ball far better than he could a note while his wife swooned with lust at her young idol.

For lust he was sure it was. What else could explain her obsession with the thin young pop singer barely out of his teens? It certainly wasn't admiration for his music, despite her protests to the contrary whenever he brought the subject up — which admittedly was hardly ever these days. The fact was that for the last few years he'd decided to go along with it. Just go along with everything.

You see, Miki whatsisname wasn't the first. Before him had been that lanky drink of water Beni something-or-other who presumed to share his distinctly unoriginal pearls of wisdom with the young women of Japan (and not so young — it seemed to Oharu that his wife was by no means the only middle-aged matron getting in a hot flush over such sweet-voiced young singers these days).

They settled in their seats, surrounded mostly by young girls in sailor style school uniforms and older office workers

in cutely exaggerated versions of the same. Oharu looked around, at the sea of smooth pubescent faces studded with the occasional walnut-skinned office-lady, and suddenly felt the desperate need for a cigarette. He pulled one from a battered pack kept in the pocket of his old windcheater but Etsuko's hand was on his before he could put it in his mouth.
"Not here, it's No Smoking."
"Wasn't last time we came!" And then the trap door opened again beneath his feet. Would he never learn? He wondered if it was like that for her. They'd never talked about it, probably never would. God, he hoped not!

It had been a while now since that last time it had happened to him. He could count it in months. To begin with of course it had been minutes, then a little later the gap had changed to days, sometimes quite a few. But that had made it worse; like a car suddenly screeching to a stop along a deserted country road, rather than the course of little judders and jerks you get in a traffic jam, the kind of thing your body gets used to if you know its coming.

"I'm going for a smoke," he told his wife.
"But he's on soon. You always do this to me! Can't you think of someone else for a change!?"
'That's rich!' he thought. Then he made the fundamental mistake of actually saying it.
"You said you wouldn't moan anymore. You promised. You never stick to your word!"
"We're bloody well here, aren't we? And the talk-show thing last month and the concert in Tokyo..." He *was* moaning.
"You're adding it all up in that little calculator in your head. If you were a kind husband you'd be glad to do these things for me." Etsuko pouted her annoyance at him and he felt for a moment like slapping her.
"I am, but we're not rich you know. The museum might start cutting back soon and I've only got another four years there as it is!"

Oharu realised that he was almost shouting. A few people, mostly young girls, looked around at him in alarm. What was this old fart doing here having a heart attack and spoiling their precious day out with Miki?

"You spoil everything!" Etsuko hissed at him.
"I'm going for a smoke."
"You'll miss him," she called almost plaintively after him.

In the hollow concrete cavern beneath the stands Oharu puffed on the cigarette in an agitated manner. He cursed under his breath. Damn! Damn her! And damn himself for getting suckered in, yet again! Life was OK if you just went with the flow, wherever that flow happened to be taking you. It really didn't matter anyway, as long as you didn't feel anything.

He laughed at himself. Who was he kidding? There was no flow, not for the last twelve years. They were both stuck like primaeval creatures in a glacier, out of their time, speeding towards death yet going nowhere.

Their purpose had been Hiro, and Hiro was gone.

They'd never really known each other anyway. She'd liked sewing and seventies pop music and gardening; he'd liked fixing things around the house and fishing. They'd both liked each other enough to agree when their parents arranged the marriage back in the days when such things were a desirable outcome for all concerned. But Mr and Mrs Oharu had never really discussed the deeper and darker aspects of life.

So when that Tuesday morning in spring arrived and the police car's blue light flashed across their bedroom ceiling as Oharu tried to sleep. When his wife answered the stabbed doorbell and made the strange little noise in her throat exactly thirty seconds later (he'd often wondered what could have been said in those thirty seconds that made her so completely understand the arc of her life was finished). When those things happened and he'd staggered down the stairs like a drunk to find her sitting on the floor with the policewoman crouched down holding her hand. That was when his wife's shocked, uncomprehending eyes had stared into his and for the first and only time in their lives something truly dark and terrifyingly deep passed between them. But they could find no words to give it a name so they never did, and never had lasted for the last twelve years.

It had seemed like both nothing and an eternity.

He needed a pee. He found the toilets and stepped inside,

the sharp smell of disinfectant battling the stink of urine in his nostrils. As he threw the cigarette stub in the bowl Oharu became aware that he was not alone. In the farthest urinal a slight figure stood hunched, his head bowed as if in prayer. For a moment Oharu failed to recognise him then it clicked; Miki-bloody-Kuroda, his wife's little toy-boy fantasy and the object of this whole pointless, humiliating afternoon. He watched the young man. He wasn't peeing; rather he seemed to be trying to make himself sick with a shaking finger stuck down his throat.

The female crowd screamed and swooned in the stadium above as the announcer wound them up, a swelling tide of nervous anticipation and oestrogen. He heard the muted noise of inflatable clap-sticks. Like the ones he'd bought Hiro on their only trip to a pro-soccer match, the sport then new and shiny and dazzlingly sophisticated in its un-Japanese-ness.

Hiro hadn't really enjoyed it as much as he'd thought he would, though. He was a baseball fan at heart. Had been a… Oharu felt a hot rush of anger, as violent as it was unexpected. What the hell was he doing here? He suddenly wanted to hit something, hard.

The Nancy boy in his silly spangled suit and floppy hair spluttering up his guts would do nicely. It was almost like slapping Etsuko, better!

He began to move across then stopped. Another man had joined them from one of the cubicles, as if he'd been waiting in there for the boy to appear. He was a big shaven-headed guy in a shiny satin suit that clashed violently with his shirt but Oharu wasn't going to tell him that, especially when he saw the vivid tattoos on the man's hands and neck.

He edged back to the washbasins, turning to view the two men in the mirror. A fat hand pushed into the boy's shoulders as he began to turn around, another grabbed his wrist and wrenched it up his back as the gangster lent into him, flattening his pretty face against the wall.

"Well Miki, it's a nice turnout for you." The voice was unexpectedly high, almost whispered into the boy's ear so that Oharu had to strain to hear.

"I said I'd pay you…"

Another thump in the back; the boy winced but didn't cry

out.

"You said you'd pay us last week. Now it's this week. It's a kind of time thing, see, and you're running out of it fast."

The man slapped the back of his head, hard. "Fulfil your obligation, yes?"

He twisted the arm again. "Yes?"

Now the boy shrieked in pain, the sound deadened by the screams of fans as the announcer read his name out yet again. He nodded.

Shaven-head pushed him one more time, turned and strode quickly past Oharu, glancing at him as if he were no more than a fly on the mirror. The boy had slipped in some pee and was on his knees holding his face, the spangled trousers now stained. Oharu walked over to him and held out a hand. He looked up, hesitated and then took it. He seemed dazed; there were flecks of blood around his mouth and a cut on his chin.

"How much are you into them for?"

The boy tried to focus. "What…"

Oharu grabbed some paper towels and tried to wipe the blood away. The boy let him.

"They're dangerous men." Oharu told him. "You'd better pay up."

"I can't." He gave Oharu a sheepish look then gathered himself. "Fuck off and mind your own business."

"You must make a fortune."

"My manager makes a fortune. I get a wage."

And he'd blown it. Now Oharu was up close he could see the little smudge of white in the boy's left nostril.

"Tell him then. He'll sort them out for you."

"It's a she, and she thinks she already has." So this was last chance saloon time then? Perfect.

"How much?" Oharu asked again.

The boy mumbled something. Oharu shrugged.

"I said four hundred thousand."

That was a lot. Oharu did some quick sums in his head. It was manageable, just.

"I want you to do a private show, you do that don't you? I know you little shits do all kinds of things the papers never get hold of."

He gave Oharu a sullen look. "When?"

"Thursday night. Then you get the money. OK?" The boy nodded. "Here's my card. Ring me and I'll give you the address."

He took it and smirked. "Security? What are you, a bloody guard?"

"Ring me, don't forget." Oharu turned and walked away. Outside he lingered long enough to see Miki Kuroda come out of the toilets' farthest door to be confronted by a small angry-looking woman in a sharp business suit, who began scolding him. She pointed to her watch and then at the stadium's main entrance where a posse of security guards was heading towards them. Kuroda had his head bowed again, as if some large weight had been placed on his back.

For a brief moment Oharu actually felt sorry for him.

He was sitting on the edge of his favourite chair, staring unseeing at the television game show that held Etsuko's rapt attention. A car slowed outside then gunned its engine. Bloody kids! Oharu wished now that he hadn't started this ridiculous farce. What had he been thinking? He wasn't going to pay Kuroda the full amount. He'd make some excuse, say the bank wouldn't let him have it all, let the guy swing; after the singing of course.

"You're very nervous tonight." She'd noticed enough to drag her eyes away from the young couple on TV trying to win a car by guessing which bizarre European country's traditions were being shown to them. "Are you alright?"

"I've got a headache." Oharu replied.

A car pulled up outside. Shoes clacked on the path then a hesitant hand knocked the door. Etsuko hadn't heard above the TV couple's embarrassed laughter.

The boy wore an expensive looking blue cashmere sweater, white jeans and spotless Nike trainers. He looked like every mother's favourite son, the one who'd done well for himself. Although Oharu had expected some kind of karaoke set-up he'd brought no equipment with him.

"Money...?" Kuroda asked.

"Afterwards, outside – what are you going to do?"

"Three songs and I'll make a big fuss of her. Is it a birthday?"

Oharu shook his head and the boy gave him a strange look then shrugged and pushed passed him. Before he could say anything they were both standing in the lounge in front of a shocked Etsuko. His wife stared up at the young singer as if an alien had materialised in her house. Kuroda bowed, took her hand and kissed it with a faint smile on his cute face then launched into what Oharu recognised as the song he'd been promoting at the stadium.

Without the flattering amplification he had a sweet though not particularly powerful voice, almost feminine.

Etsuko sat with her mouth open, one hand half covering it the other gripping a cushion to her side. Half way through the song she began to cry. Oharu tried to sit down beside her but she pushed him away, scrambled to her feet and rushed out of the room. They both heard her sobs from the kitchen.

Kuroda looked at him questioningly. "Have you been fucking someone else, does she know?"

Oharu shook his head. "Sorry. Wait outside for me, please."

He went to Etsuko. She sat at the kitchen table arms limp in her lap, staring out of the window at their neighbour's backyard. He sat down in front of her, waiting for her to speak.

She looked up at him.

"You silly man..." Her voice was gentle. "Thank-you, but you still don't understand. I thought you might have by now."

"Tell me then. I'll try."

She gave a small sigh and looked away. "It's not important who they are, I just pick one. After a while he gets too old, or he does something nasty, and I pick another. They could be anyone. They don't have to even look like him. I just imagine it's what he could have been doing now, what fun he'd be having with all the girls and the fame. He would have loved it, wouldn't he?"

She looked back at him, the question hanging in the air between them. He slowly reached across and took her hand.

"Yes, I'm sure he would. Although I always saw him as a baseball star, a real slugger..."

They smiled at each other.

Clutter

She'd heard the child crying again last night. It was more a whimper than a cry actually; an animal keening to come in from the rain. 'If people couldn't be bothered to take care of their kids they shouldn't have them in the first place,' she'd thought, annoyed. Don't clutter your life with things you can't handle – that was Kokoro Takahashi's motto.

She'd never done that, never wavered from her course.

When she started as a lowly office girl with Atonal Records in the early eighties she realised that you couldn't afford to take your eye off the ball if you wanted to match the men promotion by promotion. Female equality was mere lip service in the recording industry then, sometimes literally so. Now she'd finally made it at the agency, with her own staff and clients, Kokoro Takahashi would make damn sure she was top dog (or bitch) at Atonal for some time to come. The corporate ladder was long and slippery. Still.

But the crying was making her jumpy. Three nights of interrupted sleep meant three days of tiredness and irritation at work, culminating with a faintly ridiculous confrontation with her latest prodigy the winsome pop singer Miki Kuroda after his drug habit managed to screw up a harmless promotional appearance. But that was her job now, to guide the Miki Kuroda's of the interchangeable world of pop through the rough seas of temptation to the land of gold, or rather platinum, that lay beyond. Once that had been achieved the vessel could be discarded; there would always be another new and freshly-painted one available.

Kokoro pushed a button by her bedside and thin window blinds turned silently, allowing her the familiar silhouette of a jagged Tokyo skyline. She screwed up her eyes as a prism of morning light invaded the bedroom. As Kokoro blinked away the sun moats a blur of white passed somewhere beyond the open bedroom door. She rubbed her eyes and tried to refocus but it was gone. She turned to look for her glasses then collapsed back in bed with a grunt, unwilling to force her body into any further movement.

How cynical she had become, she thought with a sigh; how unlike her younger student self back in the days when she would follow the great rock bands from the States and Britain as they toured the world and eventually pitched up in Tokyo, Osaka and Nagoya like ancient mariners who'd lost their way.

Enough of the past! She had work to do, and the world of disposable mind-rotting pop waited for no woman. God she was tired though and, she suddenly realised, cold. There must be a draught from somewhere; she'd noticed it before but it was getting worse. Cursing the distant wailing child of the previous night, Kokoro pulled herself out of bed leg by leg. As she brushed her teeth she made a mental note to bring it up with the building's supervisor on his Monday round. Kokoro had been assured that her apartment was not only the biggest; it was, so far, the only one to be sold in the bright new complex as the downturn spread its tentacles. It had been that guarantee of complete solitude that had persuaded her to take the place. The noise had to be from somewhere else, and that meant the apartment's sound (not to mention draught) proofing was not up to the high standard promised. Heads would have to roll; after all she was the company's sole paying customer.

She had a quick shower in the immaculate bathroom she'd had specifically designed, with its sunken bath and smoked glass screens. Every morning the sheer luxury of it gee-ed her up for the day, but not this morning – this morning her body felt like it had been out running through the night on its own while she slept. It must be the stress of work what with that little shit Miki and his infantile behaviour. She was used to working with real professionals but these days...

The face behind her in the mirror made her jump.

She blinked and it was gone, but her mind's eye had recorded the image; a small girl's face, white, unnaturally so, but the long straight hair that hung down covering her eyes had been jet black, even for a Japanese. Actually covering one eye; Kokoro had seen the other through the strands, like glimpsing a still, deep pool through railings...

Kokoro got a grip on herself. It had been nothing, an image left over from last night's TV, some horror film or ghastly news report taken in at the edge of her attention and spun out of her head again as her mind raced to catch up with the day. Nothing! She would have to hurry to avoid being late for work. But then again, she told herself with a little smile of satisfaction, who would dare to complain even if she was?

It was a busy day at Atonal. She dealt with the fallout from the Miki debacle in her usual brisk fashion but the tiredness had not gone away.

"Are you alright, Kokoro-san?" Her assistant asked her. Neither the familiarity nor the question were out of place. Kokoro had a closer relationship with Mitsu than anyone else at the firm; she'd handpicked her after all. The pretty little thing was a lot like her in many ways, though not enough to be a threat. Kokoro would make sure Mitsu got her chance when she retired, if she was still around then.

"Fine, I'm fine," she told her, "Can you get me the Tina Tanaka contract please?"

The girl put a file on her desk. "Its all ready, she's coming in this afternoon to sign. It's a five album deal."

"I know what it is!" Kokoro snapped, before catching herself. "Sorry dear. I didn't get much sleep last night. It's alright for you young things." She'd expected a shake of the head and a complimentary reply but the girl just stared back at her.

"I'm sorry, Chacho! But if you don't mind me saying so, you really should take better care of yourself...Excuse me." She gave an awkward little bow and left Kokoro's office.

Kokoro was angry at the girl's impertinence. But in the lady's restroom when she studied her face under the harsh white light she saw that the skin looked patchy and dry with little wrinkles in the surface that hadn't been there a few weeks ago. Or had she missed them? The light in her apartment was kinder. A good long bath and the best moisturiser then a full night's sleep would do the trick.

But when she opened the apartment's front door that evening a chill hit her immediately. Kokoro told herself it must be several degrees lower than when she'd left. She dumped the bags of designer clothes she'd impulse-bought on her way home and grabbed her mobile, stabbing in the memory code for the leasing company. "Hello, yes hello?" She'd begun to gabble her complaint before realising the recorded voice was telling her 'so sorry, we are shut for the weekend'. She threw the phone at the leather sofa where it bounced onto the parquet floor and burst open, spilling its little electronic guts. In that instance Kokoro remembered her wall phone had still to be connected.

"Shit! Shit!" Her sudden rage surprised her; it was only a phone. The tiredness and cold must be getting to her. And that little slut Mitsu, how dare she speak to her so! She was finished at Atonal…

The tap on the door made her jump. It was hesitant, as if the tapper was unsure if they were intruding. After a pause it came again, bolder this time.

"Hello?" Kokoro heard her voice waver. No-one else should have the keys to the building. It must be the supervisor, but then how could he already know of Kokoro's complaints? She wasn't thinking straight.

She opened the door to a small bent woman in a threadbare flower-patterned dress and shawl. Though the skin on her face appeared smooth and unlined her posture and other subtler nuances told Kokoro that the woman was old, much older than her. The cracked voice confirmed it.

"I heard a noise, some shouting. So sorry for intruding, but are you having problems with her?"

"With whom? There's no-one else in here, not that that's any of your business." Kokoro felt her face flush. "I'm sorry to be rude, but how did you get in here anyway. You have to have a pass key."

"Yes, so sorry." The old woman began to shuffle away along the corridor.

"Wait! Wait a minute." Kokoro latched her door and hurried after her, catching up at the stairwell. "I apologise for what I said just now, but who are you? I haven't seen you in here before."

She turned and smiled. "I made a mistake. I thought…would you like to take some tea with me?"

"Tea?" Kokoro glanced back to her apartment door. "Yes alright. For a few minutes anyway."

The woman nodded and turned up the stairs her steps

surprisingly sprightly. She led Kokoro into an older part of the building she'd not seen before, two floors up from her own, where the walls were a chipped dark brown and the floor cheap with peeling linoleum. It was in vivid contrast to the stark white walls and polished rosewood flooring of below. Kokoro had struggled to keep up with her as she disappeared around the ends of maze-like corridors before finally slipping through a doorway.

"Here we are."

The room was old and dusty, with shoddy furniture; a dark grained sideboard cabinet, small wooden table with a couple of rickety chairs and a large armchair by a filthy window, its cover sun-faded and torn.

"Please sit down, I'll get the tea."

Kokoro sat at the table as her host busied herself in the little kitchen alcove at the room's far end. She wanted to be back in her own apartment, not trapped here with this odd person in her musty old flat. The stale smells of age made her begin to feel nauseous. She noticed photographs in tarnished silver frames carefully arranged along the dresser; a family group on an outing, a couple smiling blandly, a boy and girl clutching graduation day mortarboards on their heads and grinning. The pictures' washed-out Fuji-colour hues placed them firmly in the past.

"You have a very nice family." Kokoro told her as she brought two delicate porcelain teacups on a small lacquered tray.

"I don't see them anymore," the woman replied, and then continued, "My name is Aina."

"I'm Kokoro."

"I know, she told me about you."

"I'm sorry, who told you what about me? I don't understand..." Then Kokoro remembered the girl's white face in her bathroom mirror. "Is your grand-daughter running around downstairs in the new apartments? I really don't think that's a good idea, Aina. If the supervisor was to find out..."

"Then you have seen her. She wasn't sure but I told her not to worry, that it was only a matter of time."

"I've certainly heard her! The crying keeps me awake at night"

"Crying?" The woman looked as if she was trying to remember. "Yes, there was some crying at first…"

"Look." Kokoro found herself getting annoyed. The old dear didn't seem to realise the implications of what she was telling her. Perhaps she was senile. "I don't know how your little girl got into my room. Perhaps I left my keys in the door, I've done that before," (although she hadn't, so why was she saying that?) "I don't know, but she can't come in again. It's private property, I'll have to report her."

The old woman looked up at her then fixed her stare at the table. Her next words were spoken so softly that Kokoro could barely hear them. "I wouldn't do that. You'll just look silly, and I don't think a woman like you wants that. The girl means you no harm; she just needs somewhere to stay. She was with me for quite a long time but now that's come to an end and I have to leave her. You and I are very alike you see. She knows that. We're both on our own, both a little lonely – oh I'm sure your life is fast-paced and sophisticated; it must be very exciting. But you've got no-one to share it with, have you, no-one to talk to at night? It's empty, like your beautiful apartment. It's got nothing in it to slow you down. No… clutter?"

Kokoro found she had tears in her eyes. "I'm sorry, I have to go…"

She began to rise from the table but Aina grabbed her hand. The old woman looked up at her. "Its cold down there, isn't it? She can sense your rejection, but it doesn't have to be like that. Look at me. I accepted her for what she was and gave her a home." She took Kokoro's hand and touched the fingers to her soft cheek. "See, it can have its benefits as well. It's not just a one-way street you know. And in time you may come to love her as much as I did…"

Kokoro snatched her fingers away. "Who are you?"

The room seemed to shudder around her, as if it had become nothing more than a reflection in a pool of water, a still, deep pool that was about to close over her head. She found her breath stopped in her throat and tried to stand, but her feet slipped away and she fell, first to the floor then on, down into the silent darkness.

Kokoro opened her eyes. She was lying, fully-clothed, on the bed in her apartment and someone was banging at the door. A key turned in the lock.

"Hello? Takahashi-san?" The building supervisor stood in the bedroom doorway. "Are you alright? I was doing my weekly check-up, I knocked but there was no reply then I heard noises from inside and I thought you might... be in some kind of trouble?"

"What are you doing here?" Kokoro asked him, sitting up and rubbing her head.

"It's Monday night, as usual." The supervisor looked at her strangely.

"Monday...? God, I've missed a whole day's work, a whole weekend!" She swung her feet off the bed and tried to stand but the effort made her feel sick. For a moment the smell of the old room was back again. "I was upstairs – some old woman took me up there..." She stopped when she saw the supervisor's face. "What?"

"There's nothing upstairs Takahashi-san." His voice sounded odd. "It's all been gutted for redevelopment. Phase two if they ever get round to it. There's no money left..."

"But there was an old woman. She had a flat up there!"

"The building company bought everyone out last year. There was one old dear who refused to go but she died of a heart attack. All the stress I suppose... are you sure you're alright?"

But Kokoro was staring past him at the little white-faced figure standing in the hallway beyond. It seemed to be looking at her as if waiting for a sign.

Slowly, Kokoro nodded.

"You're looking particularly radiant this morning Kokoro-san," the company chairman complimented her as they all sat down for their weekly meeting.

"Thank-you, sir." Kokoro self-consciously touched her fingers to her cheek.

"What about that young assistant of yours, Mitsu? How's she coming along?"

Kokoro smiled easily. "She's promising sir, very promising. Of course, she's still got a lot to learn..."

Train Man

Mitsu dozed fitfully in the stuffy carriage as the hypnotic vibration gently rocked her like a baby in its cot. The mid-afternoon sun felt like a softly caressing hand as her cheek flattened against the hot glass of the train window. She moved in her seat, around and back as if her body was slowly twisting on its own invisible axis, the occasional swing of a bend or the clack of points no more than a brief pause on the secret journey back to her childhood.

She'd fallen off her bicycle, that was the image she always returned to; the wheels spinning in the heavy summer sky above her, the urgent stabbing pain in her arm and the wooliness in her head. She couldn't remember what colour the bicycle was now; if it had a basket or a bell. But she remembered the pain in her arm and the taste of blood in her mouth, the realisation that something very serious had happened to her. She couldn't just lie down in the swirling dust of the road; shut her eyes and go to sleep. She had to tell Mummy.

She'd left the bicycle and begun to run faster than she ever thought she could, back along the street with its jiggly little houses and sagging telephone wires, its barking dogs and brutal neon signs. She ran past the worried faces of strangers and older kids who laughed at her, and as she ran her arm swung strangely at her side as if no longer connected to her body, like a skipping rope twirling to its own peculiar momentum. Now the pain was gone, replaced by numbness and silence, and the sound of her feet slapping on the road's hot tarmac...Slap-slap, slap-slap...Clack-clack, clack-clack, clack...

Mitsu awoke.

Something was moving in the seat opposite her, a dark blur, its edges rimed in fierce sunlight. Somehow the movement seemed wrong. She tried to focus.

A middle-aged man's face swam before her. He had greying hair and dark eyes that stared at her trance-like as if she were invisible. Her gaze moved down over a tie-less and crumpled business suit. She saw his trouser belt undone, the fly open and a hand moving inside pale green underwear. His eyes widened in surprise.

"Oh…so sorry…!"

"What are you doing?"

"I…so sorry…"

A jolt of anger propelled her across the gap between them as she clumsily slapped his face. "You filthy pervert!" She pushed him away and jumped to her feet. "I'm calling the guard…"

"No!"

Mitsu looked down the carriage's gangway. Apart from a few old couples and some kids at the far end they seemed to be on their own. The surrounding crowd that had started the journey with her had disappeared.

"Hello, is there a guard on this train? Hello…shit!"

"No please, I'm sorry, you can't call the guard!"

She turned back to him. His eyes were wide and beseeching, his body half-raised out of the seat, hands clamped together as if offering up a prayer. Something in his expression made her pause.

"Why can't I? You were touching yourself up in front of me. I can get you thrown off this train."

"No, they'll ban me!"

"Ban you?"

"Ban me from the railway network. They'll take my pass away…"

"Good. Arseholes like you deserve to be banned!" Mitsu saw a man in a dark suit and cap slide open the carriage's far door. "Guard!"

"Please, listen to me for a moment."

Mitsu saw the guard look up at her voice then continue checking tickets. She sighed. "Quick then…"

"I'm sorry…"

"You said that, and? You've got exactly ten seconds before I shout again."

The man made a patting motion with his right hand as if to calm her. He sat back down but his body was tensed as if he might suddenly spring to his feet and leap past her. She momentarily considered tripping him if he did.

They'd both been breathing heavily. He put a hand on his chest and took a deep breath, then another.

"Heart-attack?" She asked scornfully.

He shook his head and took another deep breath. "I live on the trains." He indicated an old rucksack with a rolled up sleeping bag strapped across the top of it. "I lost my job last year; my wife left me soon afterwards taking our son. We had a company house but now that's gone too and I don't have anywhere else to go. I have this," he took out a faded season ticket in a little plastic wallet from his jacket pocket, "and that's good for another five months. After that the only trains I'll get to see will be from under the railway bridge outside Nakama City."

He saw her quizzical look. "That's my home town. I see the salarymens' camp getting bigger down there by the canal every time I go back, plastic sheets strung up like tents, old men washing their clothes in buckets. You can see the pathetic little night fires from the train. I'll be joining them soon enough."

Despite her anger Mitsu found herself intrigued. "Why don't you get another job?"

He gave her an odd grin, as if she still hadn't got it yet. "I'm a forty-eight year old salesman."

She gave him a humourless one back, "I'm still going to report you."

"Please don't." He began to blink nervously. "I get lonely that's all. You're in no danger from me."

"Apart from my dress, that is." Mitsu looked down at the smart blue outfit she'd bought in an expensive Tokyo store the previous week. "And I don't think you could even afford the dry cleaning bill."

"Who called the guard?" They both jumped. A busy-looking young man in a neat uniform seemed to have crept up on them from nowhere. He looked over at the man sitting by the window then directly at Mitsu. "Was it you?"

She hesitated for a long second then replied. "No-one here..."

The guard nodded at them and carried on up the carriage looking annoyed.

The man let out a sharp breath. "Thank-you."

Mitsu said nothing. She went over to the rack to lift down her small white travelling case.

"Can I help you with that?" She shook her head. "Would you stay then, at least for a while?" This said in a smaller voice, almost to himself.

She spun around to face him with a flash of her previous anger. "You're kidding!"

"Please. I made a stupid mistake – I... I'm very tired. You're the first woman I've spoken to for over two months." His voice had grown bolder in its pleading.

"What were you doing when the last one woke up?"

He gave her a weak smile. Mitsu looked at him, he seemed harmless enough now, and she didn't want to fall asleep again, at least until she was at the old folks' home. It was always better afterwards but as the time got nearer she would dread closing her eyes and seeing that long dusty road yet again. Sometimes she'd wake up and for a few disembodied moments actually feel the phantom pain, even though the arm had properly healed fifteen years ago. Hesitantly, she sat down by the window again.

"Thank-you, I'm..."

"I don't want to know your name!" Mitsu cut in quickly. This was for her entertainment only, to take her mind off things. It was impersonal. "What happened then?"

He took a deep breath again. Diving into the past is a bit like that, Mitsu thought, you can't go too deep but you've got to get below the surface. Stay down too long though, and you start to drown.

"I was chief salesman for my region. They made a big deal about offering me redundancy but I eventually realised it was more like an order. I could've stayed on a bit longer and humiliated myself; they'd have had me sitting in the corridor while all the young bucks sneered at me. Once you hit forty-five these days you can pretty well kiss it all good-bye. I gave my wife and kid most of the money when they left me. You see, I'm not a total arsehole."

Mitsu raised her eyebrows but said nothing.

"Anyway," he continued, "I'd just got this yearly train pass on the company. I was meant to hand it in on my last day, but..."

"...But fuck 'em." Mitsu finished for him.
He looked at her, surprised. "Yeah, that's what I thought. It's somewhere to sleep, it's warm enough, I can keep myself clean and I feel safe..." His voice trailed away as if he realised how weak the words sounded.
"No, you're right. It was a good plan. But what are you going to do when it... finishes?"
"Then I'll have to choose, won't I?"
Mitsu stared back at him without making any reply.
"How about you, then...?" he asked. "What do you do, where are you going? Boyfriend I suppose."
"No." She hadn't meant to respond. "I don't do much, really. I work for a stupid woman in Tokyo and I buy crap and drink a lot of wine at the weekends."
"Not this weekend."
"No not this weekend. I'm going to see my mum in Fukuoka City. I come from there."
"See your mum, that's a nice thing to do."
"No, its not..." The unguarded tear found the corner of her eye. She wiped it away with her wrist.
"Sorry... Shit!"
"It's alright."
"It's not alright. I get like this every time I have to see her! It's so stupid..."
He pulled out a crumpled but clean enough looking handkerchief from the season ticket's pocket.
"Here."
She took it without looking and dabbed her eyes. "She used to be a doctor but she's been going downhill for years. It costs me loads just to keep her there. See this." She indicated the blue dress. "First decent thing I've bought in months. She's got no idea who I am half the time; I could be the Queen of England as far as she's concerned."
"I'm sorry to hear that," he told her.
"You're always being sorry."
"Don't you get on with your mother then?"
"My mother's been dead a long time. I don't know who that woman is in there, but it's not her anymore.' She looked at him coldly. "And stop trying to psychoanalyse me; you don't understand."

"No, I'm sure I don't."

The man started to get up but Mitsu reached out a leg to stop him. "Don't be so boring, I thought you said you were lonely..."

"How are you then?" Mitsu asked her mother in a bored voice.

As always when she visited the home she found Michiko sitting in her shabby brown chair by the window. She perched in front of her on a rickety old stool from the TV lounge like an applicant at a job interview. Even now, with her mother reduced to her present somnambulant state, she still somehow felt like a little girl waiting for her approval.

"Food still shit as usual?"

No response. Michiko stared straight in front of her as if she hadn't heard. 'Maybe she hears alright but the meaning's all jumbled up in her head,' thought her daughter. 'Or maybe it's something else.'

"Do you like this dress? I bought it in Mitsukoshi department store last week; cost me nearly a week's wages. It had a lucky escape today, two lucky escapes actually." Still nothing. "Some old guy touched himself up in front of me on the train this morning. He thought I was asleep."

Her mother's head remained motionless but a thin blue-veined hand moved to cover Mitsu's on the arm of the chair. She pulled back quickly so that only the fingertips stayed in contact.

"I'm alright; it wasn't anything at all really. He'd lost his job, I felt a bit sorry for him. You'd probably have told him to get a grip on himself." She gave a brittle laugh. "Oh, I made a joke!" The hand withdrew. "Oh yeah, I forgot. Some things just aren't funny, are they? Most things really. Life's a serious business when you're the wonderful Dr Kimura; I must have been a big disappointment to you!" The old woman blinked once, twice, but Mitsu carried on. "Actually, I'm sick of being here for you. You never used to care if I existed and I doubt you do now. That guy on the train this afternoon said sorry to me five times, I counted them; 'I'm sorry, so sorry...' I couldn't shut him up." The little room was hot and oppressive; it smelt of urine and dead flowers and old women's underwear. "You never said that to me once, did you? I'm sorry Mitsu..." It had been a long day, a lot of miles; her head was starting to ache. She felt drowsy and nauseous. In her mind came the slap-slap of six-year-old feet on hot tarmac, the garden gate before her and the concrete steps up to the front door, the bell under her trembling finger as she pushed again and again. She saw her young self walk unsteadily around to the backyard, the locked door and the empty garage. She heard a child's words, tearful with readily assumed guilt. "Mummy I'm sorry, help me please..." Then the silence and the waiting; the waiting that went on for hours and hours...

She felt the phantom twinge in her arm again. Would it ever go away?

"Where were you Mother, seeing to your precious patients? The wonderful Dr Kimura, who took care of everyone else but forgot about her own daughter; you just left me there!"

Michiko continued staring past her through the window. She moved her hand back until it touched Mitsu's fingers again. "Blue". Michiko said the word carefully, as if dredging up a small treasure from the past.

"My dress...? You haven't heard a thing I've said!" Mitsu told her.

Her mother slowly turned to face her. "Your bicycle...was blue."

The Cat

The cat lived downstairs from the residents of the old peoples' home, curled up in its round shiny basket in one corner of the room. It was large, white and fluffy with a name Michiko Kimura could never quite catch. It would sometimes vanish for days, maybe weeks on end only to reappear on the lap of a half-dozing resident, flopping on its back for the expected caress of shaky fingers. Michiko presumed, when she still had enough energy to think about it, that the animal was meant to stimulate the sense of touch, a cheaper and more cost-effective solution than the rest of the paraphernalia gathered there. She'd used the word herself in a former life; tactile.

The nurses actually called it the Stimulation Centre as if to imply their charges were somehow otherwise dead to the world, linked only to the life force when sitting around in comfy sofas with ambient light playing off their gnarled features. At first Michiko thought the place looked less like a therapeutic centre than a cross between a third-rate disco and the lighting department of Mitsukoshi department store. As the fibre optics' multicoloured fronds layered the soft walls with gentle pastel shades and the pan-pipes whistled tunelessly to themselves somewhere off in the background Michiko had decided, in her more lucid moments, that the home's budget could have been better spent on improving the terrible food and maybe arranging a decent film channel for the TV in the residents' lounge.

She still knew words like fibre optics then, in the first few weeks when her daughter Mitsu had guiltily fussed and fretted with her room and asked her for the thousandth time if she thought she was going to be alright. She could even just about remember what they meant. But she also knew, deep in her bones, that the time was fast approaching when she wouldn't. Slow onset dementia was the specialist's opinion as Mitsu sat next to her wringing her gloves in her hands. As the young man carelessly patronised Michiko, unaware of her medical degree and forty years' practice; she had considered her options. Her work had ended abruptly, the charge of criminal negligence narrowly escaped by a hastily announced retirement. It was time for her to relax and enjoy life she had been told by colleagues who hadn't bothered to disguise their relief.

She'd felt useless then. Now she felt helpless.

The dementia had not been slow at all. It descended on her rapidly, like a pea-souper fog from her old London student days, swamping and smothering every corner of her mind. It made her a prisoner of her body; a vessel that had once served her faithfully now betrayed her constantly at every embarrassing turn.

And she was in this place. It was as if she'd woken up one morning and found herself transported to hell. The days seemed endless, all of a deadening uniformity as the nurses lulled and cooed their charges through turgid meals and soporific afternoons of bingo and sing-alongs and television soap opera trash. If the news came on they'd turn it over, if a classical concert magically appeared one evening, the girls would hastily switch channels to some overloud pop show or inane quiz. Thinking was prohibited, absorbing anything but mush likewise.

She had tried to make friends with the other inmates, tried to pass the time of day with small talk of the microscopic variety. But she had begun to find even that was a strain. Ten years ago she'd been discussing intriguing medical case histories with colleagues, five years ago sharing her thoughts on Chopin and Shakespeare with friends at dinner parties.

Now she struggled even to form a coherent sentence.

Michiko was left alone with her thoughts, and her thoughts had begun, one by one, to desert her. Mitsu still visited her occasionally but these had become strained meetings for both of them, and they seemed to tire Michiko more than if she'd just been left alone.

One night, after her daughter had left, she awoke. Usually she slept like a child, deep and dreamless, but this night her sleep had been shallow. She looked for the time before remembering her bedside clock had stopped weeks ago, its dead batteries unnoticed by her daughter. What good was time to her now anyway?

A sound, out of place and insistent, was coming from the corridor beyond her bedroom door. It came again as she strained her ears to listen in the darkness; an urgent scrabbling of claws on wood, as if something alive was trying to get in. Michiko slowly pulled back the blankets then, after a rest to gather her breath, swung her feet off the bed to place them in the slippers she always carefully positioned in the same place. She padded unsteadily across the room and opened her door just enough to peek out. The corridor was brightly lit. For a moment her eyes failed to adjust, watering and blinking in the sudden light, but then as she rubbed them she caught a blur of white tail disappearing into a crack of darkness two doors down from her own.

Michiko went back to bed. She was too tired to think about what she had seen. She accepted it as she had begun to accept everything else in the home now. Strange things happened there. She didn't know why anymore.

In the morning though, when she'd washed and was sitting in the dining room, Michiko remembered the scratching at her neighbour's door and the whisk of tail. She asked one of the young nurses clearing the breakfast things away.

"What's that, Michiko, big white cat in the residents' rooms? I don't think so. Hey Naomi, seen any white cats up here lately?"

Michiko dimly realised the girl was mocking her.

"It's the cat from downstairs, from the lights room. I'm sure of it. It shouldn't be up here…"

Naomi Kobayashi, a friendly middle-aged nurse who helped her to dress in the mornings, came over to put a plump arm around Michiko's shoulder.

"She means the Stimulation Centre," she explained to the girl. She nodded her away then beamed down at Michiko. "What is it my love? There's no animals allowed up here, or anywhere else in the place. Health and Safety wouldn't let us; we'd all lose our jobs."

"But I saw it last night. It went into Masuyo-san's room. She let it in."

Naomi's face took on an odd expression. The wide smile slipped for a moment then resurfaced. "I'm afraid that Masuyo-san won't be with us anymore, Michiko. She passed away last night. It was just her time. I'll be telling the others after lunch so please, keep it to yourself."

Michiko nodded, but when the nurse had gone she set herself to thinking about what had happened. The nurses couldn't see the cat, only the residents, and perhaps not all of them.

But her neighbour had seen it.

That afternoon she spent quite a long time in the lights room. At first, she sat stiffly, apprehensive of the cat's appearance. It wasn't in its basket, she made sure she had a good view of that; although now she looked at it again it seemed to be more like a large fruit bowl than a cat basket. Gradually the soft lights and gentle panpipes lulled her into a softly-focussed reverie.

It was Christmas, just a few years ago, perhaps last year, although maybe not as they were in her daughter Mitsu's little flat in Tokyo with her old boyfriend. She knew it was Christmas because of the large tree and bright glittery things on it, and of course the presents. The young couple were giggling and kissing together while she sat watching television, unnoticed until the smell of urine on the leather sofa made Mitsu turn angrily to face to her.

That was the night Michiko finally realised that she had become invisible.

A movement somewhere in front of her brought Michiko back to the room. Haruna Sasaki sat across the floor from her in the wicker chair, moving her hands slowly around something in her lap, as if gently needing dough. It was the eyes that appeared first, blue and unblinking, focussed on her in a mindless stare. The body seemed to grow around them, first the head, then the rest down to the tip of its tail. Haruna-san continued to stroke the soft white fur, but she never looked down at the animal. To Michiko it felt like she had just expected it to be there.

Michiko fetched a nurse, but when they returned the old woman was in a deep sleep, head lolling on the arm of the chair, and the cat was gone.

That night Michiko kept herself awake, reading the same lines of her book over and over again. They no longer made much sense to her, but it kept sleep away. Before very long the scratching sounds came. Michiko got up and went out. She followed the noise through the dining hall and beyond. Now she was in a different area, a longer corridor than her own with pictures of birds on the walls and doors either side. Near the end one of them stood slightly ajar. Michiko pushed gently on it and light rippled over the room's floor, up and onto the bed and across the form of Haruna Sasaki and the thing lying across her face. It looked up, startled, and then turned its face to Michiko. The long pointed ears jutted back on its scaly head, the sharp yellow eyes narrowed to angry slits, and Michiko could plainly see that it was not a cat at all.

"I know what you are!" She whispered, then bolder, "Get off her, go on shoo! Get out of here…!"

Michiko found herself shouting. She grabbed a heavy book from the bedside table and flung it at the creature. The light came on and there were others in the room with her, nurses grabbing her hands, pushing her back to the wall while others rushed to pick Haruna up from the floor. Michiko saw there was a red mark across her forehead where the book's cover had caught her. She was clutching at her chest for breath.

And the creature was gone.

Michiko was pulled from the room and led firmly down the corridor and across the dining hall, back to her own.

"Michiko, how could you!" as they tucked her up in bed, "Michiko, we've never had any trouble with you before," as they stroked her hair and smiled reassuringly down at her, "Michiko, was it a bad dream…? Michiko…?"

But she didn't say a word to them. What would be the use? They would never understand her, these young people with their loud friendly voices who knew nothing of life, or death, even though they saw it again and again in this place.

They couldn't see the creature, but she could. She'd seen it many times before in her long career without truly noticing it. Now, finally, she had.

Now, at last, she could see what she'd spent a whole lifetime fighting.

It had seen her too; soon it would be after her as well, but this time she would be ready for it. And she would try not to be afraid.

A Boy Called Simon

The old man on the bus from town must have been a bit lonely, Naomi Kobayashi thought. The random conversation he'd purposely struck up with her had gone from 'lovely weather' to the fact that his grand-daughter was coming to visit him, in about a minute and a half. Surely some sort of record even for old grand-dads.

She'd told him that was 'nice' and tried to look pointedly out of the window at the little squares of rice paddies climbing the hills but he'd continued anyway. Perhaps he fancied her? Who was she kidding; she was badly overweight and prematurely grey; even for a game old goat like him. That's what cleaning floors and scrubbing toilets can do to you. But he seemed harmless enough; just lonely. She understood how that felt.

"I'm Hideki Kinjo, by the way, my farm's just passed the next village."

"Naomi Kobayashi."

"Are you from around here, Naomi?"

"Fukuoka City, I'm visiting my son, he's got a new house up in the hills."

The old guy nodded and went back to the reason for their pointless conversation. Apparently the grand-daughter wasn't quite the perfect child he wanted her to be. The old fool didn't realise how fortunate he was, Naomi thought as she smiled and nodded politely.

Some people never do.

She began the slow trudge up the narrow road towards the squat modern house nestling in the hillside. More like a fortress than a house, Naomi mused, with its electronically-controlled iron gate, electrified fencing and CCTV cameras perched on poles. Its owner obviously valued his privacy, liked to be in control of events.

But then her only son had always been that way. Ever since he was little, Tatsuya had to be the one in charge, the one getting all the attention. And he always had to win.

At the gate she pushed an intercom button and spoke into a small metal grill. A man's voice answered and she repeated who she was. There was a click and she was aware of one of the cameras whirring towards her then the gate slid sideways and she was walking up the driveway and past the neatly-cut lawns to the frosted glass main entrance. Two young men in dark business suits stood waiting there to receive her. Or maybe throw her out.

She had only a few moments left to prepare herself for the first meeting with Tatsuya in five years. So many bad things had happened since then; where would she start? And how could she manage to do what she had to?

Naomi had spoilt Tatsuya after his father died. Not with money, they'd had little enough of that, but with indulgence. Exhausted after her daily work chores at the old people's home, she'd let him get away with things until it was too late. She'd been wilfully blind to his bullying and cheating at school, even after the other parents complained to his teacher. All she cared about then was that her son was exceptional. He was certainly that.

A risk-taker and naturally gifted entrepreneur, Tatsuya was running his own electronics company just a few years after leaving university. Three more years and he'd sold it to one of the giant corporations and invested the money in other profitable small businesses he'd spotted. There were fancy cars, fancier women and penthouse apartments with all the latest gadgets inside them. He'd tried to explain some of them to his mother and laughed at her incomprehension. He laughed often in those days, usually at her insistence on keeping her job at the home despite the new flat and all the other things he'd given her. That had been before the dramatic decline in his companies' share prices throughout the 'lost decade' that culminated in the charges of corporate theft. There had still been pretty girls though, although more as distraction from Tatsuya's fraught business empire than for any kind of meaningful relationship.

All that had changed with Jennifer.

Tatsuya had met the pretty English girl in a hostess bar in Ripongi one night when he was feeling down. Bright and good fun she was also adventurous, working nights in the bar to fund her continuing stay in the country she told him she loved. Jennifer had always told Naomi that it was her son's dynamic character not his wealth she'd fallen for, although Naomi had never been quite sure. For Tatsuya the attraction had been even more obvious; he'd simply never met anyone like her before.

That had been eight years previously. He'd built this house for Jennifer but Naomi had only visited it twice; once for the wedding and once to celebrate the first birthday of her grandson. His Japanese name was Souta, the one given to him by his father.

But his estranged mother called him Simon, and because Naomi had slowly come to realise over the years that she loved and cared for him far more than his father did, she had come to think of him as Simon too.

Now she had come all this way to try and bring him back to her.

The two young men took her into a large plush living room where her son stood at the window with a glass of whiskey in his hand. He was dressed in the sort of designer casual clothing only the rich can afford to wear, looking as if he'd just returned from his exclusive golf club or one of the polo matches for which he kept a string of ponies in the stables below.

Naomi thought he looked older and very tired. They'd argued five years before, she hoped they wouldn't have to today. But she was determined.

"Mother..." He came over to her and gave a little bow then bent to kiss her cheek. "What on earth are you doing here?" It wasn't the friendliest of greetings after so long.

"Aren't you going to offer me a chair?" she asked.

"Sorry, please..." He indicated a large swivel chair but she perched herself on the rich leather sofa instead. She couldn't afford to get relaxed.

"I've come to see Simon..." she started, then quickly "...I mean Souta."

"I knew it couldn't be me. Souta's fine, he's playing soccer in the yard." Tatsuya made a gesture to one of the dark-suited men who swiftly left the room. The other hovered around in the entrance lobby like a nervous bouncer, mobile phone glued to his ear. Tatsuya looked over at him questioningly but the man shook his head.

"Look mother, this is not a good day for me. Really, why have you come? You should have phoned first after all this time."

Naomi realised something was going on. He was tense, distracted, hadn't even got angry with her for turning up out of the blue. "It's the boy."

"Well what about him. He's happy enough with me."

"Really, are so you sure?"

"Yes I am. He's a lot better now he's out of that English cow's reach."

Naomi bit her lip. "She's here."

"Here?" Her son didn't try to conceal his shock. "What do you mean, 'here'? You mean she's back in Japan?"

"She's waiting for me at Narita Airport. I said I'd bring Souta to her." Naomi prepared herself for the thunderstorm.

"You did what!" His face clouded with anger. For a moment the terrible rage she knew him capable of threatened to take over. He turned away from her and strode back to the window with his hands flapping behind his back. Outside in the yard a young boy was dribbling a football head down behind the dark-suited young man sent to fetch him. He looked up glumly at his father.

"You had no right to say that." Tatsuya continued, facing her again. Some of the anger had abated.

"I promised her. She's got rights as well you know. And you did steal the child from her."

"Souta wants to be with me, mother."

"Have you asked the boy what he wants?"

"I know what's best for him!"

"No Tatsuya, you only know what's best for you! This business is wrong! The court gave her custody and you visiting rights. And it was a Japanese court, not an English one. You'll only get into more trouble if you don't give him up."

Her son gave a strange snort of laughter as if his mother had made a joke. "*More* trouble... hmm..."

The boy rushed over to Naomi as soon as he entered the room and flung his arms around her. "Oka-san!"

"Simon..." She hugged him back for a few moments then disentangled herself. "Come and sit on my lap and tell me what you've been up to recently."

"I'm too old for that Oka-san!"

He was indeed, Naomi realised with a shock. Simon had grown into a sturdy young boy in the intervening year since the kidnapping in London. The Japanese food must be doing him good, but then Tatsuya had an excellent chef.

"How would you like to come and see your mother again, Simon? She's waiting for you right now at the airport to take you back to London with her. Would you like that? I think your holiday in Japan has gone on quite long enough, don't you?" The boy looked over at his father. "Daddy agrees with me. He thinks it's time you were back with her as well. You can always stay with him again on your next visit, and come and see me as well. We'll all go to the zoo again together like we did when you were four. You probably don't remember that do you?"

He shook his head. She noticed tears welling up in his eyes.

"It's alright Simon. Daddy knows you'll miss him. Now go upstairs and pack all the clothes and toys you want to take with you. We can't take a lot on the plane so pick your best ones.

Simon looked at Tatsuya again. For a few moments the two stared at each other then he shrugged and nodded to his son. "Okasan's right, as usual Souta. Go and pack like she says and I'll get one of the boys to drive you both to the airport. Hurry up now son."

As Simon ran upstairs the man in the lobby with the mobile shouted across to Tatsuya. "The money's in boss! It's transferred OK, we've got it!"

Tatsuya gave an audible sigh of relief. His whole body seemed to deflate. He sat down heavily in the swing chair and put his head in his hands.

"Who is it this time, Tatsuya?" Naomi asked.

He took his hands away and looked across as if he'd forgotten for the moment she was there. "It's nothing mother, just a transaction to secure a loan – standard business stuff."

"Its yakuza, isn't it?" He didn't reply but his look told her. "I hope you know what you're doing son."

"Don't worry mother, I can look after myself," he told her, but added, "Maybe it's a good time to take the boy though."

Naomi nodded. "I think so too. I'll tell Jennifer that you're OK with it then?"

Tatsuya looked as if his thoughts were far away for a moment. Then he shrugged again and gave Naomi the sort of cheeky smile he used to in the old days when he was a young man with everything before him. "Yeah, tell her that if you like. I'm always OK..."

In the departure lounge at Narita airport Simon had rushed into Jennifer's outstretched arms in the same way he had Naomi's. The tears had already started to flow when there was some sort of scuffle at the gate, then a man was running towards them with two security guards trailing after him.

It was Tatsuya. 'Oh no', thought Naomi, 'he's going to ruin it all!'

Her son stopped short of the little group and the guards bumped into his back as they grabbed him by the arms.

"It's alright," Naomi told them hurriedly, "He's my son; this is his ex-wife and child..."

The two guards looked at Jennifer and she gave them a little nod of confirmation. After giving Tatsuya a few words of advice they slunk away.

"I'm sorry," Tatsuya told Jennifer, glancing away from eye contact with her, "but I wanted Simon to have this." He awkwardly held out a dark red passport to Naomi. "It's his Japanese one; he left it behind in his room."

She hesitated for a few moments then nodded and took it. "Thank you..."

She gave Naomi a hug and whispered her thanks. At the gate the boy waved back at Tatsuya then looked up at his mother and said something. Seemingly reluctant, Jennifer waved too – and they were gone.

"Come on, you can buy me a coffee," Naomi ordered her son as he stared at the empty departure gate. "Come on, he'll be back one day."

He continued to stare.

"Does this mean there may be some danger of you finally growing up at last son?" she asked.

Tatsuya finally tore his eyes away. "Don't push your luck, mother…"

Keeper of Lost Things

Chika's spiky little voice interrupted Hideki Kinjo's thoughts again, this time to the extent that he actually opened his eyes and stared up at his persistent grand-daughter. She wore her sulky face with the pouty mask of personalised injustice that all girls seemed to have refined to perfection by the time they reach fifteen. He sighed and sat up a little in his comfortable leather armchair.

"What's the matter now?"

"I'm bored, I want to go home! When's mum coming back, it's been ages?"

It had been less than two hours since Akiko had driven into the small town a few miles away to buy provisions for him. He hadn't asked her to, that was his weekly task on the local bus and he was quite prepared to do it this weekend.

"The doctor told you to rest, didn't he?" she had said.

"He said 'avoid anxiety'. Your fussing around only makes me more anxious."

It wasn't the most gracious of replies but the dull throbs beneath his rib cage that would spring into stabbing pain without warning were making him a grumpy host. Even by the severe standards of their past history.

What was it that annoyed him so much about his only daughter? That she'd stupidly lost her husband? That she was raising his only grandchild as a spoilt and troublesome brat? That she'd never managed to make the most of the opportunities her natural intelligence and ability had laid before her?

Or was it just that she was plain unlucky?

Yes, he had to admit to himself. Deep down inside he knew that to be the real crux of the matter. She was unlucky; unlucky and careless. She lost things – husbands, advantages, chances. She'd been well-educated; got a good degree from university and married a man she'd convinced herself she loved but then she'd done a silly, almost unforgivable thing that had hurt him and her mother. Now Akiko lived in a small flat in the port city of Kamisu and worked too hard at a job beneath her capabilities while her daughter steadily grew away from her. She'd lost the chance of a better life, and he had lost the chance to be able to finally stop worrying about her.

Hideki's wife Mina, the grandmother Chika would never know, had left him some time ago. If any death can be considered fortunate then surely a gentle one must be. Mina had slipped away from him one night in a hot and balmy July; she'd kissed Hideki as she always did, turned over into the darkness and never woken again. He'd found her body cold beside him in the first filtered light of dawn, still facing away, eyes staring sightlessly at their two forms reflected in the dressing table mirror. He'd like to have said that he held her once more in his arms. In truth he leapt off the futon and sat on the carpet in the corner until gaining enough composure to stand up, reach across and push her eyelids closed.

But that had still been a lucky thing, a painless, private exit from a long and fulfilled life. It was how he would have wished to go before his present problems arose. Now, who knows what would happen? The doctor had given him tablets for when the pain got really bad. A bypass operation was discussed with Akiko and himself but no date decided on. It would take a good deal of money to get it done quickly, probably most of his and Mina's savings, the money they'd been keeping back for Chika's university education. See, luck again. It looked like Chika would inherit her mother's unfortunate relationship with the gods of fortune.

Maybe it all came down to him after all, but he'd always told himself that he'd had the best life he could have hoped for. There had been Mina, and the farm she'd inherited and they'd both worked at for many years to make a go of. Tough, back-breaking work, but they'd survived and eventually prospered.

And they'd been blessed with Akiko, and now Chika, although Chika was going to be a problem, he could see that clearly. The girl was angry and restless; she had a devil inside her that would not bring anyone peace.

Maybe it was him, maybe he was the carrier; the bad luck giver.

A memory came to him out of nowhere in particular. Akiko had been given her report card on the final day of term at her high school and they'd all gone out to the cinema and then an expensive sushi restaurant to celebrate. It wasn't her finals; that would be in another year's time, but even so the results were good, in fact very good. He'd tucked the report in his pocket as they left the house and read it again out loud after they'd eaten. Akiko had blushed with embarrassment at other tables overhearing her father, but he'd carried on. One of the waiters had taken their picture with Akiko's camera and they'd all grinned up at him, the sake loosening their reserve.

It had been the perfect evening. "Your poor old father and mother are getting old Akiko," he'd told her in relaxed philosophical mood. "But you've got your whole life ahead of you, remember that. You're a lucky girl!"

The pain was thumping again. He really should take a tablet. He focussed on Chika's face again, with some difficulty. He found he was sweating, a salty drop running down his forehead and into his eye. He blinked it away.

"What?"

"Where's mum got to? I want to go out tonight and see my friends. We're going to be late back at this rate." Her voice sounded peevish, her little face pinched. He fought down the urge to reach out a hand and slap it.

"Don't talk to your grandpa like that, Chika!" His own anger surprised him. His whole body felt hot and he tried to readjust himself in the chair. His joints were stiff and unresponsive.

The girl shrugged. "I was only saying..."

"Well don't. I want you to go up to my room and get my pills. They're on the bedside table. Hurry up for me, will you?"

Chika gave him a sullen nod. She silently turned and went out of the living room. He heard heavy feet trudging up the stairs, kicking each one as she went; bang, bang, bang...

BANG!

Something inside him exploded.

BANG!

And again... his body jolted upwards then slumped back down. He felt winded, then suddenly very cold, as cold as before he'd felt hot.

This was it then. It was now.

"They're not here!" Chika's muted voice came from upstairs.

A shot of pure stripped-down pain coursed through the left side of his body and punched deep into his chest below his heart.

"Grandpa? I said they're…"

BANG!

He clutched at his chest with a claw-like hand, the other gripping white-knuckled to the arm of chair. His head fell to one side as he felt his mouth begin to drool, the saliva gathering on his chin.

Hideki steadied himself for the final jolt then blacked out.

"Sir…? If you're ready…?"

He opened his eyes. It had been a man's voice, not Chika's. Sure enough a pleasant looking young man stood before him. The room was dark now and night had fallen with just the soft moonlight through a window to pick out the stranger's details. He wore a smartly tailored suit and bore an expression that was neither smile nor frown but somewhere quizzically in between, as if he was used to patiently waiting for people to notice him.

The young man leant over and put a steady hand on his shoulder. He spoke slowly in a relaxed but firm voice. "If you'll just come with me Kinjo-san I think we're ready for you now."

Hideki heard the words but found no meaning in them. The pain below his heart had stopped though, and he pulled his hand away. He wiped his chin. He managed to sit up.

"With you…?"

The man turned away, looking back over his shoulder as if expecting Hideki to follow. "If we could move things along sir…"

"Yes…alright…"

He got up and stumbled after him through the darkened house.

He found him in the back garden. What had been the back garden anyway, now it had disappeared under rows and rows of…things.

The young man turned to address him. "If we could make a start sir, only time is pressing." Hideki noticed a clipboard in his hand with a pencil tucked under a large bulldog clip holding reams of list-filled papers.

"What's all this?" He heard himself asking without consciously forming the words.

The other smiled indulgently at him. "I thought you'd realised. It's the Lost Things checklist. Your lost things I mean."

"And you are?"

"The Keeper sir, at your service. Now if we can begin? Start along the left hand side and work your way around to the right. I only need your recognition." He made a self-conscious ticking motion in the air.

"The Keeper…?"

"Of Lost Things, sir. Rules are rules I'm afraid. Loose ends need to be tied up."

Hideki looked around him at the neat piles of formless clutter that stretched away into the night. "But if they're already lost… and it's a bit dark isn't it?"

"They're only lost to you, sir. We have to reset their status while there's still time. Would this help?" He shone a powerful torchlight on the ground.

Hideki bent over the objects spotlighted in the beam. Some items had been arranged into collections, old pens and chewed up pencils, worn paperback books some quite new ones, a pile of misplaced work tools, another of cutlery he hadn't missed for years, scraps of written notes, a mountain of newspapers and magazines, small pyramids of paperclips, nails, drawing pins, watches, a pile of individual socks and shoes, a mountain of shirts, trousers and jumpers he barely if ever remembered wearing, hats, coats, scarves…As he recognised them one by one he was conscious of the young man ticking off his lists a few paces behind.

Hideki stopped, so abruptly that the man bumped into him. He bent down. From a box of old photographs he held one into the torch's beam. Three happy faces looked up at him, red-eyed and grinning, surrounded by the other restaurant diners.

He turned to show it to the strange young man. "I want to take this with me. Is that possible?"

"Yes sir, of course. I thought I'd already mentioned that you're allowed one excess item. But I would have thought you'd have preferred those…"

The Keeper swung the torch away to pick out a white plastic pill box sitting on top of an old radio. Hideki gasped then rushed over to pick it up. Holding the box in one hand and the photo in the other he turned to see the Keeper silhouetted beyond the ring of the torchlight. Hideki held up the hand with the photo to shield his eyes.

"It's a difficult choice isn't it Kinjo-san? A very difficult choice…"

"Grandpa...! Open your mouth Grandpa!" Hideki felt something bitter on his tongue. He tried to spit it out. "No Grandpa, swallow!" He felt water splash inside his mouth and gulped it down automatically.

"That's right, now another. Come on Grandpa!" It was Chika's voice. Her face swam into focus behind two fingers holding a little white pill. He opened his mouth and swallowed again.

"That's it Grandpa, well done. You'll be alright now won't you?" She sounded desperate.

He slowly gathered his wits together. The thumping in his chest had subsided. There was feeling coming back to his limbs. His body was still cold but he began to feel warmth slowly flowing from somewhere. His breathing was becoming steady again.

"They were in your pocket Grandpa," she jabbered excitedly at him. "I thought you'd lost them, but I found them in your pocket…"

He saw she'd been crying and put a hand to her cheek to calm her down. "Yes, I know. Thank-you Chika, I'm feeling much better now."

"It wasn't my fault…"

"I know it wasn't Chika. We don't need to tell your mother about it do we?"

She looked away from him for a moment. After a pause she shook her head. In that moment she seemed much older than her fifteen years to Hideki.

"Good." He tried a smile. "Let's go and see a film together the next time you two come up. And maybe a nice meal afterwards…"

Unlucky

She had to admit it, Akiko Kinjo had got herself well and truly lost. She'd been driving around central Kobe for what seemed like hours but was probably no more than forty-five minutes. The traffic system turned back on itself along the narrow strip of land between the sea and the mountains like a snake swallowing its own tail.

Ren Shimasaki's import-export business was meant to be somewhere in the south of the city, down by the docks, but the area he'd mentioned in their occasional correspondence contained neither the building nor even the road mentioned on the impressive company letterhead.

It was no use. She'd have to stop and Google him on her iPhone, something she should have had the foresight to do before setting out this morning. She'd been in such a rush to get that lazy Chika up and off to school.

Akiko smiled at her daughter's vain attempts to tell her about some crazy dream while she struggled into her uniform, still half asleep while her mother fussed around her. Twice she'd managed to bang her knee on the open drawers as she helped/got in the way of Akiko's panicky search for a clean blouse. It was sadly true that neither of them were particularly well organised when it came to the slog of everyday life; like mother, like daughter.

At least they had each other though, and Chika's morose personality had taken on a slight improvement since the visit to her grandfather the previous weekend. Perhaps her old man had said something to make the girl pull her socks up at last. Akiko could only hope.

But back to the problem of the disappearing Shimasaki-san; she tapped his name into a local businesses site but nothing came up except a plastics company and a noodle bar, nothing to do with any trading corporation in the financial district of Kobe. She was about to click back when something caught her eye. Under the 'Golden Prawn' noodle bar were two names, presumably the proprietors. One was a woman's she didn't recognise but the other she most certainly did:

It was Ren Shimasaki; Chika's father.

"You say you're looking for Ren?" The girl asked Akiko as she brushed past her in the bar's narrow entrance. The three bowls of ramen destined for a table of noisy young salarymen seated under the plastic awnings outside clinked dangerously together on the tin tray. One of the diners broke off from his mates to take a worried glance at their meal's progress.
"Yes, I'm... an old acquaintance. Just thought I'd look him up seeing as I was in Kobe. What time did he say he'd be back?"
The girl returned and stood directly in front of Akiko as if to appraise her. Behind her the ramen-eaters were now making satisfied slurping noises.
"He didn't, but he won't be long. Gone to the fish market, we're clean out of salmon and roe. I nagged him to get some in this morning – probably all gone by now."
Akiko looked at her watch. It was still only ten thirty.
"We start at six," the girl answered the unasked question. "That's just washing the place down though. We don't actually open till eight."
"It must be exhausting." Akiko nodded, trying to keep the girl in conversation. "What time do you close up?"
"Eleven; plenty of time left to go clubbing."
"Ren goes clubbing?"
The girl snorted a laugh. "I'd like to see that! No he's too old, poor thing. Excuse me." She went back to get the next order from a tiled counter where a bulky looking young man was using a very large knife to do something impossibly delicate to squid. Steam rose behind him as a kitchen door banged open and for a moment he looked like a rock star surrounded by dry ice. Two vicious and deliberately aimed chops from the gleaming knife immediately dispelled the image.
Who was the young clubber? Akiko wondered. Might she be Ren's daughter? No, too old. She looked about twenty and any kid of Ren's would have to be less than Chika's age. But then how did she know he hadn't already had kids somewhere before they'd met? The short answer was that she didn't.

The long answer was a bit more complicated.

Akiko had met her future husband in her final year at Tokyo University. She was a Science major, he a Law. They'd married almost exactly a year later, with her parents' grateful approval of her ambitious fiancé, and rented a tiny flat two hours train ride from the city. He'd commuted every day to the law firm where he planned to become a junior partner; she'd caught a number of buses to the public relations company that had taken her on their graduate training scheme. All was going to plan in their exceedingly well-planned lives, nothing could go wrong to spoil things.

But then, Akiko's husband hadn't been Ren Shimasaki.

It had been in a noodle bar, of course, where they'd first bumped into each other – literally so.

She'd been there with a crowd from the company after the signing of a big contract she'd had nothing whatsoever to do with. She'd still allowed herself to be dragged along to the celebrations though.

After their first clumsy coming together that night Ren had apologised profusely for spilling his beer on her dress, although in truth it had been more her fault than his. Sake tended to make her giddy and they'd drunk quite a lot of it in between toasts to the brilliance of the company, the company's chairman and each other.

In fact, as the evening wore on Akiko was starting to feel a bit left out. She'd only been with them for six months and was yet to make any friends in the frighteningly competitive atmosphere the others all seemed to thrive on. So when the mutual apologies and recriminations were finally over Ren and Akiko found other things to discuss while their separate groups got on without them.

Much later someone had suggested a party that they might gate-crash. It sounded like fun; Akiko's serious new husband was away on some course or other and the tiny flat felt depressing on her own. As she hardly knew anyone who was going a tipsy Akiko decided to ask her new friend along for company.

Nine months later, to the day in fact, Chika was born.

It hadn't really been all Ren's fault that night. Such things go on all over the world, and probably always will. The

Americans have a phrase for it; 'shit happens'. She never thought of it that way though, because it had given her Chika; the moody, difficult and quite wonderful child her life now revolved around.

It had also given her the shame of her parents, a quick divorce, and the end of any career in public relations, or anything else that mattered in the immediate future. After a cooling off period for his anger, Akiko's father had let her move back to the farm until she managed to find a poky little flat and a badly paid job in the nearest town along the coast. Then Ren began sending regular maintenance checks after she'd found the courage to tell him about his unknown two-year-old daughter, and things gradually began to straighten themselves out again.

The money had made enough of a difference to their lives for Chika to keep up with her friends on school trips and with extra tuition to scrape her through her exams. Now though, Akiko was going to need more from him. After all, she'd supposed, he could afford it being boss of his own company and all. Her daughter was falling behind again and tutors were expensive, there was a new laptop to buy, new school sportswear and uniform. Chika was rapidly growing into a young woman, and she did mean growing. So money was the reason for today's trip to Kobe to see the man with whom she'd spent one drunken night, sixteen years ago, that had changed her life.

In fact, the very man now squeezing past a young couple hovering in the bar's tight entrance while trying to balance two plastic ice-filled buckets of fish. He was shorter than she remembered; his face was lined, the wiry hair going prematurely grey.

The deep eyes hadn't changed though. They were exactly the same.

"You were wrong as usual, Yoko. I got them..." He looked up at Akiko. The expression on his face was hard to read. Surprise certainly, maybe annoyance? There was fleetingly something else as well.

"Oh... It's you. Err..." He dumped the buckets down slopping the ice, and the girl he'd called Yoko came forward to manoeuvre them awkwardly around the bar into the steam-belching kitchen. Akiko noticed her giving him a raised eyebrow as she went. The pair seemed close. Akiko thought, more than just workmates or friends.

As if noticing her glance, Ren said, "I see you've already met my young partner Yoko, I hope she's been looking after you."

Akiko nodded. This was weird; the girl was no more than twenty and far too young to be with Ren, but then up until ten minutes ago she'd had no idea he co-owned a noodle bar in the back streets of Kobe either. She suddenly felt an irrational anger towards him. He should be Chairman of Shimasaki Trading Corporation like it said on the emails where he asked about Chika's progress at school between matters of her upkeep. Was he was married to this girl then? What exactly was going on?

Ren wiped his hands on a stained apron and pointed to a table wedged into the bar's corner.

"Please, let's take a seat and I'll get us something to eat and a drink; Sake or beer? I'll get us both. Then we can have a chat."

"Oh...that's alright, really. I only came to ask about... look I'm sorry, I didn't know you'd switched jobs. You must be very busy." She saw him studying what must have been a bemused expression on her face. She felt awkward but carried on. "How long have you been a restaurateur?"

"Quite a while really, let's sit down shall we?" He stood self-consciously by the table while the girl began preparing it for them with mats and chopsticks and a couple of bottles of Kirrin.

Ren shrugged as if to say 'look you might as well now we've made the effort'. He pulled the chair back and she reluctantly sat down.

"Good, well then..." Two bowls of ramen instantly appeared before them out of nowhere. They smelt delicious and Akiko had to admit that despite her confusion she was starving.

"Well..." Ren started again as they began eating. "It was pretty soon after I moved here actually. I'd bought all the start-up stock I needed, spent the entire budget and then some. I'd just been trading a few months but things were still going pretty well considering. Then..."

"Then...?"

A shadow passed across his face. "Then it was five forty-six on the morning of January the seventeenth, 1995. I lost everything in the fires; the whole lot. The warehouse was insured but not the stock, I couldn't afford to so I took a gamble. One I lost as it turned out."

"But I thought... I mean your letterhead. And you never told me anything of this. I was worried at the time but you seemed to indicate everything was alright."

"It was, eventually." He knocked his bottle against hers, "Kampai!" and took a thirsty gulp.

"But what about this place...?" Akiko asked.

"Yes, well that's a bit of a story. I helped a girl who'd got trapped in her own house later that same day; I suppose I kind of dug her out, her kid as well. We both had nothing left so we hung around together for a few days helping out as best we could, then a few days turned into a few months and one thing led to another. One night when Yoko was asleep between us in the emergency tent and we were both pretty drunk Susi decided she was going to buy a noodle bar with the little money she'd managed to save. I'd learnt enough about her by then to realise she was a lousy cook, and told her so. She replied, and I quote; 'I'm not doing any fucking cooking! That'll be your job'." Ren smiled at the memory. "I guess she meant it as a kind of payback to me, y'know... for helping them out."

"She sounds like a tough lady." Akiko told him. "I'd like to meet her."

"Yes, she was." Ren's voice took on a distant tone. "Susi died a couple of years ago, Cancer of the throat. She smoked a lot, I always told her to cut down and she always swore she would..."

"I'm sorry, Ren."

"Yeah, well... Anyway, I promised her I'd look after Yoko and she left the place to the two of us, so that brings us up to date."

"Why didn't you tell me any of this before? Why the deception? I thought you were some kind of rich business man and all the time you were..."

"Look, apart from the first couple of years we've done alright. You never get the chance to find out, but I'm actually a pretty good noodle cook and Yoko's a great manager. We get by just fine."

"Yes, but the money you sent us. It must have been tough for you."

His face took on a firmer set. "I took advantage of you that night. You were little more than a kid and I knew you'd just got married, you told me all about what's-his-name while you were still sober. I was the one who suggested we went to your friends' party – you don't remember but then you were far more pissed than I was. You lost everything and I just walked away from it all. When I finally got your phone call I felt sick at what I'd caused. I know my responsibilities Akiko, I'll always be there for the two of you."

She stared across the table at him. "You've never said this to me before. I hated you to start with, even after you agreed to pay your way. I hated having to swallow my pride and call you."

"I know. That's why I've always kept things business-like between us. Why I didn't tell you."

Akiko lowered her gaze. "You didn't even ask me for a DNA report." Suddenly she couldn't look Ren in the face.

"I knew you weren't the kind to lie about such a thing. And if you thought I was doing really well you wouldn't feel so bad about taking the money."

"How...? How did you know that much about me from just one night?"

He shrugged. "Some people are just like that, I knew you were a serious person straight away." He glanced past her then got to his feet. "Would you excuse me for a moment?"

She turned in her chair to see him put his arm around an old woman sitting on her own at the bar's only window table. She was staring out at the afternoon passers-by while he bent down to say something in her ear. She looked up at him and nodded absently then continued to stare. As Ren sat down at their table again the old woman suddenly got up and left.

"What was that all about?" Akiko asked, intrigued.

"Nothing, she's a bit lost in the head these days poor thing. We've known Maya for quite a while; apparently she used to come in here regularly with her husband before Susi took over the place. That was their favourite seat." He pointed at the window table. "Lately she's been coming in again and just sitting there. We bring her tea and a bite to eat and eventually she remembers and leaves, or I give her a gentle reminder."

"About...?"

"About the fact that her husband's been dead for the past sixteen years, so he probably won't be meeting her. He died in the 'quake."

"Oh...that's so sad!" Akiko was momentarily stunned. "It's nice of you to care about her." She thought he looked embarrassed.

"I guess the old dear puts things into perspective for me. I lost a lot that day, but I never lost anything really important. That was still safe."

Akiko bit her lip. For a moment she didn't trust herself to reply. "You know, my dad used to say I was unlucky. He wasn't being nasty, just matter of fact in his own stubborn way and I always believed him. I'm not so sure now, though. I think maybe he was wrong about that."

Ren smiled. "So, what's Chika doing for her school summer holidays this year?"

"No plans at the moment," she told him. "Why?"

"I just thought she might like to spend them in Kobe that's all. What do you think?"

"That's very kind of you, but I couldn't let her go on her own."

"Of course not, I've got a spare room for the two of you upstairs. It would only be for a few weeks."

Akiko automatically began to shake her head then thought 'why not?' Chika would have to meet her dad sometime. She'd asked her enough questions about him in the past.

"Yes, OK," she told Ren. "I'd like that, if it's alright with you."

"Brilliant, that's sorted then." He grinned and lent back to shout at the counter. "Yoko!"

"What is it Ren? Can't you see I'm busy....?!"

"It looks like we're going to get some extra help for the summer season; Chika's coming!"

"Great, does she like clubbing?" Yoko yelled back.
Akiko and Ren looked at each other and laughed.

Aftershock

Maya heard the car pull up outside and the engine cut off as she washed the rice in the rice cooker for the third time. It was an old cooker and sometimes it overheated and the rice stuck to the sides and burned. She hoped that wouldn't happen today.

"They're here," her soft lilting voice told no-one in particular.

"About time...!" No-one answered her back.

She smiled to herself. She'd missed them last year when they'd decided to go off to Europe in the summer then somehow found themselves much too busy to visit her at New Year: Junko's school skiing trip, Goro's new job, Kaori's choir concert and the Neighbourhood Association's party to organise. They'd had a busy time of it alright.

"They couldn't have used the Hanshin Expressway, must have come through the city."

"Don't be silly, they fixed that years ago."

"I knew that!" his voice sounded put out, pride wounded. "I meant traffic and such..."

"You're getting senile," she told him as she switched on the cooker.

"So are you!" She had an image of him sticking his tongue out at her like he used to, his cross frown smoothing into laughter lines.

The back door rattled open and her daughter stood in the little kitchen.

"Oka-san." She took two steps forward and gave Maya an awkward hug. Maya smelt expensive perfume. "Who were you talking to just then?" Maya watched as Kaori stepped back and looked around the dingy room.

"Oh mum, it smells in here. Let's get a window open and some light on things shall we?"

Maya cursed herself for not turning on the fan. It did indeed smell as the strips of beef teriyaki and stir-fry vegetables sizzled and sent up wisps of dirty smoke. Where had her mind been?

Now Kaori was joined by her husband Goro and a pretty young lady, with dyed-blonde streaked hair, wearing a tight-fitting green summer dress. Maya started at the stranger before recognising her grand-daughter.

"Junko…? Why how you've grown! Your hair…"

"Hi Grandma, long time no see!" She gave Maya an enthusiastic squeeze, almost knocking her over. "Sorry Grandma, you've got so much frailer…"

"Junko!" Her mother cautioned. "Sorry mum, look why don't you go and sit down and we'll finish the cooking. Goro take her through will you?"

Her son-in-law obediently took her elbow. Why were they treating her like a child, had it been this way on their last visit? She tried to remember.

They'd all been looking at Junko's graduation photos in the rice-paper walled living room after lunch when the doorbell rang.

"I'll get it Grandma." Junko came back followed rather sheepishly by a woman who bore a striking resemblance to Kaori.

"Hello mother…"

"Mariko…what are you doing here?" She hadn't spoken to her other child since the funeral. Some argument over money, Maya had forgotten the details long ago but remembered the pain.

"Kaori asked me to come along."

The other two glanced at each other then left the room.

"I don't know what all this is about but it's good to see you again Mariko."

The woman wouldn't look at her but Maya could see a tear slide down her cheek. She put a shaking hand up to catch it. "There, it's alright. Whatever it is can't matter that much."

Her face still turned away, Mariko held out her arms and the three women embraced. After a while Maya said she'd make some tea. She heard their whispers from the kitchen.

"I'll start it off and you back me up."

"Are you sure it's ok?"

"Well you can't do it, can you? We've been over all this."

"Ok, ok…"

Maya smiled. They must think her deaf.

"It's good to have her back again," she told no-one in particular.

"Can't see what all the fuss was about." No-one replied, in typical grumpy fashion.

"You weren't here to judge, were you? It was horrible…"

The two women broke off their sotto voce conversation. "Mum, did you say something?" Kaori's voice sounded startled.

"I said, would you like some sweet-bean curd?"

When she entered again they were all there waiting for her, half-kneeling on tatami mats around the little kotatsu table in the middle of the room.

"Please sit down, mum." She joined them. "Mum, Goro and I would like you to think about coming to live with us."

"Live with you? Where…?"

Kaori kept a patient smile. "In our house in Takatsuki City, it's not too far from Kobe and we can all visit the place at weekends. We just think it would be easier for you." She turned to indicate her sister. "Mariko agrees with me." Mariko gave a helpful nod.

"Oh…"

"It's just that we've had some calls from your neighbours recently. You've been wandering around asking for dad, if they've seen him. Dad's dead, mum."

"I know your father's dead!" She didn't remember doing that. She would've remembered such a silly idea, but so many things slipped by these days. What was Mariko doing here? She hadn't been at the funeral. That had been a long time ago though, hadn't it? She wasn't sure anymore.

"What about your father?"

"Mum…" both sisters together.

"I know, I know, I didn't mean…" What did she mean?

The floor seemed to move around her legs, like a giant snake was rippling beneath it. She felt the wall's wooden frames judder around her, there was a deep crack in one of them that began to widen until daylight spread through it. Distant screams and muffled bangs came from the street. Her nose tingled with burning smells; wood and tarmac, plastic and paint. There was a crash from somewhere upstairs. A voice she recognised whimpered nearby but she couldn't go

to it, couldn't move her arms or legs, couldn't breathe...
The others were all staring at her.
"Mum, are you alright...?" Mariko asked.
"Yes."
"Well then, what do you think?"
She looked around at her family, then at the figure standing silently in the doorway behind. He smiled at her and slowly nodded his head.
Maya found she suddenly had tears in her eyes.
"Yes," she told them hesitantly. "I think maybe it's time.'

Tap – Tap

The doctor had come down to meet Goro at Reception, his young face bearing the neutral expression of professional concern.

"Can I see my mother please?" Goro asked.

"Of course, Rin-san, but first I think I'd better warn you. As you were told on the phone she's managed to survive the stroke and we've stabilised her. However, there's been massive haemorrhaging to the brain causing extensive tissue and nerve damage."

"What does that mean?" Goro asked the doctor. He was still out of breath after his dash from the hospital car park.

"We think your mother may be virtually brain dead, I'm sorry."

It took a few moments for the words to sink in.

"You mean she's...?"

The doctor met Goro's desperate gaze and shook his head. He motioned to someone behind him. "The nurse will take you through now."

Goro could hardly recognise the woman he'd last seen at the old people's home that weekend. The area of her face still visible beneath the tubes and wires was sallow and bruised; the cheeks red-veined and sucked in. Her eyes were shut tight. She seemed to be struggling for breath, a continual dry rasp from beneath the little plastic mask counterpointing the rise and fall of the oxygen machine's bellows. She looked a shrunken husk of her former self, Goro thought. He turned to the young nurse standing at his side.

"Can she still hear me if I say anything?"

"Doctor Hidaka thinks she's totally unresponsive, I'm afraid." She smiled sympathetically at him.

"Mother...?" There was no reaction. "Mizuki...?" A few seconds, then an eyelid twitched.

"I think she heard me." He told the nurse. "Mizuki, its Goro. The eyelid twitched again.

"Excuse me Rin-san, I'm going to get Doctor Hidaka."

He looked round to see the door shut behind the nurse.

When he looked back he caught a ripple of movement on his mother's face. It came again. Her arms, varicose veined and dappled with liver spots, lay resting on top of the fresh white sheet. He watched her wrinkled fingers.

Suddenly the forefinger of her right hand twitched.

Instinctively he reached over and put his palm underneath it. The finger twitched again.

"Mizuki...? Can you hear me love?"

Nothing. He waited for a minute which began to stretch into two.

Then the finger moved, but not a twitch. This time it rose and fell deliberately. It did it again, quicker, a tap, then two more like the first, slow and deliberate. There was a long pause, as if the old woman was steeling herself for the effort, then a short tap. Again a pause, then three more taps on the sensitive skin of his palm. The eyelid twitched again.

He sensed she'd finished and squeezed her hand to let her know he'd understood. Five minutes later Hidaka returned with the young nurse in tow. Goro thought the young man looked annoyed, as if he felt he'd been dragged away from something more important for no good reason. The nurse seemed embarrassed.

"Rin-san, I'm afraid the fact that your mother twitches occasionally is irrelevant considering her condition. I doubt very much if she's aware of anything that's going on around her."

"My mother has just communicated with me using Morse code."

Hidaka gave him a patronising smile. "I think that's extremely unlikely in the circumstances."

"Mizuki worked as an operations girl for the Japanese Air Force during the war. They taught her Morse code and when I was a child she taught me. She just signalled the word 'yes' when I asked if she could hear me. That means her mind's fully functional."

"Impossible, I'm afraid."

Goro tried to get his mother to repeat the message but the doctor was already looking at his watch. "In catastrophic cases like these the body often leaves one small nerve out of the total shutdown but it's just a physical reaction, nothing more."

He put a hand on Goro's shoulder. "There's really no will involved you see. I'm afraid sooner or later you're going to have to admit to yourself that your mother is to all intents and purposes gone. Now I really must be getting along."

Goro was back at the hospital the following afternoon. The preceding twenty-four hours had been spent laboriously checking the internet for any Morse-related PC software he could find. He'd finally located a small company in Nara. A long drive later Goro sat poised with his laptop on the bedside table. He put a thimble on Mizuki's index finger and a small sensor pad beneath her hand that was plugged into the laptop. He clicked the software icon and a blank page appeared on the screen with a cursor flashing in its top corner.

"OK, Mizuki. We're going to see if this will work. Understand what I want you to do?"

For a few moments the frail hand remained motionless. He was about to ask again when the finger began to flick at the pad.

"Y E S"

Goro clenched his fists. It had been a tiring day but worth it a hundred times over now. But what to ask her...? He hesitated. What can you ask someone who's quality of life has just been reduced to zero? What could he say to her that wouldn't sound trite or pointless?

He lent across to stroke her brow. "Are you in any pain, dear?"

The finger moved again and he looked back at the screen.

"Y E S"

He bit his lip. This was awful. "I'm so sorry, mother. I'll try to get them to make it better. Where are you hurting you most?"

The cursor moved again.

"Y E S"

The young doctor, looking flushed and annoyed, entered the room. "I wish you'd informed me before starting this." He frowned at him then glanced at the laptop screen. "Is that it so far?"

"We've only just started." Goro replied. He was getting annoyed at the man's negativity.

Hidaka strode to the bottom of the bed. He pulled back the sheet and gently kneaded the sole of Misuki's left foot with his thumb. "Can you feel this Mizuki?" He asked. There was no response. "OK, let's try something else shall we? Do you know where you are?"

There was a long pause. *"YES"*

"It's the same thing again and again," he told Goro in an exasperated voice. "I told you Rin-san, it's just a nerve in the finger jerking away to some random pattern you've decided to decipher as a word; the same word!"

Goro gazed down helplessly at his mother then at Hidaka.

"I don't believe you. Please, let's just give it one more go...?"

"It's hopeless!" The young man stared scornfully at Goro. "Oh, alright! Mrs Rin, do you know who I am?" There was no response. "You see...?"

But then the finger began to move. This time it kept on going. Goro could feel the huge effort his mother was making.

Finally, she finished. Both men looked down at the screen.

"YES," it read, *"YOU BASTARD"*.

Shrine

Hayate Hidaka's disciplinary interview with the Director of Human Resources at Takatsuki General Hospital was meant to be for five o'clock. He'd arrived flustered and late but the man still wasn't ready for him. He perched nervously on a face-saving chair found for him by one of the cleaner's, too distracted to thank her for it.

Some while later there came the sound of raised voices from inside the office culminating in a female one saying, "Well we should at least try!" followed by a muttered response. "Well screw the budget, that's all you people ever think of!"

A handsome woman in her late thirties wearing a white lab coat burst out of the office, slamming the glass door behind her.

He heard a faintly sarcastic, "Thank you for your input Doctor Sasaki," then "Would you come in now please Doctor Hidaka".

Hayate felt the pins and needles in his legs as he stood up quickly. It had been another long day, first in surgery then prepping for a difficult procedure the following morning. The tiredness that was always there had begun to dull his apprehension: now it stabbed right back. He couldn't afford to lose this job.

A nondescript young man almost as young as him in a sharply pressed grey suit ignored him as he took his seat. Instead he made a show of continuing to read and sign various reports in a plastic file. Finally he closed it and looked up.

"Doctor Hidaka, sorry to keep you waiting, lots of paperwork to get through as usual. Actually, some of this is about you." He ignored Hayate's embarrassed shuffle and continued, "Or to put it more precisely, Mizuki Rin; your case I believe?" He paused as if expecting Hayate to confirm.

"Why am I not seeing the Head of Surgery about this?"

"New Hospital policy; he's far too busy to waste his precious time dealing with such matters. It's our role to discipline staff now." He said the word 'discipline' with a flare of the nostrils, as if an unpleasant smell had leaked into room. "So, the Rin-san case you misdiagnosed as…" he theatrically flipped opened the file and pretended to run a finger down the page, "…ah yes, an Intraparenchymal haemorrhage when in fact it turned out to be a…" he did the finger run again, "…Subarachnoid one, caused by a ruptured cerebral aneurysm. The far more commonplace version in fact – usually recoverable from if operated on immediately. You, however, chose to wait – worse, you misread the CT scan and didn't refer it to a senior surgeon. Consequently, we are now being sued by her son for malpractice; quite a day's work on your part."

Hayate began to protest but the young manager held a hand up. "I'm sorry, we try to protect our staff but this case has been reviewed thoroughly by the board and it's been decided to issue you a final warning. One more slip and your contract will be terminated immediately. You'll also be relived of all medical duties until the case is heard."

He waited for Hayate to slump back in his chair before leaning forward to speak in a softer, more mollifying voice. "I know the hours you juniors work are tough, Hidaka-san, but it's the same for all. You're a technically gifted surgeon. What you're lacking, it seems, is heart; you just don't care enough. A surgeon has to care. Take Doctor Sasaki for instance; she's been a senior here for a number of years, she could rest on her laurels but instead she still fights for every life placed in her hands. She never gives up on anyone. That's what we want from our doctors: heart, and care. We want them to care. Think about that."

Hayate was driving back on the freeway to his postage stamp flat with the Director's last words still echoing in his mind. Although he lived in nearby Shimamoto it took hours to get through the morning rush hour traffic. At night though, he could open up the throttle on the Honda GT86 and put some speed behind his troubles. The dark red sports car served to prove, at least to him, that he amounted to something more than a complete non-entity.

As the miles increased so his grip on the wheel began to

relax. Hayate loved the speed, loved being in control at least here in the darkness as the sodium street lights swept past, a soothing blur in perfect time with the giant pulsing heart of the one continuous city.

Neon splayed across the dark hulk of anonymous buildings to either side of the raised freeway, garish advertisements for perfume and golf clubs, jewellery and whisky; the dream of successful lifestyles at odds with the lattice work of tiny roads and drab compacted housing spreading out behind the office blocks and warehouses.

The drops of rain he'd felt in the hospital car park had quickly turned from shower to driving squall, pinging off the car's bonnet and spattering the windshield.

Despite his shock at the interview's outcome Hayate felt even more exhausted than usual, the confrontation draining his last reserves of concentration. He was unaware he'd closed his eyes until the car swerved wildly across another lane, slithering in the wet as he over-compensated. He forced his eyelids open in an unblinking stare.

The signboard for Shimamoto flashed by overhead, telling him there was another half mile to go. There was a giant billboard advert wrapped around the next corner that either hadn't been there before or he'd missed it. A pretty young girl's face gleamed out at the swishing cars as a delicate disembodied hand held a Diet Coke bottle dripping with rain to red lips. A neon eyelid suddenly winked down at him as he sped past; he glanced up at the movement then quickly back at the road as a blur of something struck the passenger side a glancing blow. The vehicle gave a slight wobble. For a moment Hayate carried on then his brain caught up and he stabbed the brakes to slither the car to a halt on the hard shoulder. A driver directly behind blasted a protest as he swerved around him.

"Shit!" Hayate swore aloud, thinking 'I must have hit a dog.' He waited impatiently for a swarm of cars to pass then backed up to where he'd felt the impact. There didn't seem to be anything there; no pathetic bundle of bloodied fur and guts smashed across the ribbon of concrete curling back into the night. There had been a bump though, he was sure of it, and the blur had had a head attached to it. Not a dog's head though…

He'd just hit someone.

He scrambled out and followed the crash barrier, hugging its side as juggernauts crashed past him. It had been a child; that second unavoidable truth surfaced next in his consciousness. He'd killed a child. Then a third unworthy one rushed into the vacuum left by the other two; he would lose his job, worse, lose his licence to practice. He would be disbarred!

In that moment of sickening realisation he noticed a distant figure on the highway's central reservation. Hayate put up a hand to shield his eyes from the rain sheeting into his face. The shape was vague, outlined by a thin electric frisson of industrial light, but it was indeed a child. It moved in a confused way, a few haltering steps forward then a twist of the head as if seeking its bearings. It looked lost but not particularly hurt. Hayate gave a sigh of relief; his career might be saved after all.

If the child was alright, if it hadn't seen his car properly or read the plates...

He stopped and stared off into the darkness. 'You callous fuck,' he thought, 'has it really come to this?' Hayate reached to somewhere deep inside himself, the figure an unfocused mote at the edge of his vision. With a feeling of almost overwhelming relief he found that it hadn't.

"Are you alright?" Hayate's shouted words were whipped away on the storm. The boy made no sign of having heard them, or any acknowledgement of his presence. "Hello, can you hear me? Are you hurt? I think my car struck you."

Two saloons whipped by trailed by a van then a giant articulated lorry with a random collection of popular TV personalities plastered across its side. A deafening horn-blast ripped the night as the van hurriedly moved out of its path. When he looked back the boy was gone.

Hayate felt a presence behind him and turned around.

He stood no more than a few feet away, so that Hayate could now clearly see every detail. The boy wore green shorts and a black Batman t-shirt, wet socks clumped around new-looking trainers. The skin had a porcelain quality that almost shimmered in the streetlights. The age was anything from six to nine, the features anonymous apart from the large mordent eyes that stared fixedly at him. Something beautiful deep inside them made it hard to look away.

Then Hayate noticed a dark stain spreading slowly into the gold Batman logo. A tick of red appeared in one corner of the lips and began to dribble down the chin. The boy still hadn't moved.

"You're hurt..." This time Hayate felt no urge to run; he wouldn't need to fight that demon again. "Come over here and let me see what's happened." The boy stepped back as he moved toward him. Hayate opened his arms. "It's alright I won't hurt you anymore, just need to take a look..." The boy made to move past him. Hayate reached out to try and grab the tiny frame but found his fingers clutching only air. The child dashed across the road, almost under the wheels of a truck which Hayate was sure had crushed the little body until he saw it standing over by the freeway wall.

Again he waited for a gap in the traffic then walked as slowly as he could towards the child. "Wait, please. I'm a doctor, you've been hurt and I need to take you to my hospital to make you better." He pointed to the Honda GT86 still parked with its lights on fifty yards away. "That's my car, see, the red one. It's a sports car, very fast; I can take you for a ride to the hospital in it." He began to walk towards the car, hoping the boy would follow. No footsteps sounded behind; at the car he turned back but found the road empty. Hayate let out an exasperated sigh. The police would have to deal with it. He slid in and reached for the phone. Sitting up he found the boy staring at him in the mirror. There had been no click of a car door.

He nodded back, not wanting to frighten him again. "Good boy, you'll be OK soon now, I promise. Better do your seat belt up." His passenger didn't move. Hayate shrugged; at least he was in the car. "OK, hold on tight."

Hayate drove to the next gap in the central reservation and swung the vehicle around then put his foot down.

He was off the freeway and pausing at a set of lights when he checked the mirror and found the back seat empty. Craning his head around there was no sign of a child along the sidewalk of noodle parlours, tobacconists and electrical stores. He parked hurriedly and got out to search. After half an hour's fruitless questioning of shop-keepers and their customers he was about to return to the car when a local newspaper headline in a Seven-Eleven caught his eye.

Hayate waited patiently on the hard shoulder just down from the winking girl advert. He'd been there for almost four hours, the car's heater keeping off the chill. Occasionally he'd rev the engine to stop the battery going flat. A cop had pulled up to ask what the problem was and he'd made a big enough fuss about a breakdown truck being late to send the guy on his way with a 'that's life' shrug.
   It must be some random pattern of events, he mused to himself, a matter of perception set off by the distraction of the advertisement so that you only see it on the peripheral. Then once you've got the focus, it sees you; the two planes interconnect, lock together somehow. Did that make any sense?
   He gave a rueful smile of exhaustion. Not really.
   In the mirror he saw a car driving towards him give a sudden jerk, as if dealt a glancing blow. It swung wide and slowed its speed for a few moments then sped past him. Hayate switched his view over to the central reservation to be sure then got out of the car. He walked across the now deserted highway.
   "Hello again, I've been looking for you." He saw recognition then wariness in the large eyes. "Don't worry, I'm not angry or anything. I think I understand now. I'd like to show you something if you'll come with me. It's a kind of secret message from your mum and dad, just for you." Hayate saw interest spark then a hesitant smile start to spread across the wane face. "That's right, they haven't forgotten you." He beckoned to the boy. "This way..."
   Again, no footsteps but when Hayate stopped again he was at his elbow. They both stared down at the bedraggled bunch of flowers tied half way down the concrete pillar. The picture in its rain-streaked cellophane wrapper had already begun to fade.
   "See, they haven't forgotten."

A small hand reached out to touch the petals. He grinned up at Hayate and the pale lips moved soundlessly. Then he was gone.

Smiling to himself, Hayate walked slowly back to the car and drove away into the spreading dawn.

Seconds

Chiyo Sasaki heard a hesitant footstep outside her office then the click of the door. She turned at her desk to find a middle-aged man with a balding head of wispy white hair hovering in the doorway, as if about to exit again at any sudden movement from the surgeon.

She was annoyed at his obvious reticence then remembered the particular case circumstances and relented. Bedside manners had never been top of her priorities but she would need to find some now. She'd done this before of course, many times in her long and successful career. She could usually give a slight hope, a small rock of a chance to cling to amongst the raging waters. Sometimes miracles happen. Not this time though.

"Abe-san isn't it? You were sent to see us by your local doctor two weeks ago I believe, a priority assessment. Chiyo tapped up a file onto the laptop's screen. "We gave you an EEG scan and..." she tapped some more, "...apparently a psychiatric assessment as well. Would you care to come in and take a seat?"

The man shuffled a little further forward, his left hand still trailing behind on the door handle.

"I think...I may have made a mistake coming here."

"Why do you think that?" Chiyo asked, trying to keep her voice patient.

"Because I think you're going to tell me it's no good, that you can't help me." He began to back away to the open door again.

"Wait! Please, we need to talk." She caught herself and took a deep breath. It had been a long tedious day and her temper, never at any perceptible length, was shorter than usual. "Look, just come in and we'll go through it together, OK?" She added, helpfully. "I have the results of your scan here. We need to discuss it, calmly."

"My... scan." He said the word as if it might explode in his face.

"Yes, I have it here." She tapped up another file, this one an image of concentric tree-ring like blotches. "Please Abe-san, take a seat and I'll go through what we've found. I'm afraid..." she turned back to him again "...the news is not what we would have hoped for."

"What do you mean?" He asked.

"Well, that the tumour is inoperable. I thought you'd realised that when you said you didn't think we could help you."

"What tumour?" His eyes darted to the blotches. "What are you saying?"

"Abe-san, you have an inoperable brain tumour, in the hippocampus region to be exact." Chiyo pointed to a seahorse-like shape with a large dark lump attached. "I'm very sorry." His face had whitened with shock.

"I... I thought you wanted to talk to me about the other business."

"What other business?" Chiyo asked.

He stared past at her at the shape she'd pointed out. "The memory thing I told the doctor about. I thought we were going to talk about you curing that."

It was getting late but Chiyo still hadn't gone home. She was busy studying Katsu Abe's psychiatric report in a lot more detail than the brief read-through that morning. She'd been under intense pressure all day with surgical procedures to prep and rounds of check-ups. How she'd missed the Psyche's conclusion of mild paranoia she wasn't sure, but it seemed clear enough.

"...patient shows clear signs of paranoid delusion...believes himself to be victim of some bizarre shift in the timeframe...would suggest long-term chemical based treatment programme if not for the particular facts in this case..."

For instance, the fact he was about to die in the next few months. The meeting that afternoon had got no further than her look of stunned surprise.

"You don't know what I'm talking about, do you?" he'd asked.

"I..." She'd been lost for any coherent reply.

"I thought not. I told the young doctor everything but it was obvious he didn't believe me and you've been no help at all. Anyway, I have to go..." He'd stumbled clumsily to his feet, knocking his chair over. At the door he turned to face her. "I'm not going to die you know. I've only just got here."

'It was a strange thing to say,' she thought, 'especially by someone who'd just been told they had an inoperable condition.'

It hadn't been Dutch courage either; he'd seemed genuinely convinced. Nevertheless, the result would be the same. She studied the conclusions of the medical team that had assessed the case:

Large swelling left side hippocampus causing dysfunction, high rate of dopamine release in basal ganglia etc. May affect integration of information in prefrontal cortex leading to...

Leading to madness perhaps? Maybe that would be a blessing in disguise. There was something else weird as well, evident in the waves on the man's EEG chart. A normal Theta rhythm should be between three and ten Hertz but these were a tsunami-like fifteen to twenty with some spiking even higher.

She shook her head, stood up and stretched, then snapped the laptop shut and pulled on her coat. That was it for today. There would be a whole ton of fresh problems tomorrow but they could wait. She had a half bottle of rosé demanding her attention at home, and a very hungry cat to feed.

The railway station was almost deserted by the time Chiyo had taken the longish walk from the hospital. She had a beautiful new Honda Civic in the garage of her condominium in Osaka but hated driving on the crowded freeway every day. And besides, she could work on her case files with her hands free. Her time was far too valuable to waste sitting behind a wheel.

As her tired eyes adjusted to the harsh fluorescent lighting she realised with a start that she recognised a hunched figure sitting at the far end of the platform. What was he still doing here? He'd left her office hours ago. After a few moments hesitation she walked along the platform. Katsu Abe looked up at her approach.

"Ah, hello Doctor..." He seemed slightly embarrassed, as if

caught out doing something he shouldn't.

"Abe-san, you should have been home hours ago!" She realised her voice sounded chiding. "Forgive me; it's been a long day. I'm sure you..."

"Have a lot to think about?" he finished her careless sentence. "Yes I do."

"I don't wish to disturb you..." She began to edge away but he held up a hand.

"No please, I'd like someone to talk to." He indicated one of the scooped-out plastic seats next to him.

"I really don't... my train will be here soon."

"Please. I apologise for losing my temper earlier." He dipped his head in a self-conscious bow. "You must understand I was under a good deal of stress."

"Of course, I'm sorry..." Chiyo took the proffered seat.

"It's a pleasant evening, isn't it?"

She looked out across the cityscape to the last rays of the sun as it slid behind the starkly vertical hills. There was a light breeze blowing lengthways along the track that mingled with the dusty vestiges of the last Shinkansen to have thundered through.

"Yes it is," she agreed.

"You probably think I'm mad." She said nothing. "Perhaps you're right. I think you probably are. You know more than me about these things."

"It's not madness. Your memory is being affected by the cancer; throwing up false data, confusing you. It's not unusual in cases like..."

He smiled sadly and gazed at the last remains of the sunset. "I'm going to die, aren't I?"

Chiyo nodded, even though he wasn't looking at her.

"Quite soon...?"

"A few months or so."

The last sunray turned green and fringed the horizon before vanishing into the earth.

"Thank you for being honest."

She nodded and made to go, but he continued:

"You see, I woke up one morning a short while ago and found I'd lost the last forty years of my life. Oh, I can remember the details but it's like they happened to someone else, as if I read about them in a book or saw them in a film. One moment I was sixteen, the next I'm an old man. It's like everything has been taken away from me and put behind a glass wall. I can still see it but I can't get to it anymore. I've still got friends and I remember how we all met over the years but they mean nothing to me now." His voice had taken on an odd flatness, like a rundown battery.

"Are you married?" Chiyo asked, self-consciously. "What about your wife, do you feel the same way about her?"

"I thought you said you'd read my file. No, I'm not married. Never had the time to find anyone who'd put up with me. No kids either, I'd have liked some but..." He shrugged.

She studied his face sideways to see if he was faking but the perplexed expression seemed genuine. "I see that you're a lawyer", she tried again. "Has this loss of... focus affected your work?"

"That's the one thing that hasn't changed. My job is just facts; the condition made no difference until the headaches started."

"You don't enjoy it then, the law I mean?"

"My father was a lawyer and he always wanted... I've got a kind of knack for it. I don't enjoy it though, not for one second. I really wanted to paint, you see."

"To paint...?"

"Landscapes. It's too late now though, isn't it? Too late for a lot of things..."

Chiyo instinctively put a hand on his knee then quickly snatched it away. If he noticed the gesture he didn't react. After a short silence between them he spoke again. "I'm a Christian, did you know that at least?"

"Yes," she blushed slightly at his reprimand, "I do remember that bit."

"You're a Buddhist, presumably."

"I'm not really anything."

"So what do you imagine happens to us when we die?" he continued. "Where does all that consciousness go?" She shrugged. "Some vast pool of thought-waves out in space maybe, awaiting rebirth...?"

"I don't know. Probably nowhere; this is it."

"I don't believe that, you see. I believe our souls go to heaven, even yours."

She gave him a rueful grin as she got up to leave. "That's a nice thought. Thanks for including me."

He gave her a tired nod then a slight wave of the hand, as if dismissing her. When she looked back he was staring out at the darkening hills again. As her carriage pulled away ten minutes later he was still there.

"Are you sure you still want to do this, Chiyo?"

The hospital's Chief Surgeon, Rikuto Fujiwara, had mentored her meteoric career since her internship so his use of her first name wasn't out of place. She knew he only did it when concerned his protégée might be making a mistake. Like right now for instance.

"Yes Sir, I do," Chiyo nodded vigorously to emphasise her decision, "it's worth a try. Since the collapse he's remained in a deep coma so we can try things we couldn't before. Take a risk. We've nothing left to lose and nor's he."

"You certainly have got something to lose; your reputation. You've already made a perfectly viable decision and now you're backsliding. It looks bad."

"But it's a very interesting case Sir; you've seen his file. It's unique."

"The hippocampus is swollen by the tumour. So what?" the old man replied.

"But what about all the neural activity, the intense dopamine release?"

"He's your patient not your guinea pig, Doctor Sasaki. Let the poor man go." Chiyo gave an annoyed shake of the head and continued prepping for surgery. "Then I may as well join you, if your brilliant career is about to disappear down the toilet we might as well make it worthwhile. Just like in the old days, eh?"

"Thank-you, Rikuto," she replied, failing to keep the relief from her voice.

"I don't know what the hell you expect to find though," he told her grumpily.

Chiyo was back in her office after the operation, slumped in her seat. She was exhausted, physically drained, devoid of all emotions bar one; frustration.

Utter damn frustration.

There was a slight knock on the door. She ignored the knock and a heavier one replaced it. She sighed. "Come!"

The Chief Surgeon stuck his head into the room. "OK? Need to talk?"

She gave another long sigh. "Yes, no... This damn thing...!" He came in and stood behind her chair as she pointed to the image on her laptop screen.

"That's the MSI display I take it."

She nodded absently, not looking back at him. He placed a hand on her shoulder. "Let it go, Chiyo."

"I can't. You know that, you saw it too. Look..." She pointed to a sudden flare of bright energy that rippled outward from the same swollen seahorse-shaped lump she'd shown its host in this very room. That had been barely two months ago, now here she was watching his final moments drain away to nothingness. She clicked on the screen and played back the short passage again; *flare, ripple, dissipate.* And again; *flare, ripple...*

"Stop it my dear; don't torture yourself. You did all you could, more than you should have done to try and keep him alive. It was an impossible procedure; too much sensitive tissue, far too many vital nerves. You would have destroyed the whole synaptic region, even if you'd got the cancer. He would have been a vegetable, you did him a favour."

"So what's all that?" She made a stabbed gesture at the ever-repeating lightshow. "You saw the readings; for a few seconds they went right off the scale. His last dying moments then...bang, zoom, everything's gone haywire."

She felt him remove the hand. "I advise you to drop it, Doctor. Something happened in theatre that can't be rationally explained. It's not the first time and it won't be the last. Get over it!"

But Chiyo's mind scarcely registered the old man's rebuke. It was too busy racing a spark along the neural pathways of Katsu Abe's disintegrating brain, leaping the synaptic gaps at each neuron end. What would he have seen, experienced, in those dramatic last few seconds? Another life perhaps, the one he should have lived? Just a few short seconds, but dreams only last that long and they can seem go on forever…

Could you fit a whole lifetime into a dream?

Chiyo played the dazzling images through one more time then shut the laptop lid with a studied finality. She turned to face her old mentor. "Do you believe in Heaven, Rikuto?" He smiled down indulgently then shook his head. "No, neither do I. But sometimes I wish I did."

The Last Protester

The metallic panelling along the outside of Gifu-Hasima station reflected the harsh afternoon sunshine into Rikuto's eyes. He hoped he'd got the time right. Miu had told him to wait at the main exit; he hovered around outside it, kneeling to fuss with the zips on his overnight bag, fruitlessly searching for the sunglasses he knew he'd left on the kitchen table of his small flat back in Takatsuki.

The flat was functional in the same way his life was five years after the divorce from Yoko. Situated near the hospital, it meant he could continue to work the long hours his exalted position demanded. Did all work and no play make Doctor Rikuto Fujiwara a dull boy? he mused as he zipped up the bulky pockets again. Probably; he'd become a workaholic bore, an old one at that. No doubt his young interns silently agreed.

Was that what this slightly crazy trip was about then; his self-respect?

Rikuto had his grandson to thank for his current situation. Masaru had introduced him to Facebook and Skype six months previously as a means for them to keep in contact. His dad's new job had taken the family to Tokyo the year before just as the boy was reaching an age when Rikuto was beginning to find him interesting. He loved Masaru of course, but had never felt like playing the doting grandfather. He told himself he simply didn't have the time: a lazy lie.

His daughter Akemi had certainly never accepted it. "You were the same with me," she'd told him during a slightly drunken goodbye meal that had inevitably turned into an argumentative one. "It was always work, work, work; you missed I don't know how many school plays and prize-givings, you'd have even forgotten my graduation if mum hadn't dragged you along. You probably thought I'd let all that go by now, well you don't forget that sort of thing. I'm not letting you do it to Masaru as well!"

But their year apart had seen Masaru blossom into an intelligent, confident boy who could hold his own in their playful weekend chats. Although Rikuto was loath to admit the fact, they were often the only thing that was pulling him through the week. Yoko would have rolled her eyes at his admission if they'd still been on speaking terms; "So, it's still all about you then?" He could just imagine the scornful words in his head.

So, to start with, the new on-line world had just been about keeping up with Masaru. Gradually though, Rikuto began to investigate its full potential; he contacted old colleagues and high school friends, even some junior doctors he'd had under his wing, especially the pretty female ones. Why not? He was a single man now living on his own with too much time on his hands. Why shouldn't he cultivate a new circle of 'friends' with a tap of his finger? It might seem a bit sad but what harm could it possibly do?

That was how he'd found himself talking to Miu again. He'd leant back in surprise as she peered out of the screen at him, the once familiar face blown up and slightly blurred as if framed in some fairground mirror. Rikuto had wondered how it was conceivable that forty-odd years had passed between them.

"Hello?"

"Yes, it's me, thank-you for responding to my message." There was a long pause while he'd groped for the words he wanted to say. 'Sorry' sounded incredibly weak, but she'd responded before he could even say that.

"It's been a long time; I can't believe it's finally happened." He'd given a secret sigh of relief, hoping she'd take command of the situation. Excitedly, she did: "I've been waiting for this day…"

The once light and breezy voice was now the husky one of a smoker. Large eye's he'd once loved to distraction blinked and grew larger still in the thin face. They were even more heavily shaded with kohl eyeliner than he'd remembered. It had given her a rather clownish appearance.

"I mean, I never thought we'd speak again," she continued more evenly, "it's wonderful to hear from you after all these years. How are you, are you well? I'm sure you must have a lovely family; children, grandchildren even! How nice…" Her words tailed off and there was a longer pause. What he

could see of her slight frame appeared even thinner than the twenty-year-old one that had thrust itself to orgasm on top of him in his dingy campus room. "I'm sorry, I'm gabbling aren't I? It's just shock, that's all."
"No, I apologise. I just happened to come across your name on Facebook. Actually that's a lie; I was searching for you. You're looking great, Miu-san."
She'd given a deprecative shake of long grey-streaked hair. "Now you really are lying." The kohled eyes had blinked gratefully none-the-less.
Another awkward silence this time broken by him. "Actually, I'm divorced."
"Oh... I'm sorry to hear that."
"Yeah, well life... look, we should meet up sometime. I mean, if you're free to do so. Obviously, I don't know your situation but maybe just for a coffee; have a chat about the old days." He'd immediately felt a fool for pushing her too far. She must have a family herself, a man; not some sad old fart like him though.
"The very old days I'm afraid." She'd made a joke of it as if to mask her embarrassment. He'd expected her to make a face-saving excuse and click off. "Actually that's a lovely idea. I see you live in Takatsuki; a little difficult for me to get to, but perhaps you could come up to Gifu. I've got a flat in the city, quite near the station. I can pick you up from there. What do you think?"
Lonely and bored with his own company, of course he'd agreed. He hadn't had sex for quite a while either, hadn't dated in ages apart from a few miserable attempts directly after the divorce from Yoko. Miu had made him feel flattered, excited even; perhaps they could start something new, or better still carry on from their lusty student days. They arranged a day and a time.
Now here he was outside Gifu station, squinting into the slanting sunshine for a blue Mitsubishi Jeep. He turned away from the glare for a brief moment. When he turned back it was there waiting for him, the passenger door open.
Like a lot of things, he hadn't seen it coming.

She really was thin, even more so than she'd appeared on

Skype. When they'd been medical students living in the same accommodation block in the University of Tokyo her frame had been slim like many young Japanese before the national diet became subtly westernised.

Rikuto leant across to give her a clumsy peck on the cheek. Framed in the Jeep's side window the once beautiful face now seemed out of proportion. She'd lost her small but perfect breasts; the top half of a drab un-pressed trouser suit hung straight down the bony chest.

He must have changed in her eyes, the spare body of his youth long ago succumbing to takeaways on late night shifts. He caught his reflection in the car mirror; jowly and red-faced, hair greyly receding across a bald spot made pink in the sun. He was no prize draw; a fact Yoko hadn't been slow to remind him of in their last bad-tempered years.

"It's good to see you again. You're looking really good," she told him.

Even without the Internet's distortion the voice still had an unexpectedly deep rasp. 'She'd been twenty though, just a kid – you were just a kid,' he reminded himself. 'Everything was different then.' He remembered the last words she'd called out, edged with panic as they echoed down the stairwell walls... He shook himself back to the present, realising he hadn't replied. "So are you Miu, so are you. You're... you're looking amazing."

The black-flaked eyes glanced quickly across at him as she pulled out into the mainstream of traffic. For a moment there was something indefinable in them, a hardness that had been undetectable on the laptop's screen. Then it was lost in a thin lip-glossed smile of yellowy teeth. "So, tell me all about yourself then..."

Miu's flat was near the top of a nondescript block somewhere down the backstreets they'd been following since turning off the main road out of the city. He'd only previously zoomed through Gifu on the Shinkansen so, once they'd begun to head away from its raised outline, he was immediately lost. The warren of roads grew ever tighter, their small neat houses crowding in on him as they left the anonymous offices and department stores behind in the evening haze.

She parked underground and he followed behind her to the lifts. She had a slight limp, he noticed. He had a touch of arthritis himself; 'No-one's as young as they used to be,' he thought. He stared at Miu's reflection in the lift's dark glass panels until she caught him and smiled, the harsh lighting throwing the planes of her petite face into stark contrast.

"Well, this is it." Miu rustled her keys in the lock and pushed open the door.

He quickly took in the flat's collection of nondescript rooms leading off a narrow hallway. All had their doors open except one. He glimpsed a sliver of narrow living room with a bowl of fruit and vases of dried flowers on a dresser, garish plates hung on a wall along with various faded photographs in bamboo frames. The rest of the furniture looked old and worn, the carpet threadbare in places half-covered with what appeared to be off-cuts. There was a stale smell hanging in the air; noticing his reaction Miu moved into the kitchen to open a window and the distant drone of traffic invaded the flat. He followed behind her. An ancient grease-stained cooker was wedged into one corner by a chipped Formica work-surface, beneath which a washing machine leaked suds across a patchwork of curling plastic floor-tiles.

He turned to the sun-burnished city skyline so she wouldn't see his face. "You seem well set-up here." It was all undeniably shabby.

"Well, I've done my best, considering." There was something bitter in her voice that made him turn back.

"Considering?"

"You know. It was a long time ago though, things change with time don't they? Some things anyway."

"What do you mean?" he asked.

"Well you've done pretty well for yourself from what you told me in the car. Head of Surgery; that's a big deal. The boy I remember wouldn't have wanted all that."

He thought it was an odd thing for her to say, almost a sneer. Something in her attitude had subtly altered. But then she gave him another toothy smile.

"Go and make yourself comfortable and I'll make us some green tea. I've got some sweet mochi in the fridge. Please, I'll just be a couple of minutes."

"OK, thanks. Through here?" He indicated the narrow room and she nodded.

He studied the photographs on the wall; mostly groups of young people waving lurid banners on various protest marches and sit-ins, taken sometime in the early to mid-seventies judging by their appalling fashion sense. The men wore flairs, big pointy-collared shirts and denim jackets; the girls virtually the same, all angrily demanding something or other with expressions of grim conviction. Miu could be spotted in each one if you looked carefully, the beautiful dark features contorted in photogenic rage. One picture was missing that should have been there.

There seemed to be a gap between these and others of a now middle-aged Miu with a smaller number of mature banner-wielders, dressed in sensible anoraks and duffle-coats outside what looked like government offices. The rage-full expression on the pinched face was still there though.

"Fight the good fight." Almost at his elbow, she'd silently entered the room without him noticing. She set a tray of tea and two plates of mochi down on the coffee table crammed between the sideboard and sofa. "Please, sit with me, you can tell me some more about your wonderful job and lovely family." Again, he sensed her sneering but the smile seemed genuine enough. "Did you tell them you were coming to see me today? I wouldn't want, Yoko was it? I wouldn't want Yoko to be jealous on my account. After all, this is just for old time's sake."

"Erm... As I said in the car, we're divorced now. We don't see that much of each other unless it's something to do with my daughter and grandson." He lowered himself awkwardly beside her, feeling almost elephantine next to the pencil-thin figure.

"Oh yes, divorced, that's right. And your daughter's name's Akemi, and your grandson's Masari."

"Masaru, yes."

"But you haven't told them you're coming to see me either?"

"No, I don't see them so much since her husband's office moved to Tokyo."

"That's a shame; I'm sure he's a nice little boy. Drink your tea; it's a special local blend I bought for today."

The green tea had an unusual, almost nutty, taste: an odd combination he'd not tasted before. Green tea should be thin and bitter; who knows what this stuff was. He sipped at it to please her, though it made him slightly queasy

"What about you then, Miu? I can see you've been busy on the erm... political front, but what about your career? I mean, did you stick with medicine or..." He suddenly realised he knew nothing whatsoever about her. She'd been a keen student before all the political stuff got in the way; more able than him certainly. He glanced around the room searching for a clue; she obviously hadn't made any money. Nursing maybe? Even then she'd have made at least Ward Sister or Matron by now; quite well paid these days. Maybe she'd simply retired? He'd be doing the same himself in a few years.

He somehow sensed it wasn't like that though.

"I never went into medicine. I... lost that chance. Something happened to me. You were there weren't you, remember?"

"I don't know what you mean exactly. Last time I saw you..." He stopped. The last time he'd seen Miu had been that awful day in the Yasuda Auditorium clock tower; why had he blocked that out until this moment?

There had been many other memories of Miu and the others; lounging around the campus together in big friendly groups, playing Frisbee on the lawn over the long hot summers, the parties and the drinking, the intensity of exams and the exhilaration/suicidal depression of their results. Then in '68 it all changed as the conflict from the outside world ruptured into their cosseted lives; Grosvenor Square in London, Berkeley in California, the Sorbonne in Paris – it seemed the old ways were finished; everything around them was going up in flames and they'd all gleefully determined to be part of the conflagration.

Miu joined the All-Campus Joint Struggle Committee. Her boyfriend Daisuke was already one of its leaders, fighting for campus democratisation and an end to the U.S. – Japanese Security Treaty she'd proudly told Rikuto. Yes, she had a boyfriend then, but not him; never him. Apart from that one drunken night of course when she shared his campus dormitory bed to try and make Daisuke jealous; to force the fool to love her as much as she loved him. It hadn't worked; he was handsome and magnetic, the golden-voiced campus big shot every girl worshipped from afar. He could have had anyone he chose, and did. His sleeping around had broken Miu's heart. The timid Rikuto had never told her how much she'd broken his.

It had been a clichéd love triangle of children playing dangerous games in an adult world. But in the winter of '68 they'd all grown up fast. The conflict with the authorities was spreading throughout the universities of Japan but Todai was its main focus; the Diet passed bills giving the boards sweeping powers and the police began zealously to enforce them.

It had all come to a head one January morning in '69 inside the Yasuda Auditorium when the riot squad, camped for weeks on the circular quad outside, had finally broken in. He'd been inside the old building with all the others waiting for the endgame; so had Miu and Daisuke. Now the two of them were amongst the mass of bodies on the eighth floor of the central clock tower. Rikuto remembered hearing the police copters' whirring blades, seeing them through the tower's broken windows as they hovered menacingly outside. Around him the batons rose and fell, pushing the shouting students back up the stairs as they tried again and again to break through of the thick ruck of police. Rikuto had been on the seventh floor; looking up above him he could just make out Miu standing at Daisuke's side. The peace-lover had a bloodied baseball bat in his hands as he screamed down at the throng. Figures behind him were frantically lobbing Molotov cocktails through the windows' shattered glass. Rikuto had started to choke on the waves of tear gas wafting up the stairwell.

Then, with a sudden clarity of mind, he'd known it had all gone too far; why was he getting mixed up in all of this? As he began to squirm back through the mêlée the yellow helmets pushed on through the last resistance, smashing it out their way. Knocked to the floor and trampled, he'd looked up through the legs to see Miu's long black hair and kohled eyes, heard her cry out in defiance as the first policeman reached out to drag her down the stairs; heard the crack of the baton against her beautiful head as she fell...

Yes, that had been the last time he'd seen her.

How long had he been sitting there in silence, her question hanging in air?

He began a stuttered reply but she cut him off:

"I remember someone hitting me. A cop dragged me downstairs, smashing my head against them one step at a time, something in my leg snapped and the pain felt like an explosion, blood ran into my eyes so I couldn't see properly. Then I was outside lying on the lawn, clutching my leg, holding my head in agony; I had a fear my brains were poking out; that I had to hold them in somehow. I was sticky all over in my own blood; I'd pissed myself and I couldn't tell the piss from the blood; it all ran together and the smell made me vomit but I couldn't let go of my head to wipe the sick away. Then I was being thrown around inside an ambulance with some stupid fuck of a nurse trying to strap me down. Then there were bright lights and a trolley bumping beneath me, my leg was on fire, my mind was screaming. I was screaming..." She stopped.

After a long pause he said "Miu, I'm so sorry. I hadn't forgotten..."

"I was in the hospital for three months," she continued. "They monitored my visitors, questioned my friends. Soon everyone stopped coming apart from my parents then even they stopped. You never came. I got out eventually and tried to apply to re-take my final year but they'd told the board not to let me back. You could have said something to them but you never did, never lifted a finger. They got to my parents too, made them disown me. I had no money. I had to find a way to pay the hospital bill, to live somehow. The first years were very tough, but I survived. I made new friends, people like me; outsiders. We did things that made a difference, took the fight to the authorities. Even when they arrested me again and tried to convince me I was mad my new friends still waited for me."

She raised her head to stare at him. There was something disconnected in the stare, as if she were looking through a sheet of opaque glass at him.

"You never waited for me, Daisuke."

He tried to swallow but his throat felt dry. "Miu...I'm Rikuto."

"That's a funny little name you've given yourself. I understand, so your pretty wife and lovely children won't know about us. We don't have to keep up that pretence anymore my darling. They don't know you're here with me; we're together again and that's all that matters. The past is the past; I won't hold it against you but I just want to understand why you didn't wait for me. That's reasonable, isn't it?"

"Miu, this isn't funny..." He found it difficult to get the words out. His tongue was swelling in his mouth, his throat suddenly closing up. He tried to suck in air but an invisible barrier seemed to have formed itself around his mouth.

"What have you done to me...?" Rikuto flung the tea across the room. "What... what's in it? What did you use?"

"It's alright Daisuke, you won't feel any pain. I'll be with you."

"What the fuck did you...? I'm Rikuto, I'm not Daisuke you mad bitch...!"

He tried to get up but she was quicker, pushing him back, moving her thin frame across him as the skeletal hands thrust his head down into the sofa. He felt his chest muscles cramp and tighten; his arms and legs fail to respond to his mind's panicky instructions, as if they'd been severed from his body. He gagged for breath but found none. The dusty, dirty stink of the sofa in his nostrils would be the last thing he'd ever smell, the grainy groups of angry students in their bamboo frames the last he'd ever see.

He began to lose consciousness... then one last thought: Masaru. He hadn't said goodbye to Masaru.

Rikuto balled up every last pitiful ounce of strength that remained in his body and focussed it in the base of his spine. Then he pushed against the sofa.

He rolled out from beneath Miu's paper-thin body and hit the carpet with a dull thud. Frantically commanding his arms and legs to work in tandem he began to worm his way to the door only to sense her drape herself across his back again. He rose up on his knees with her still clinging on then toppled over sideways into the coffee-table. There was a splintering sound and he felt something sharp slice through the back of his hand. He crawled around to find Miu lying in the bent metal frame with a mustard coloured lump on her forehead. Her eyes were shut but the blood seemed to be mainly from him.

He pulled himself up and lurched out to find the bathroom. Two fingers down his throat brought up the scummy green liquid. He drank some water and splashed his face then walked slowly back to the sitting room. She was still where he'd left her. He bent to feel for a pulse; she was still alive. If he left now that would be it. She had no idea where he lived; he'd only told her Taksutski city in the car, even if she found the hospital no-one there would take her ramblings seriously.

Rikuto grabbed up his jacket and made for the stairs. In the corridor he saw the other room, the only one with its door shut. Somehow, he had to look.

It was filled with junk; stacks of political pamphlets, some curling with age. Various banners were rolled up and propped along the walls; he opened one up that read 'STOP THE AIRPORT – NARITA FOR THE FARMERS' in faded red paint. There was a close musty smell like an old storeroom nobody visits anymore. On a writing desk full of half-written scrawls of paper stood a framed picture; the one missing from the living room wall. Again, it was a group of long-haired student protesters, shaking their fists and mouthing demands at a row of riot-shielded police. His young self was there, slim and almost unrecognisable. Along the frontline from him was Miu, her face beautiful in its intensity, her arm draped almost casually around the neck of another. The young man's face had been crudely cut out, replaced by the cardboard back of the frame.

Rikuto could still clearly see it was Daisuke.

He heard steps to his right and turned. She stood in the doorway, dishevelled and disorientated. The kohl had run into tear-streaks down her face so that now she truly did have the appearance of a mad clown. He pushed past her. For a moment he was unsure which door was the exit then he was out of the flat and staggering down the stairs.

"Daisuke!" He stopped half way down the stairwell at her

voice. "Wait, I'm sorry..." He heard desperate footsteps then a cry followed by a slithering, bumping noise.

Cautiously, he began to climb back up.

She lay sprawled down the steps, one foot caught in the railings to that the whole leg was twisted at a bizarre angle. Confused eyes stared up at him. A dark patch of blood from her forehead began to stain the stair carpet.

He heard doors opening along the upper corridor and backed carefully down again. Random voices echoed.

"What's happened?"

"She must have fallen, somebody call an ambulance."

"She's still breathing; can someone help her, please! We need a doctor, does anyone know...?"

Rikuto shut the back door to the car park as quietly as he could. He wiped the blood off the door handle with his sleeve. Then he turned and ran blindly in the direction he imagined the Shinkansen station to be.

A girl, her coat dripping wet from the thunderstorm, stepped into the lift just as the doors were shutting. Startled by her sudden presence he momentarily imagined a young Miu had somehow followed him to Yoko's apartment. He shook the irrational thought away. Although small, her dark hair was short and she looked nothing like Miu. Rikuto noticed she was shaking, a hand held to her head as if in pain. He'd managed to clean himself up in the train, change into a clean shirt and find a large enough plaster in the washroom's first aid kit to cover the cut on his hand. The girl didn't seem to notice it.

"Are you OK?" he asked. It was a relief to speak to someone normal again. "Can I help? I'm a doctor."

She grimaced. "Migraine; I'll be alright thanks."

"I passed a chemist a couple of streets away. I think they were still open. 50mg of Sumatriptan should do it; I've got my prescription pad with me..."

"Its fine, I'll be OK. I've got something upstairs that usually works."

"Well, if you're sure?"

"Yes, thanks anyway." The lift doors opened. "This is my floor." They slid shut again as he watched her walk away.

Rikuto tapped his ex-wife's apartment door gingerly. He thought she hadn't heard then the door opened a sliver against the chain-lock.

"What are you doing here at this time?"

"Sorry, I need to see you."

"I wish I'd never given you that damn key code."

"Please Yoko..."

There was the sound of the lock sliding back then Yoko was standing in front of him in the silk dressing gown he'd bought for her fifty-seventh birthday.

"Are you completely mad?" She sounded more tired than angry.

"Sorry, I just... I've had a very bad day. Can I... I mean would it be alright... I don't want to stay by myself tonight you see. Just tonight, put me up on the couch. I don't mind."

"Why should I... what's that on your hand?"

"I was cut. I mean I cut myself..." He saw her look. "Not like that, it was an accident. I can't explain it tonight, maybe tomorrow after I've had a rest."

"You've got a bed in your own place I presume. I suppose you don't get much rest in that either, knowing you."

"Please Yoko, not tonight. I just want to stay with someone I trust."

"Someone you...? What's happened Rikuto, you're starting to freak me out."

"It's just... I met someone I hadn't seen..." He stared at her. "She didn't remember me Yoko, she didn't even know who I was! She thought I was some sort of... ghost, from her past; not me at all. I thought... I thought for a moment I wasn't going to see Akemi, or Masaru, or... or you... ever again." He felt tears sliding down his face but didn't try to stop them. "She wanted to drag me down with her, Yoko, drag me back into the past. I'm not a ghost, I have a life...!"

He felt Yoko's arms around his waist, pulling him to her; he bent his head to her shoulder. Suddenly he was clinging to her the way a drowning man holds on to his last breath, still praying for another.

The Girl Downstairs

Manami Ochi's headache had begun to subside at last. It had been a particularly bad one this time, like a drill bit tearing through her head; worse than all the others she'd suffered in the last few weeks. There had been a storm earlier that afternoon, battering itself against the windows of her trendy new apartment. But as the storm cleared, so did the pain in her head; as the pattering rain on the condo's walkways stilled, so did the confusion in her mind.

She began to feel at peace again.

She perched on her smart leather sofa to take in the beautiful apartment. She was so lucky to live here. It had everything the agency had promised: a concierge, a kitchen with waste disposal unit, electronic toilet, both induction and under-floor heating, although both seemed to be failing at the moment. Even a dry cleaning service, plus it was situated in the trendiest area of Mishima City.

No people though, it didn't seem to include people; or friends. The few occupants she'd come into contact with had been distant and distracted, unwilling to make eye contact. Even the concierge refused her shy attempts at friendliness. The woman would unexpectedly let herself in without bothering to use the intercom or even knock on her door. Just barge it open with her plastic bucket banging against her knees slopping pools of water across the deep-pile carpet. When she remonstrated with her, the tired old eyes would turn in Manami's direction and blink uncomprehendingly.

She shivered in the apartment's chill.

Despite the beautiful surroundings she felt isolated and lonely. Perhaps she'd always been this way: even when surrounded by those claiming to be her friends. They'd been no more than passing acquaintances, never managing to stick for very long. Only once, maybe once... She found it hard to remember. An unbridgeable chasm was filled with a swirling mist her memory could no longer penetrate. Vague shapes moved on the other side but she'd left them all behind. Here was where she belonged now.

A sudden movement in the corner of the room caught her eye; a blurred figure crossed her vision. Manami glimpsed another room slipping by filled with pulsing primal colours, as if about to spill into her own. The image disappeared abruptly. She stood on the spot it had vanished. For a few moments she imagined she could hear indistinct echoes, random bangs and screams.

Manami sat down heavily on the sofa again. Was her new apartment haunted? She tried to rally her senses. It had obviously been a trick of the twilight; some garish neon reflection, maybe the projection of carriage lights from a distant Shinkansen. She'd just imagined it, noises and all. She was suddenly very tired, and cold; it would have to wait till morning.

All would become clear then. Manami closed her eyes and laid her head back on the smooth leather.

When she opened them again it had grown dark outside. She really should go to bed. She pulled herself reluctantly to her feet and walked over to look at the nightscape. Laid out beneath her, strings of streetlights marched up through the city to the distant purple hills. She reached to close the blinds then jerked in surprise at a knock on the door. Who could it be, she knew no-one here; and why so late? It came again, heavier.

Manami hesitantly crossed the room. "Who's there?"

A muffled voice said. "Miss...?" Then, louder, "Open the door please Miss!" She paused for a long moment then turned the handle.

There was no-one outside in the corridor.

Manami awoke to a bright crisp morning; strong sunshine rippled across her slender form from the half-drawn blinds. She felt a sudden surge of expectancy as her senses attuned themselves to the new day; something wonderful was going to happen, she was sure of it.

Sometime later she decided to go out, maybe take a walk amongst the temples and shrines of Rakujuran Park. She loved the Sakura trees there, although their beautiful cherry blossom had long since been swept away. She'd gone there on her first night in her new city, glancing at the lovers strolling hand in hand with shared smiles of intimacy. Soon they'd be returning to the bedrooms they'd left that morning. She'd felt jealous; she wanted a smile of her own, a promise of fulfilment. It wasn't fair.

At the end of the building's concrete walkway there was a small rock garden then beyond that a high wooden fence with a gate. Manami pushed the gate but despite a dry squeak it refused to move. She pushed again and a sliver of path appeared in the gap.

"Hello." Manami turned at the girl's voice. "Hello there, going for a walk?"

Manami had never seen her before. She was quite tall, much taller than her anyway. Long straight hair dyed a light brown, layered severely, cascaded over the shoulders of a smart tweed-style jacket. Manami's eyes followed it down a partially buttoned white blouse to a swell of creamy breast that rose and fell, as if the girl had been running to catch up with her. She turned to push the gate again.

"I'm Kotone," the girl said breathlessly, "apartment thirty-two, one floor down from yours."

Still looking out at the path Manami replied, "You know my apartment?"

"I… passed you in the corridor once, is it a nice view from your balcony?" Manami nodded automatically. "I expect it's very modern, they're all so lovely aren't they and this little garden is so pretty? Sorry, I'm babbling. I was a bit nervous to say hello to you. I wondered..."

"You wondered?"

"If you'd like to have a coffee with me; or I have Jasmine tea. I've just bought some in case... in case I ran into you."

Manami turned back to face the girl. "I was going to go for a walk in Rakujuran Park."

"It's lovely there in the summer isn't it? Although not so nice in autumn and it's going to rain soon. You'll get ever so wet without a jacket or coat."

Manami looked down. She wore only a thin blouse, a red one, tucked into a tight pair of blue jeans turned up above her thin ankles.

Her feet were bare.

She saw the Kotone girl looking at them as well. "You'll

hurt yourself like that." She turned and headed briskly back up the path towards the walkway. "Number thirty-two, third floor; I'll put the kettle on for us."

The apartment was smaller than hers. It had the same basic layout but the window wasn't as big and showed a sprawl of office buildings and a car-park. It looked clean and tidy enough but neutral and characterless. There was a bookcase, almost empty of books and a wooden shelving unit with various vases and little painted boxes plus a couple of fussily-dressed dolls arranged randomly. She noticed one box in particular, a bright blue plastic one with a picture of Mini-Mouse on it. Then she realised the dolls were Disney characters as well. There was just a small sofa and a coffee table in the meagre floor space but no television. The whole place had an air of impermanence.

"Here we are, please..." Kotone laid a tray with two porcelain cups of dark tea on the glass coffee table and sat down next to her on the sofa. Jasmine prickled her nose as the girl handed one to her. She felt odd, dizzy: momentarily disconnected from the room and the girl. She put a hand to her face as the tea's aroma swum inside her head.

"Oh, I feel..."

"Are you alright, Manami-san? It is Manami, isn't it?"

"Yes...I feel a little faint." She shook her head; how did the girl know her name? "It's nothing, how silly."

The girl reached across to place a hand on her brow. Her fingers felt hot on Manami's skin. "You're cold," she told her.

"Yes, I suppose I am." But Kotone made no effort to get up and switch the heating on. It was even more cold in this apartment than in Manami's own but the girl didn't seem to notice. She took the un-drunk cup from her hands and set it back on the tray. Manami's head began to clear.

"Maybe we should do this another time, when you're ready."

"I'm sorry..."

"It doesn't matter, there's plenty of time to get to know one another. It's lonely up there on your own, isn't it?"

Manami nodded and felt an irrational tear creep into the

corner of her eye. She got unsteadily to her feet. "I'd better go."

"I'll be here when you need me." Kotone told her as she shut the door.

She was staring at the ceiling in the darkness, watching the reflected glare of car headlights from the highway flash across it. She didn't know what time it was; the clock on her bedside table seemed to have stopped. Something was wrong but she didn't know what; something to do with the girl downstairs. She couldn't get the smell of Jasmine tea and the blue Mini-Mouse box out of her mind. She wouldn't go there again, avoid the girl if she saw her. That would be less confusing.

Out of the darkness there came the sound of a girl crying, so close it seemed to be inside the actual room with her. It came again, shrill and desperate, then suddenly stretched into a scream.

Manami sat up in bed, shaking. It had happened again.

The apartment door opened to show Kotone's fulsome figure swathed in a white nightdress almost transparent in the half light. Manami gave a little bow of apology then spoke hesitatingly. "Please, I'm so sorry but something happened upstairs, there was someone crying, a girl...I don't know who but she was inside... I mean she couldn't have been..."

The other girl put a gentle arm around her. "You had a bad dream, is that it?"

"Yes... a dream... but it seemed so real."

"They always do." She suddenly gave her a hug. Manami tensed. "Why you're shaking. It must have really scared you. Why don't you come in for a while?" The hug tightened. Manami started to respond then pulled away. "It's alright Manami."

"I'm being stupid. I shouldn't have come."

"Yes you should. Let me help you." Kotone's hand held on to hers. "Come."

She found herself being guided through the same room, now in darkness, to another, half-lit, at the far end. This one had only enough space for a small wardrobe, dressing table and single bed.

"I'm afraid this is all I've got. Let's get some sleep and we can talk about your dream in the morning."

"I really should be getting back," Manami heard herself reply.

"Stay here just tonight, please. We're both a little lonely, aren't we?"

Without waiting for an answer Kotone slipped in beneath the bed's duvet then held it open for her. "Why don't you make yourself more comfortable?"

Manami nodded shyly and unbuttoned the red blouse, then peeled off the jeans. She shivered then felt Kotone's body warmth surround her. It was like being inside a cocoon.

The two women lay together in the narrow bed, not quite touching. Manami reached up to turn off the bedside light. She felt a hand on her wrist.

"Leave it on." Kotone whispered. The touch was as hot as before; hotter. "You're still so cold, let me warm you up."

Manami felt Kotone's hand move to rub her bare arm while her other began a circular motion in the small of her back. Both were almost scalding as their heat gradually diffused inside her skin. She arched her back and sighed. The hand left her arm and reached around to cup her small breast. Its fingers pushed up under her bra to squeeze the nipple. Now the other hand was moving further down inside her pants and between the slender cheeks, forcing her legs open. Manami sighed again then automatically clinched her thighs against Kotone's probing fingers. She cried out then turned to kiss the girl's warm mouth, carrying on down to her full breasts. The nightdress lifted over Kotone's head and the long straight hair fell in sweet smelling waves across Manami's back. Both girls were moving in time with each other now, a perfect interlocking jigsaw of flesh. As the other's sweat mingled with her own Manami felt a searing heat start to build inside her body. Then, suddenly, it exploded in a fireball of sensual fury. She gave a little cry and lay back exhausted. Too stunned to speak, she felt the last of the clinging chill finally slip from her skin.

Manami opened her eyes. She was lying in the bed on her

own. The sound of water from somewhere else in the apartment told her Kotone was taking a shower. She decided to join her but then another sense held her back. The feeling that something was wrong came again, much stronger this time. It wasn't just in her place but down here with this strange earthy girl as well, outside in the little rock garden, down by the gate that wouldn't open. The sliver of path she'd managed to see through the gap had been unfocussed and somehow threatening, as if warning her to stay within the confines of the apartment block. The girl had caught up with Manami just as she'd begun to take a step outside; what would have happened if she'd completed that step? Did the girl know?

Suddenly Manami had to see inside the blue Mini-Mouse box. She hurriedly pulled the red blouse around her and made for the living room; she found a standard lamp and turned it on then crept softly across to the shelving unit. The Disney dolls stared accusingly at her in the half-light as her shaking fingers picked up the blue box and prised open its lid. There was a photograph inside; two framed figures on a mechanical ride caught shrieking and laughing, their hair flying out behind them. One had much longer hair than the other. She took the picture over to the lamp and stared down at its contents.

She could see the details quite clearly now.

"Yes, it's you and me. I was wondering when you'd find it." Kotone stood in the doorway with a towel wrapped around her. Light brown no longer, the wet hair hung in black snakes across her shoulders.

"I don't know you..." The statement sounded false in her ears.

"Yes you do, you've just forgotten me. It's alright; I didn't expect you to remember. Maybe next time you will."

"Next time...?"

"Or the time after that... We're not going anywhere, you and I; we've got a whole lifetime left for you to remember." Her words sounded somehow bitter.

"Remember?" Manami's mind was in freefall. Why was the girl saying these things to her? Who was she?

As if reading her thoughts, the other moved quickly across

the room and took Manami's hands in her own. "To remember me, remember yourself... for God's sake try to remember us Manami my love, remember and wake up!"

She was crying now, Manami saw. Big brown eyes red-rimmed in pain blinked tears away to run down the beautiful face; the face next to hers in the photograph, the one she somehow knew she loved. She wanted to lick the salt tears away, swallow them like tiny pills to *make* her remember.

She reached up to hold the face still. "Help me, then."

Kotone took her hands away and nodded. She went out to the kitchen and came back with a small tin of tea. She opened the lid. "Smell..."

A wave of Jasmine hit Manami's senses as a whirlwind of memories unleashed itself:

She'd just moved in to her new apartment, tired, head throbbing, more than throbbing – splitting in two. It was worse than in the weeks before, far worse – she was shaking now, crying, down on her knees in the deep-pile carpet, hands pressed against the pressure inside her head as she screamed in pain; "Ow... Ow! Help me! Oh my God somebody please help me...!" A banging noise, then; "Miss? Open the door Miss, Police." Blue lights from outside swirling around her, she was lying on her back as they flashed across the ceiling, "Miss...? OK, stand back inside!" There was a stabbing pain between her eyes, everything shot through with primary colours, a splintering of wood and a crash... and then the cold, the terrible cold; and the darkness...

She felt herself about to collapse but Kotone caught her, wrapped her arms around her. "Remember Manami? We'd make love in the afternoons and I'd bring you Jasmine tea. It was your favourite; remember? You must try to remember, to wake up my darling! You must, you really must...!"

Manami sat on her smart leather sofa staring out at the chill autumn sky. There had been a storm earlier that the afternoon, battering itself against the windows of her trendy new apartment. But as the storm cleared, so did the pain in her head; as the pattering rain on the condo's walkways stilled so did the confusion in her mind.

She began to feel at peace again.

Sometime later she decided to go out for a walk in Rakujuran Park.

The Cop and the Monk

The new Kinki Regional Police Bureau's headquarters was a vast white square building situated just across the road from Osaka Castle and its dark wide moat. The giant building was as imposing in its own way as the famous old landmark itself – both strongholds of power, both symbols of law and justice. It had a heliport, a pretty good restaurant and miles of offices and meeting rooms; and, of course, a large holding jail. The building was situated in Chou Ward alongside the city's financial district and its various national embassies. Yuuto Kikuchi had thoroughly enjoyed his last three months there doing his National Police Agency training programme. It would all end next week though when he returned to his home city of Kyoto and, of course, Chihiro.

That was the problem. He'd have to work out what to do about Chihiro in the next few days. Did he still love his wife? Perhaps even more pertinently, did she still care about him?

He sighed inwardly as he pushed the chrome and glass doors and walked past the main desk to the locker room to clock off. Apart from all the martial arts, first aid and firearm training the prefectural officers were given, they also went out on patrol with the station's regular officers. Yuuto had just finished his shift and was looking forward to a beer with the friends he'd made on the course. Someone had earlier mentioned a nightclub they knew of a few blocks away and he'd agreed, somewhat guiltily thinking of Chihiro, that the suggestion was definitely worth consideration. Actually, he'd been looking forward to it all day.

A call from behind stopped him in his tracks. "Officer Kikuchi?"

He cursed silently, spun on his heels and saluted. "Sir...!"

The Training Inspector favoured him with a mirthless grin. "I heard about the little expedition tonight Officer. I'm afraid that place has been declared out of bounds for the trainees. Not good for the Bureau's image in the city; I'm surprised Personnel didn't tell you guys that in the induction meeting three months ago. Or perhaps some of you missed that bit."

"Yes Sir. I was forgetting." Yuuto kept his eyes trained on a patch of wall to the left of the Sergeant's head.

"Well don't forget anything else Officer Kikuchi. Your final interview is next Wednesday; I suggest you spend your downtime preparing for that."

"Sir, yes Sir."

He walked over until he stood next to Yuuto's shoulder. "Don't fuck up son, you'd be better than most of the rest if you could just learn to focus. We need serious people." Yuuto said nothing. "By the way," the Inspector continued, "well done on that Mishima City incident with the girl last week. The report's on my desk; you acted quickly, its good to see the medical training we give you isn't going entirely to waste."

"Thank-you Sir." Yuuto beamed inside. "Do we know…I mean is she…?"

"That's not our business anymore, son. Right, I know it's the end of your shift but I've a little job for you first. You can claim it on overtime. The Desk Sergeant has the details."

"Yes Sir." Yuuto gave him an awkward sideways glance with the salute.

"Good lad, carry on."

'There's always a catch…' Yuuto thought as the Inspector walked away.

He went over to the desk. "Officer Kikuchi?" Yuuto nodded then remembered to snap out another salute. "He's over there. Just take him to this address." The Desk Sergeant pushed a print-out across the desk. "Try not to get lost, OK?"

"What's he done, I mean what's the case? Sir…?"

The man looked up from his laptop screen. "Not that you need to know but he's a witness to a suicide. We can't keep him for questioning any longer so you're taking him home."

"What kind of suicide?"

"The messy kind; some idiot jumped in front of a train. He was the last guy to talk to the jumper a few seconds before. That's all I know."

"Which one is he?" There was a small group of miserable-looking people dotted around the reception area. Some had their heads buried in magazines, most stared vacantly around them at the general bluster in the busy office. The Desk

Sergeant lifted a bored finger to one of them. "Says he's a monk; doesn't look like a monk to me."

"A monk...?" Yuuto followed his direction to a small squat man in a neat blue business suit. He was reading a golf magazine. The only thing monk-like about him was the completely bald head gleaming under the office lighting.

"Take a car from the pool, they've been told to expect you. And don't take all night; we've got better uses for them than taxis."

Yuuto looked at the address on the printout. "Shitennō-ji temple in Tennoji Ward."

"It's the Ward directly south of Chuo. Just take a right outside and go straight down Uemachi-suji until you see a big temple on your right. You'll have to go round to the main entrance at this hour. Apparently he's one of the night watchmen there so he can let himself in. Drop him off and put the car back in the bay then you can piss off home."

"I thought you said he was a monk?"

"They're very adaptable. It's probably a noble calling, just like our job."

Yuuto returned the Desk Sergeant's good-natured grin and strode across to the man who failed to look up at his presence. Yuuto tapped the golf magazine. "I'm to take you home. Let's go, I should have been off duty ten minutes ago."

The man slowly lowered the magazine to stare up at him. He had a round, almost child-like face, but the eyes immediately held Yuuto's own. There was something both calm and dangerous in them, an indefinable strength that he found difficult to look away from. It was so unexpected that he realised he still had his mouth open and shut it quickly.

"What's your name?" the man asked.

"Yuuto..." Yuuto answered, before realising that he had. "I mean Officer Kikuchi badge 13250, Sir. I've been asked to take you back to your place of residence."

The man stood up, smoothed his immaculately-creased trousers then buttoned his jacket. "Good. Shall we go then, Officer Yuuto?"

It was almost ten-thirty by the time he'd finally driven the black and white patrol car up the car pool ramp onto the road that went directly south to the temple. His guest remained silent in the back, slumped a little in his seat as he stared out at the busy Friday night traffic. 'All going out drinking and clubbing or home to their kids', Yuuto thought, 'and I'm doing neither.'

After this pointless errand he would be back in his tiny room in the trainee's accommodation block with the rest of the weekend to worry about his impending interview. He'd phone Chihiro when he got back; talk things over with her. Or maybe not: he'd better wait until he had something to say, one way or another. He'd have to make up his mind about her before the end of next week…

"Problems, officer Yuuto…?" For a moment Yuuto couldn't work out who'd spoken; he was so wrapped up in his private thoughts he'd already forgotten his odd passenger in the back seat.

"What?"

"I said problems; you seem to have some. I can always tell."

"That's none of your business." Yuuto snapped back.

"Women are always a problem, one way or another," the man continued as if not hearing, "you either love them too much or not enough. I think maybe with you it's the latter."

Yuuto felt his face flush with anger. Who was this pretentious little bastard pretending to read his thoughts? He'd throw him out right now but that would mean more trouble than it was worth if the guy made a complaint.

"Why don't you just keep quiet until we get to your address? That would be my advice Sir."

He saw the round moon-face nod in the mirror before turning to stare out at the spot-lit hulk of Osaka Castle as they crawled past.

"You could do worse than ask my advice though," he spoke as if addressing the words to the driver of the car beside them. "People ask me things like that all the time."

"Just keep quiet." Yuuto advised him.

They made the lights this time and he opened the car up a little before slowing down to join the queue edging towards the next intersection.

"Did they tell you why they hauled me in?" He was still staring vacantly out of the window.

"None of my business; I'm just driving you home." Yuuto replied evenly.

"Oh, it's not my home."

"Your work then, night-watchman isn't it?"

The man gave an odd little laugh, more a snigger like a naughty child. "Is that what they think I do there? How ironic..."

"That's what you told them, apparently." Yuuto answered, against his better judgement. This guy was an obvious creep, he'd be glad to get rid of him.

There was another silence between them as the patrol car inched along. Just as the lights finally changed to green, his passenger's high-pitched voice came again.

"They think I'm responsible for his death."

"Sorry?"

"The guy who threw himself under the Shinkansen at Osaka station; they think I said something to him. They showed me the CCTV footage, told me they'd brought a lip-reader in to find out what it was."

There was a long pause while he seemed to wait for an expected response. When none came he added, "They were wrong of course, it was entirely his own choice."

"Of course..." Yuuto replied dryly.

"You don't believe me?"

"Oh, I believe you Sir. All very mysterious I'm sure; sounds to me like you were wasting police time."

"I'd say it was more a case of them wasting mine. I have things to do at night in this city; important things. Lives depend on me."

"Really, Sir...?" 'The poor deluded fool,' Yuuto thought. 'No wonder they were in a hurry to get him out of Headquarters.'

The man straightened the blue jacket, self-consciously brushing the lapels. "You think I'm joking?"

"No, I'm sure you're serious. But I'd advise you to leave upholding the law to us in future. We're trained to do it properly; vigilantes just get in our way."

Yuuto saw a tick of anger cross the bland face; the eyes

sharpened in the mirror, the fat lips pursed themselves petulantly. "Your people miss nine-tenths of what goes on in this city; you always have. I've always had to clean up the mess you've failed to deal with. Take this man today; you had no records of him, no idea of the things he did to the young women here. The way he tricked them into being his lover then forced them to have sex with degenerates. The way he made them kill their babies so they could carry on working for him, making him money. You had no idea, but I did. Someone told me; a girl's mother. I went to him, gave him a choice. He saw the situation could have only one outcome if he wanted to keep his soul. Better be a dead man in this world than an animal in the next; a real animal – not the human dog he already was."

The young patrolman's passenger had been leaning forward, almost shouting the words into his ear. Now he slumped back in the seat again as if the outburst had exhausted him. He wiped a hand across his brow then turned his head to gaze out at the neon-lit shops and arcades as if nothing had happened.

Yuuto's mind was racing. The sheer unpredictability of the guy was starting to shred his nerves; one minute calm and sardonic, the next raging madly at imagined injustices. Was he actually dangerous? Another thing; he'd almost just admitted he'd somehow been responsible for the victim's death, even though that was certainly un-provable. He'd admitted to threatening the man, but with wild ramblings no jury would take seriously. Should he report the conversation to the Training Inspector on his return; would he just get laughed for his naiveté? He determined to dump the man as soon as possible and sped up to the maximum speed manageable in the cramped lane of cars.

Then, despite his attempts at concentrating on the road ahead, something made Yuuto look up at the mirror again. He saw two slits of white in the darkness, the black dots inside them trained on his own eyes as if by some kind of magnetic force. The dots had an intensity that made it impossible to look away. For a long moment his vision was stuck on them then a car horn's rasp broke the connection and he reacted automatically to swing the vehicle away from

another.
When he glanced back the black dots in the mirror hadn't moved. They continued to stare directly at Yuuto. He saw the mouth below them open to speak. This time though, the words seemed to form themselves directly inside his mind; all his senses told him there was now total silence inside the car, but still the words came:
"You people are weak – you always have been. You need our strength and guidance to help you find the path. Never forget us; we protect you from the darkness of your desires, the terror of your emptiness. We are the guardians of your soul, Officer Yuuto. Lose that and you lose everything..."

Yuuto didn't know how long he'd been driving; it felt like hours but couldn't be. The journey was no more than a twenty minute one, even with the busy Friday night traffic. With a start he checked the mirror; the little man was gone! Then he heard a gurgling noise and craned his head around. The plump figure lay across the back seat, eyes tight shut, fleshy lips spluttering a wet snore. Yuuto gave a sigh of relief. Realising he'd been holding his breath he let it out in a gulp that appeared to wake his strange charge.
"Officer Yuuto..." He stretched and yawned "Are we there yet?" He swung himself up in the seat, adjusting his jacket then smoothing down his trousers with the palms of his hands.
Yuuto saw a jagged outline of darkness split the evening sky on his right. He slowed the car to find an exit. As they drove nearer he could make out the shape of a five storey pagoda tower, behind it a larger, longer building with a series of slanted roofs. Their spiky silhouettes seemed alien in the midst of the surrounding block-shaped offices and high rises.
A high concrete wall ran around the buildings and he left the main road to follow it until his passenger grunted, "Here," at a small pagoda-roofed gateway. There was no actual gate, the narrow road just passed through it to a shadowy complex of temples beyond, but there did appear to be a modern cabin nearby with a light showing a figure in its window.
Yuuto rolled to a stop. "I guess this is it then."

"Thank-you Officer Kikuchi, badge 13250. I hope I didn't spoil your evening too much."

Yuuto sat still and said nothing. With a shrug the man opened the door and climbed out. He made a show of brushing down his suit yet again then turned towards the gateway.

Yuuto lowered the passenger side window. "Did you say something to me just now?"

The little man hesitated. "I'm sorry if I got a bit worked up. It's been a long night and I tend to run off at the mouth after I've had a few drinks. I hope I'm not in any trouble, Officer."

"I didn't smell any drink on your breath." Yuuto told him. "And it wasn't that, it was after; I thought you said something strange to me, well stranger than the rest of it. I felt you said something more."

"Felt...? That's a strange word. I've been asleep. I hadn't realised the city was still so busy at this time of night. Please forgive my outburst earlier. I'm sure the police are doing a wonderful job."

He gave a slight bow then walked away into the shadows. Yuuto stared after him then up at the pagoda tower wreathed in night clouds. As he prepared to go, his eyes caught a stray gleam of light from the car's back seat. He reached out and found his hand clutching a smooth cold object; the guy's phone. Yuuto grunted in annoyance. On a whim he flicked quickly through the contents until he found an index of men's full names with another list of male and female first names tagged to each. He somehow had the impression these were all children's. This was strange; was the guy some kind of vigilante after all? He'd report it anyway.

And he supposed he should give him his phone back. Yuuto reluctantly got out and walked towards the cabin, cautiously finding his way in the darkness.

He gave the plastic door a load wrap. A large man in some kind of security uniform opened it immediately, almost hitting him in the face. Yuuto stepped back. "I'm a police officer; I've just delivered a crime witness to this address. He's forgotten his phone; can I leave it with you?"

"No-one's come past me. This is my watch; I'm the only one on tonight Officer." He sounded affronted, as if he

thought Yuuto doubted his ability to handle things his own.
"I'm sorry, I don't know what you're talking about."
"I saw him walk in just now!"
"You're mistaken Officer. Excuse me; I have to get back to my job." The door slammed in his face.
Yuuto swore, shook his head then put the phone back in his pocket.

A few days later Yuuto decided to call his wife. They'd spoken almost every day at the start of his training course but lately it had been reduced to only once or twice a week. He'd felt guilty, sometimes missing her calls on purpose when out on patrol. "Don't you want to get that?" his partner would ask, to which he'd reply, "Later."
But 'later' couldn't keep being put off, and he was coming home next week. The course would be finished a few days after his final interview.
"It's me," he told her, unnecessarily.
"Oh, hello..."
"How are things," he asked, 'is mother alright?"
"She's a handful but I suppose she's OK in general. She doesn't appreciate me though Yuuto."
"I know; I'm sorry..." There was a long pause as both struggled to continue the conversation. "We need to talk, Chihiro."
There, he'd said it.
"Talk about what?" But he could hear the resignation in her voice.
"Things, us..."
He heard a sigh. "We've done all that before."
Another long pause; this wasn't going to work on the phone. "Anyway, the interview's on Wednesday so I'll be back Monday week. I'll have a word with mother then if you'd like."
"Thanks..."
"I had a... something funny happened the other night." He needed to tell somebody about the little man in the blue suit, the 'monk'; someone who wouldn't laugh. Chihiro always listened to him about work. "There was this guy, a witness. They told me to take him home but..." He told her the rest.

It was the day before the interview. Yuuto should have been studying, preparing himself for their questions, especially the trick ones he knew were coming. Instead he felt listless, uncertain. He'd not spoken to Chihiro again after his confused and gabbled tale of Friday night's events. She'd asked him a few questions but even as he gave faltering replies he'd become aware of how ridiculous the whole scenario must sound to another. It had already taken on the aspects of a dream encounter, a half-remembered anecdote for a party or bar told for amusement at his own expense.

He still had the phone. Halfway through the afternoon he knew he needed to get out of his oppressive room in the police trainee's accommodation block.

A random idea came out of nowhere; he would walk to the Shitennō-ji temple. It was a straight route, maybe forty-five minutes. He'd be back in a couple of hours, the edginess gone. Or perhaps he'd find a noodle bar on the way, have a few beers, try to chill out and forget about his interview nerves.

He grabbed a light jacket and pushed the phone into a pocket.

The day was overcast, the light already fading when he reached the walled complex. He found the small temple gate again and entered amongst a small stream of obvious tourists and general onlookers. He walked with the throng towards the buildings he'd glimpsed in profile that night, past the cabin that now seemed empty. Yuuto joined a crowd hanging around a pretty girl in a smart green suit wearing a white hat with 'guide' labelled onto it.

"So, we've entered through the Nakanomon Gate and now we will see the first hall on our right, a Jizo hall. As many of you probably know the Jizo bosatsu is one of the most beloved of Osaka's seven deities. Traditionally he's the guardian of children who died before their parents although in modern Japan he's also worshipped as the guardian of the souls of the stillborn, the miscarried or aborted foetuses. These are some of the many statues left by parents."

Yuuto saw row upon row of concrete shelves stacked one above another. Each carried a line of small stone statues of stylized babies with brightly coloured clothing painted onto most. There was a long list of names fastened onto the bottom shelf. He bent to read it. Halfway down the second column he saw an unusual name he thought he recognised, then a little way on another and another... They'd all been names on the monk's mobile, the list he'd flicked through.

"Let's go inside, follow me please." Yuuto tagged onto the fringe of the sightseers as they pushed inside. The guide led them through to a small courtyard. "All the temples in these grounds were rebuilt in 1963, but the statues themselves are, of course, many hundreds of years older. This one is of Honzon Tatsue Jizo, the bosatsu so many bereaved parents come here to pray to."

Yuuto stared up at the life-size stone statue on the concrete plinth and the hooded eyes in the round child-like face stared back. The fat lips had a serene, almost mocking smile on them. For a long moment Yuuto continued to stand still while others bumped passed him, then he shrugged his shoulders and took out the mobile phone. Stepping carefully forward amongst the smaller statues he placed it in the upturned stone hand.

Then he bowed slightly, returned the smile and turned to go. It was a long walk back to Headquarters.

Whispers

Chihiro Kikuchi switched off the vacuum cleaner. "What, Oka-san?"

The machine's steady whine had camouflaged the din of the subtitled American crime drama from next door. Now it flooded back in, the alien rhythms immediately out of sync with the serenity of the sparsely classical room. She popped her head around the living room door. Natsumi sat in her old armchair enwrapped in the 49 Precinct's latest homicide. She hadn't heard her.

Chihiro shrugged and went back to the vacuum cleaner.

Her mother-in-law's house was old, even by western standards. In Japan it was considered ancient. It had four main rooms, two up and two down, plus a kitchen, toilet and washroom built clumsily onto the back of the building. The ground floor was actually one large space with a fusuma, an opaque sliding partition, dividing it into two: a guest room which doubled as Natsumi's bedroom, and a living room. The living room had long ago surrendered its simple clean lines to a junk heap of furniture, including a big ugly leather armchair where Natsumi took her afternoon nap beneath a crocheted blanket. A hulking sideboard full of big china plates and lacquered vases and bowls and a cupboard stacked with ragged old paperbacks left little room to squirm past. The giant old Sony lodged in one corner and a rug-covered kotatsu leg-warmer took up what space was left.

The two bedrooms upstairs were almost as crowded; one was Yuuto's old room, left almost shrine-like since he was a boy, the other the one they'd somehow managed to exist in without killing each other during the first year of their marriage, before they'd moved to their present apartment in central Kyoto.

In contrast, the room that Chihiro was now cleaning, exactly the same size, was an empty plain of ancient calm and tranquillity. A series of tatami mats fitted the floor-space like rows of perfectly positioned dominos. The beige-coloured walls were blank apart from two bamboo-framed portraits of serious-faced ancestors in ceremonial clothing, Yuuto's grandparents apparently. There was a rolled up futon on the floor with a small electric bedside light next to it and an old leather-bound book. Diffuse daylight struggled to penetrate the shoji blinds covering the large window. Their white screens held the outline of a balcony rail with a faint shimmer of treetops beyond. Yes, the house was so old it actually had its own garden, not a narrow yard with a few pot-plants like modern houses but a proper raised one with little rock islands and miniature trees surrounded by its green carpet of moss. It was dominated by two large pines.

Like many old people's houses, it was totally impractical for someone of Natsumi's advanced age. Cold in the winter, with no heating other than floor heaters and the kotatsu, stifling in summer with no ventilation other than sliding open the outer door to the raised porch which immediately let the mosquitoes and dragonflies in. Natsumi had lived there all her life, but Chihiro was determined to change that.

She ground her teeth at the war of attrition she knew was coming to get her mother-in-law out of her nest for an hour so she could clean that too. It hadn't always been like this but as age took its toll the old lady's ability to care for herself had gradually faded in direct proportion to the dust-trapping flotsam and jetsam Chihiro had to manoeuvre her duster around. Quite frankly, she'd had enough. Actually, she'd had enough a year ago.

Now she was pissed off well into overtime.

The role of 'dutiful daughter-in-law' had never been one she'd agreed to but apparently it was one she now filled. She'd talked to Yuuto about putting his mother into an old people's home many times recently but it had always ended the same way:

"She won't go," he'd tell her, "she'd rather die than leave that place."

"You have to convince her then Yuuto, for her own safety; she could hurt herself on her own there and we can't move back in to look after her. I need to be in the middle of Kyoto, not stuck out in the sticks. My clients expect me to be somewhere reachable; that place doesn't even have a good Wi-Fi connection. And you need to be near the precinct not having to drive all the way out here after a nightshift." Yuuto would automatically nod in agreement to pacify his young wife. "And the neighbours told me she's been out wandering again; they've had to bring her home twice in the last few weeks."

"I know, you told me before."

"Well then!"

"Well, we could talk to her..."

The discussion would carry on around the circumference of the problem like it always did.

'We' meant 'her' of course. For a tough cop Yuuto was an incredible mummy's boy; probably the result of being an only child growing up with his mother in this fusty old museum of a home. Yuuto's father had succumbed to cancer when he was just two; Natsumi had done well really, considering. But she would never take advice from Chihiro, the lucky girl who'd somehow managed to bag her wonderful son. The girl she probably suspected of scheming to sell her house out from under her and keep the money for herself.

So, they were all at an impasse until something changed. Until then she'd 'dutifully' make the trek out to Natsumi twice a week to shop and clean and dust and wash her smelly old clothes, and grin and bear it whilst swearing grimly to herself under her breath. Unfortunately her mother-in-law still had all her hearing faculties despite the deafening effect of the TV.

Chihiro shut off the vacuum again; the old woman was definitely calling to her now. She'd already made her dinner. Cleaning the guest room was her last job before rushing home to do the paperwork she should have done today.

"What is it Oka-san?" she asked. Natsumi began jabbering excitedly at her. "I can't hear you, please turn the television down." She scrabbled for the controls and the American actors lapsed into silent emoting.

"I said, did you hear it that time?"

"Hear what dear?" Chihiro stole a look at the time; she didn't need to get involved in some new distraction now.

"What I mentioned to you earlier at lunch." Although the weather had been a little chilly they'd eaten out in the small high-fenced courtyard beneath the protection of the pine trees' dense branches; anything to get her out of that stultifying room for a while.

"What are you talking about Natsumi-san?" She glanced at her watch again.

Natsumi made an irritated 'oh really' gesture. "The whispering noise, the one I told you I'd been hearing lately. I just heard it again."

"I'm surprised you can hear anything above that row. I had the vacuum on as well, how could you..."

"I'm telling you I heard whispering!" Her face had grown suddenly angry, confused, distrusting.

Chihiro didn't want her to get into a state just as she was leaving. She'd been too distracted by all the arrangements she had to make for her main client Hotaru's upcoming tour to listen properly. Perhaps she should now? It might save time later if the delusions got any worse. She perched on the arm of the sofa, ready to make a quick exit, and said, "Please tell me again about the whispering noises, Oka-san."

"Maybe it's just the pipes, an airlock or something. They're so old. Can you get a local plumber to have a look?" Her husband's voice sounded tired. It would be good to have him home again from his training course with the Osaka district force. He'd told her enough times staying in the poky police accommodation was driving him crazy, perhaps too many. There had been something in his voice lately, a false note the sharpness of the phone connection seemed to amplify. Who knows what cops get up to off duty? And Yuuto was a good-looking man... They'd grown increasingly distant over the last few difficult months; the actual physical separation paralleling the more intimate one. Would she actually know if he were seeing someone else? Would he ever tell her?

Or would it be like the last time?

She tried to shake the thought away. "Okasan's worrying herself about it. I think she's quite frightened really but she won't show me. Everything I do's never good enough for her."

He ignored the last bit; she knew they'd danced around that one enough times already. "Have you heard anything?"

"Of course not, it's in her mind! There may be some noises

at night but old houses have old plumbing and you've told me before that the place hasn't been touched for centuries; there's probably rats scurrying up and down the pipes. She says it happens in the daytime as well but I can't hear it."

"What does she think it is?"

"I told you already: 'whispering', whatever that means. I just don't want her neighbours involved again; I had to sort it all out last time, remember?"

"I know Chihiro, sorry," Yuuto sounded placatory, "I really appreciate your patience with her..."

"We really have to get her into a home!" his wife snapped. "I can't stand it."

"I... I'll call her, promise. I'll try to find out what's going on. As you say it's in her mind but if you could just get it checked out to stop her worrying..." There was male laughter on the other end of the line then it sounded like someone had slapped Yuuto on the back. "Got to go, love you Chihiro."

"I Love..." The line cut her off. She gave an irritated sigh and threw the phone across the kitchen table.

She'd had to take time out from her busy schedule to let the man into the house. It would have confused Natsumi to do it, even if she'd managed to remember why he was there after Chihiro had explained it to her three times.

"Glad you found the place alright, please come in." A small man in a blue boiler suit shuffled off his shoes in the genkan, but shook his head at the slippers proffered.

He stepped up into the hallway. "I'll need to have a good look around."

"Of course, through here please." Chihiro showed him first to the bathroom and toilet then the small washroom at the back.

"OK, leave me to it. Wouldn't mind some tea..."

She nodded and went to placate a worried Natsumi then put the kettle on.

Half an hour later came the report. "I've checked all the water pipes on both floors, checked the one leading outside to the plastic tank as well (Yuuto had put it in to water the garden), there's a bit of knocking when the hot-tap's on full, I've reduced the pressure but it's nothing really. The connection to the kerosene heater outside's tight enough. No leaks anywhere, I've bled any air out of the system that might have been trapped. Basically if you had any problems before you're fine now. How do you want to pay?"

After he was gone Chihiro told Natsumi, "We won't be getting anymore whispering, Oka-san." 'And if you say you can still hear it', she thought, 'maybe that will prove enough for Yuuto to finally sort out the main problem once and for all.'

She sat on the futon in their old bedroom, remembering with a smile their increasingly desperate attempts at sound-proofing their love-making from Natsumi, asleep directly below them in the guest room. The itinerary and contracts of Hotaru Sasaki's upcoming world concert tour were arranged in neat piles before her as she double-checked the pages.

As she was turning the last one Chihiro felt something on her neck. It had been like a sudden release of trapped air from somewhere directly above her. She glanced around then up at the ceiling but it had been much closer, as if someone had breathed down on her. Damn that plumber, he'd messed something up. And he'd been smoking as well; her nostrils picked up faint shreds of rich pungent tobacco.

She got to her feet and stared around the room. It was still crowded with boxes of unlikely wedding gifts they hadn't managed to find a home for yet in the small Kyoto apartment.

Chihiro sat back down on the futon and began putting the pages back in order. She was still fiddling with their plastic file when the voice whispered in her ear.

"What...?" She span around. "Who's there?" She put up a hand as if violated. There was no-one else in the room. Of course there wasn't! Chihiro shook her head to dislodge the last vestiges of the sound. She began to put a finger in her ear before catching herself. What was she doing? It must be the tiredness and the concentration; she always got stressed out with Hotaru's itinerary. Although a personal friend, the maestro was by far her most important client. She couldn't afford to lose her through some careless slip-up.

She went down to the bathroom to wash her face. It was a long journey home and she'd let it get far too late already.

"I'm going now, Oka-san."

When there was no reply she found Natsumi already tucked up asleep in the guest room, the moonlit shadows of the pines playing across the lumpen figure curled up on the futon, like giant caressing fingers.

Chihiro bent to kiss her cheek then close the shoji, before quietly shutting the front door behind her.

She was almost half-way home when she received the text from Hotaru-san.

"*Still on for a.m.?*"

She thumbed a reply while balancing the wheel one-handed.

"*Update me re. Munich.*" Hotaru-san responded.

"*Ok, no problem.*" Chihiro replied.

"*Thanks – c u.*"

As Chihiro returned the phone to its holder she felt a sudden stab of anxiety. The plastic file with Hotaru's tour itinerary, the one she'd just spent the last three hours making notes in. It was on the back seat, right? She'd automatically picked it up?

A quick glance told her she was sadly wrong on both counts. She'd have to go back. Damn!

Thunder drummed overhead. 'Perfect', she thought, 'that's all I need!'

As Chihiro absently tapped the wheel in frustration and the wipers slapped away the curtain of rain she thought about the voice. She'd imagined it of course, but it had felt so real at the time, so...there. It had been a man's, soft and wordless yet somehow urgent; she didn't know why she knew that, she just did. And the smell had been like the kind of thickly sweet tobacco her great uncle used to smoke. As the other lane whined by and the honking juggernauts splashed surface water across her windscreen Chihiro replayed the moment again and again.

Twenty-five minutes later she was pulling up outside the old house.

Apart from a nightlight in the porch the whole place stood in silhouette against the angry storm clouds fringing the hills. Rain ran in torrents off the guttering and flushed out of drainpipes, almost as if the great hulk was crying to itself. Behind the house the darkened shapes of the pine trees fought against each other in the whipping wind. Lightning cracked the horizon as another great boom of thunder echoed overhead. Chihiro fiddled with her key, eager to get out of the storm then hurriedly shook off her shoes in the genkan.

She padded as quietly as she could along the corridor, past the sleeping Natsumi and up the stairs. The plastic folder was still on the futon exactly where she'd left it. She'd had an illogical fear the old woman would wake up and tidy it away somewhere then instantly forget about it.

She was halfway back down the stairs when the whisper came again, this time from directly behind her:

"Get her out..."

The shock of the words inside a rush of air almost made her fall. Chihiro grabbed the stair-rail and twisted around. "What...?" She stumbled backward a few steps in confusion. "Who are you... where...?"

"Get her out...!"

There was a loud crack from somewhere outside then what sounded like a rustle of branches. Instantly Chihiro knew what was about to happen. She dashed down the rest of the stairs and into the guest room. Etched on the shoji screens a dark monster was twisting and writhing in its death-throes. There was the sound of tearing and snapping above the rushing wind.

She bent to pull the old woman out of the futon, grabbing her under the armpits as Natsumi awoke in a spluttered a cry of confused indignation. Chihiro managed to drag the struggling figure halfway down the hall when the cracking sound came again, this time like a rifle shot. There was a crunching noise then sounds of splintering wood and breaking glass. Plaster fell on their heads as two large beams crashed down on either side, one of them scraping Chihiro's shoulder. She cried out in pain as she fell. Somehow she managed to find her feet again in the thick swirling dust. She groped for the front door, then carried Natsumi's frail figure outside before collapsing in the road. Choking and fighting for breath she looked back at what was left of the house.

Behind it the two pine trees had been reduced to one.

Chihiro and Yuuto were picking their way through the wreckage two days later. Most of the roof was down as well as a large section of the back wall. They'd decided Natsumi would stay in the Kyoto apartment with them until a home could be found; they'd already put her on a waiting list. Chihiro had cuts and bruises on her shoulder and arm but nothing broken. The old woman was still in shock but they'd arranged for a private nurse to look after her that morning so they could assess the damage. Yuuto thought the whole structure looked unsafe; they couldn't afford to rebuild and would have to get the site cleared before they could sell it.

Yuuto stood next to her in the wrecked guest room looking forlornly around at the house he'd spent his life in. There were splintered pieces of wood and smashed tiles everywhere. The tree's mangled branches filled half the floor space. Its long bulk ran from the mound of tangled roots at the top of the moss garden and across the courtyard to end with its tip flattened against the far wall. The ripped shoji flapped against it like a pathetic sail caught in the breeze.

Natsumi's futon still lay beneath it.

Chihiro had told him nothing of the sounds in their old bedroom, the whispered voice on the stairs. If he didn't know she might be able to forget about it herself in time, pretend it never happened. The mind will do what you command it to if the alternative is... what? A kind of madness? Was that the same way Natsumi saw the world now? She shivered in the chilly room, its classical perfection already a fading memory.

Her shoe crunched on broken glass. She bent down. "There's something trapped underneath it."

"Be careful!" Yuuto warned her. "I don't you to get hurt again."

She looked up, directly into his eyes. "Don't you...?"

Something unspoken seemed to pass between them. She tugged a mangled bamboo frame out from under the main trunk. The stern old man's picture had lain almost exactly where his daughter's head would have been.

They both stared down at it.

"You saved her life."

"I'm good for something then." She hadn't meant her reply

to sound so bitter.

"Chihiro, I'm sorry if I've been..."

His words tailed off and Chihiro nodded. She fought back the urge to ask him if his grandfather had smoked a pipe; he would only have stared at her, especially if she'd suddenly broken into hysterical giggles. Instead, she took a calming breath then reached for his hand.

"I think we'd better have that talk you wanted tonight."

Empty Seat

As the last notes dissipated into the air in the surrounding auditorium Hotaru Sasaki remained still, her slender hands resting gently on the piano keys as if one slight movement could still jar their resonance. The spell was broken by clapping from the wings and she slowly turned to face the noise as if surfacing from a dream.

"Magnificent!" a voice shouted, echoing around the empty hall. An attractive young man in an expensive business suit strode across the stage towards her, hand outstretched in greeting. Smiling, Hotaru half rose from the stool to shake it then gave him a hug.

"Jiro-san, its good too see you again! I got here a bit early so they let me get on with it. Your staff are as delightful as the last time I met them."

"That was two years ago, Hotaru-san, but you will still see the same old faces. Our people remain very loyal to us at the NHK."

"They've got a good manager."

The dapper young man smiled self-consciously and nodded his head. "You're too kind."

"Have we got time for a coffee?" Hotaru asked.

"Of course, I was just about to suggest it."

Hotaru sat at a booth in the plush cafeteria as Jiro brought them both espressos. She sipped her drink.

"So," he continued, "has Cologne changed much since my last visit? You were here in the spring, weren't you?"

"Cologne is always changing but the old city is still there underneath. And of course there's still scaffolding around the Dom." She rolled her eyes and laughed. "When will there ever not be?"

It was their private joke about the old cathedral. She had played there a few times now and the place was still as dark and foreboding as always, its air cold and heavy. This last time the concert had been recorded and in the long wait between the sound check and that evening's performance Hotaru had decided to visit the famous Shrine of the Three

Kings, the reliquary supposedly containing the remains of the three wise men who attended Jesus' birth.

She'd found the gilded sarcophagus by the large oak crucifix and walked slowly around the box. It was beautifully engraved, the gold shining out in the muted lighting, but it was still just a box; a box full of old bones. She couldn't see what all the fuss was all about.

There was a lesson in this. 'Once a thing's dead, it's dead,' she told herself. 'There's no resurrection, no second coming.' If only that were true...

Later, Hotaru began to think about the coming night's performance. It had been in the back of her mind since Hong Kong, but the last few days had sharpened her focus. That morning's run through had been unsatisfactory. The Chopin was alright of course, nothing would affect that, but it was a side show to the main event.

She had undertaken to perform all of Liszt's twelve Transcendental Études, a task that her agent, Chihiro, decreed as 'madness' when Hotaru asked her to go ahead and arrange the tour schedule.

"Nobody's done that for years," she'd told her. "You crazy woman, you'll wear yourself out!"

"I need a challenge, Chihiro. I'm bored."

"I've told you before what you need," the mousy-haired little woman had replied in a careful tone. Her client was her best friend but she would only be teased so far.

"I'm OK. You're lucky you've got Yuuto; not everyone can get someone special."

Her friend and agent had given a little shrug but said nothing.

Perhaps Chihiro had been right about the Études; they were famously difficult to play, even for the world's top pianists. Written for solo piano by the great man in 1852 they were a revision of an even harder set of pieces that were near impossible to render on anything resembling a modern grand piano.

They were all in different keys, a collection designed to show off the flamboyant young maestro's performing genius at the keyboard – so fast, varied and complex that he was virtually the only one at the time who could play them. But as age mellowed Franz Joseph, he reshaped the pieces so that some of his contemporaries could join in the fun. All except the fourth Étude that is; the Mazeppa in D minor – that he'd made even more difficult.

Based on Victor Hugo's cruel poem, it told the tale of a Ukrainian pageboy, Mazeppa, being strapped to a horse set free to gallop across the tundra until both man and beast are near death. Only then is the boy freed, and at the end of the piece crowned king. The final frenzied 'Allegro Deciso', as the horse makes its last desperate bolt, was enough to ruin the reputation of the world's finest pianists. It was almost unplayable.

And Hotaru would be performing it that night.

This was the second date of the tour, next would be Munich then three more European appearances before finishing at the Barbican in London. Although she had spent months preparing the material Hong Kong had been difficult and she had nearly slipped a couple of times, especially in the Mazeppa. Only Hotaru knew this at the moment though; she must conquer her nerves before playing the piece again.

And hope that he appeared again that night, as he always did.

The vast indoor stadium of the Budokan where Hotaru had earlier rehearsed to an empty hall was now swarming with eager concert-goers anticipating the night's coming performance. Many had already taken their places amongst the high bank of seats.

A short while later the one minute bell rang in Hotaru's dressing room. She stood up nervously, smoothed down the sleeveless black satin dress, took a deep breath and made her way to the short flight of steps that led to the wings.

Jiro was there waiting for her, looking as calm and in control as usual. He put a reassuring arm around her shoulders.

"OK? Ready?"

She nodded, not letting herself speak. He gave her shoulder a little squeeze then strode confidently out to face the audience. He waved down the applause.

"Tonight we have a major treat in store for you all. Ms

Hotaru Sasaki, one of the most talented concert pianists of her generation, will play Chopin's mazurkas Opus 17 Number 4 and Opus 33 Number 2." The applause began again. "And then after the break, ladies and gentlemen, Ms Sasaki will give you Franz Joseph Liszt's twelve Transcendental Études in their entirety." The fervent clapping welled up inside the huge octagonal hall until it threatened to take the roof off.

Hotaru peered out at the auditorium, to the seat down at the front of the central row she'd selected to be in her direct eye-line when she sat at the Steinway. The one she'd asked Jiro to reserve for her.

It was still empty.

Back in her dressing room at the break she composed herself. The Chopin had gone well, as she knew it would, but…

But this had never happened before. She felt like a crutch had been kicked from under her. Dare she go out to face them again? She knew she had to, that even her outstanding reputation would not survive a refusal. It was too late to claim she was unwell without arousing comments of unreliability. There were younger, prettier and, dare she admit it, more talented performers to take her place.

Her thoughts were interrupted by the trill of the bell.

Eyes fixed steadfastly in front of her, Hotaru made her way to the piano. She would not raise her head until the final moment, not until she had composed herself, fingers at rest on the keyboard ready to begin.

It was the only way. Whatever happened next was beyond her control.

"You were brilliant tonight Hotaru, the Mazeppa…wow! But then I expected nothing less."

"Why, thank-you Jiro."

They were sitting at a small cocktail table in the members' bar. Most of the audience had left and the staff had already started clearing up. A few hopeful fans hung around in little groups glancing her way, some of the bolder ones approaching with embarrassingly fulsome praise.

Hotaru reached up to sign another autograph, hopefully the

last of the night.

"Who shall I make it out to?"

A gaunt looking man in his early forties indicated an old woman standing a few paces behind him. "My mother, Etsuko."

Hotaru, on her fourth glass of a particularly fine red wine, gave 'Etsuko' a friendly wave.

"I was talking to Chen on the phone this afternoon while you rehearsing." Jiro told her as she turned back to her glass. "Chen Li, the concert arranger at Hong Kong City Hall, your last venue."

The smile remained on Hotaru's face. "I didn't know you two were acquainted, he's never mentioned it."

"It's a small world in the concert business. He thought the Études were marvellous, by the way." Jiro hesitated and she thought he'd finished. "I um... I asked him about the seat you booked with him. The one that nobody used, like the one tonight..."

"How did you know that?" Hotaru felt her face flush.

"I just guessed you had. A hunch, you've done it before at other venues."

"Been checking up on me?" She felt angry with this smooth young manager, as if he'd somehow betrayed her trust. She suddenly wanted to be back in her hotel room, packing for the flight to Munich.

"You probably think I've been spying on you."

"Haven't you?"

"Not like that," he told her. "I was concerned. I consider you a good friend as well as an artist."

Perhaps it was the wine, but something snapped inside Hotaru. "So you want to know about the empty seat, the one I book for every performance I give?"

He looked at her steadily but said nothing.

"I've never told anyone else about this so consider it an honour. My father was a pianist as well." She put a hand up to halt Jiro's enquiry. "You wouldn't have heard of him, Daddy was that thing that damns all would-be maestros; he was just 'good'. He was also a sadist. I'm older than you but when I was a youngster the term 'child abuse' was only used for men in dirty raincoats doing filthy things to little children.

Not for fathers bullying their daughters into being the great maestros they never were. See this?" She showed Jiro a thin scar running along the top of her left hand. "One day he forgot to flatten out the metal ruler he used to teach what he called my 'lazy hand' to keep up. I was seven at the time. My mother said nothing to him about it." She gave Jiro a brittle smile.

"Anyway," she continued after a pause, "six months after I was accepted at the Paris Conservatoire he dropped dead in the street of a heart attack. After that I started to fail, to lose focus. They told me I was more than good enough but that I needed to find an edge, something outside myself to 'fulfil my true potential'. I started to imagine he was standing behind me, ruler poised." Hotaru shuddered slightly as if ashamed to continue. "After a while I mentally moved him to a space in front of me, an area of the room or better, an empty chair. Something I could focus on before I began to play, to keep in my mind's eye."

She looked up at Jiro. "And I never gained the courage to stop you see. So now you know; big mystery over." There was a tremble in her voice; she suddenly felt awkward, absurd even.

He seemed embarrassed. "Come on, I'll take you back to your hotel."

The lift doors opened. "Thank-you for seeing me home, Jiro."

He moved to follow her out but she held up a hand. "Really, it's alright. I'm fine now."

"I don't think so. I think you need somebody with you tonight." Jiro replied softly.

She forced a self-deprecating laugh. "Jiro, I'm a thirty-eight year old woman. I think I can take care of myself!"

His expression didn't change but she saw hurt in his eyes. "Of course, I just, you know…"

Hotaru gave him a stiff little wave then quickly opened the door to her room and shut it behind her. She leant against the wall for a moment, drained and suddenly sober. She reached for the light switch but her fingers failed to find it.

As her eyes adjusted to the dark the shadows seemed to rise

up from their corners, oppressive and threatening. The voice in her head began its familiar tirade, the same words again and again:

"You were weak again tonight, sloppy, lucky to get through it. What did you think you were doing, you were close to messing-up! You'll never be any good Hotaru! Never be..."

She put a hand up to her mouth as if to stop them. "Shut-up...! Shut-up! You're just bones, just a pile of old bones!"

"Hotaru...?" She heard Jiro's voice from the other side of the door. Her hand reached back blindly for the handle and twisted. Then she was in his arms.

"I... I came back to apologise..." he started.

"Take me to your place tonight, please..."

He nodded. "Yes. I'll get your things."

"I'll get them in a minute. Just hold me a while."

She felt tears on his cheek and realised they were hers. "I would have done anything for him, Jiro – anything. If only just once he'd told me..." She faltered as he raised a hand to brush the hair away from her eyes.

"Hotaru, my love; it's time you had someone else to tell you that."

The Fox in the Park

He first saw it as a small blur from the car when his mother picked him up from their local station. That had been four days ago. He was back at home living with her, a condition of his early release into the community. They'd made it sound like he'd be stuck there indefinitely.

"What was that, on the corner of the park?"

The 'park' across the road was only a park in Japanese terms: an area of scrubby grass between an apartment block and a row of shops and tiny noodle restaurants. It had some neat little bushes along a winding dirt path and a couple of cherry trees severely trimmed back in obedience to the surrounding city.

"I didn't see anything."

"It looked like a fox."

His mother squinted in the rear view mirror as she slowly swung the car around into their narrow street. Now the park was behind them.

"It can't be. You don't get foxes in the city."

Kenzo turned to look back.

"Do you remember that story I used to read you about the fox god," she continued, "how it pretended to be a young woman to tempt men, how it liked to trick and deceive them?"

Kenzo silently glared at the back of her scrawny old neck. How could she say such idiotic things to him of all people, even now? Her crass stupidity never ceased to amaze him.

"What are you doing?" His mother's sharp words made him jump. It was two days later and he'd been leaning over the sink staring through the glass, a hand stretched to pull the net curtain aside. The kitchen window at the side had a direct view of the park, in between the intervening gardens' sagging washing lines and plastic fences. He'd been there maybe three minutes.

"Nothing..." Kenzo sat down at the kitchen breakfast table. "I thought I saw it again."

"Saw what?"
"Nothing."

She shook her head and went to sit down beside him. Already, he wished she'd leave him alone. In the prison people had left him alone. He'd heard about other cases like his: warders putting shit in your food and passing you soap with razor blades in it; beating you up if you complained, or even just looked at them. But it hadn't been like that at all. He'd been put in a special unit with other sex offenders, some of them quite young. Most had seemed very ordinary, even nice. It hadn't been particularly difficult, and he'd had his privacy.

Now he'd begun to think he'd swapped one kind of prison for another: a much worse one. He felt under constant surveillance; by the social services, the police, even his own mother. It had made the final decision seem even easier than it might have done.

"What is it, Kenzo-chan?" She still spoke to him as a child, still her little boy from the fresh-faced school photos that sat on the dresser in the living room with the sunlight fading their Fuji-film colours a little more every year.

He wanted to get up and look out of the window again but realised there probably wouldn't be anything there. It only seemed to appear when he wasn't thinking about it.

"Nothing, I'm OK..." he dragged the sullen words out of his mouth then turned around to face her. She'd become an old woman while he'd been inside, the once thick black hair now thinning and grey-streaked, the face lined and pinched by worry and incomprehension.

He'd done that to her. He was glad of it as well.

Mrs Tanaka had two main rooms in her old-fashioned house in the middle class Tokyo suburb of Jiyugaoka. One was a western-style living room but the other was a traditional Japanese one, complete with rice paper screens, a kotasu table and tatami mats, and a wall shrine to Kenzo's family ancestors. His great grandfather's samurai sword hung suspended from a hook above the ancient silvery photographs of young men and women in silken robes and strange headgear. Below them, in a mahogany display case surrounded by beautiful porcelain dishes, lay his ceremonial knife in its lacquered white scabbard propped up on a little black stand. The fierce-looking old man had used it to commit seppuku at the end of the war, had taken his own life the way a defeated Naval Commander of Nippon should.

Etsuko Tanaka had eventually inherited the home she'd grown up in and married a rather intense young man who worked in the office next to hers. A year later she'd given birth to their only son.

"Isn't it today the Social people come round?" She made them sound like a group of friends.

"I believe that the nice people from the Child Protection Unit will soon be here to check I'm settling in. See that I'm being a good boy."

She gave a sigh. "I wish you wouldn't talk that way..."

He shrugged.

"I still don't understand why all this had to happen, why you're like this. You're forty-three!"

"Don't you mother? I mean really, don't you?" He couldn't rouse himself to anger anymore.

"You made a mistake that's all. It's something all the teachers have to be careful of but it wasn't your fault. That girl...the lies..."

"She was fourteen years old," he said the words matter-of-factly, coldly even.

His mother began to cry but Kenzo knew it wouldn't last. She'd be back in the living room later that afternoon surrounded by her collection of porcelain dogs, with her feet up on the sofa and her woollen shawl wrapped tight around her wiry old frame. She'd probably be playing her 'proper music' on the old stereo, the western classical records she'd always used to escape from things she didn't want to deal with or think about. The woman had spent a small fortune on fruitless piano lessons for him as a child, failing to understand or admit that his talentless fingers would never be capable of producing anything of beauty.

Kenzo had hated those lessons. They'd made him feel clumsy and stupid; that dry old bitch of a tutor would shout at his fumbling efforts and make him cry. And when, during the long cold evenings in the draughty house, Kenzo finally realised his father kept an ear cocked for any break in the sweeping cadences of Mozart and Liszt from downstairs while he did all those bad things to him, he began to hate the actual music itself.

"He's getting much better," she'd tell her husband at the breakfast table, and he'd absently nod his head behind his paper, reach over and ruffle his son's hair. And the nine-year-old Kenzo would feel he must be mistaken, that things were as they should be after all; that it was just him.

Even all these years later, long after he'd left to pursue his lonely life in the city and the old man had died of a stroke in bed, she still hadn't got it. Kenzo's mother had bought tickets for her favourite pianist Hotaru Sasaki at the Budakan as a 'first night home' treat for both of them. He'd made it to the first interval before rushing to throw up in the toilet.

"I'm going out, Etsuko," he told her.

"Where...? Where are you going?" She shuffled after him in her slippers into the cramped little hall as he pulled on his jacket and bent to tie his shoes. "You're meant to stay in the house. What if they catch you not here?"

"I'll be back before then. Don't worry." He shut the door before she could reply.

Kenzo walked down the road to where the animal had been. He'd seen it the previous evening as well, its shadowy little body forming itself in the space between the two trees. It had given him a long look then turned away. There had been some kids in the playground at the back of the park, their swinging bodies silhouetted in the garish lights of a distant pachinko parlour, but they didn't seem to notice as it slunk past them in the twilight.

Kenzo wasn't meant to go anywhere near there of course. He'd been told specifically to stay away by Michiko, his personal case-handler. She'd warned him at their first meeting in her cramped downtown offices that he was on a list to be 'tagged'. Kenzo had hoped that it proved to be a long one but now that ceased to matter either way.

They'd given him special pills to take twice a day as part of his supposed 'treatment'. They gave him constipation and turned his piss a funny colour. And he seemed to be tired all the time as well, finding his sudden 'freedom' paradoxically exhausting.

Kenzo was back a good half hour before Michiko showed up. Although she'd usually been late for their 'case conferences' in the prison visitors room, he couldn't take a risk on her slackness today. It must all go smoothly so that she wouldn't suspect.

"How are we then, Mr Tanaka? Everything OK, adjusting well?"

"*We're* fine, thank-you." He'd never liked her patronising manner; it was bad enough being spoken to like a child by Etsuko. Perhaps she'd got used to talking that way in her job; he could appreciate the irony in that.

"What do you think you'll be doing for work now?" Michiko asked him, her brow furrowed in serious consideration. "If you hadn't thought about it we do have an outreach programme..."

"I thought I'd ask for my old job back." He kept a straight face at her expression.

"I...I don't think that would be possible Mr Tanaka."

"Really...? Well, then..." It had been another hour of smug lecturing and form-filling before he'd finally got her to the door.

"Good luck, Mr Tanaka." As she returned to her car he glimpsed a movement in the shadows on the far side of the street. Two small bright eyes blinked at him then with the swish of a bushy tail something scuttled away.

Later that night he was staring out of the kitchen window again. His mother had dosed off with the headphones on, the sounds of Richard Strauss scratching tinnily in her ears. He couldn't settle though; he'd sit down at the table to read the evening paper then five minutes later be on his feet again. Something was coming and he knew what it was; this time it couldn't be avoided. He thought about what he'd tried to do in his cell, the 'incident' as Michiko had described it in her case notes. That had been clumsy though, as clumsy as his childhood piano playing. Tonights would be a more assured performance.

At just gone two o'clock there was a scratching sound at the front door. He listened in the stillness and it came again, this time the scrabbling little claws more insistent. He got up and moved into the darkened hall, but by the time he'd got his shoes on the noise had stopped. Kenzo opened the door a sliver and looked out down the street.

The fox sat in the middle of the road half-lit by the end streetlight, its pointed shadow elongated across the path and up a garden wall. As its shiny little eyes looked up at him Kenzo saw that it had something white clasped sideways in its mouth. Before he could identify what it was the fox turned and trotted away down the dark tarmac towards the park. Kenzo hesitated for a moment then followed. The animal was waiting for him by one of the bushes on the side of the path. As he approached it dropped the thing in its mouth. Kenzo saw the knife glitter in the grass.

"What are you? Are you her?"

The fox backed away then sat under the bush, its long tongue lolling in its mouth, the tiny yellow eyes sharpened unwaveringly on him. Kenzo knelt down in the dew-soaked scrub and picked up the knife. He unbuttoned his shirt with one hand and pulled up his vest to reveal a slight paunch hanging over his trouser belt. He undid that as well then slid the white lacquered scabbard off the knife blade. It came away smoothly in his hand.

"Is this what you want?"

The fox sat panting to itself in the darkness. Kenzo grabbed the curved handle of the knife with both hands and turned it around so that the tip of the blade rested on the naked flesh of his stomach.

"Is this it…?" Kenzo was sweating despite the night's chill. His arms began to shake and he couldn't stop them. He grasped the knife even harder, the cord of the handle biting into his fingers.

"Will this do it? Will it…?"

He took a last deep breath but, before he could move his hands, the animal sprang at him clenching its jaws around his wrist. With a shriek of pain he let the knife go and it span away to be lost in the darkness. For a few seconds the pungent smell of the creature filled his nostrils then it suddenly loosened its grip, kicked out its hind legs at him and disappeared back into the night.

Kenzo sat winded for a few moments, then got shakily to his feet. He looked down at his wrist but it was unmarked. He found the knife after a short search and carefully cleaned the blade on the grass. His trembling hands slid it back into its scabbard. Back at the house he quietly opened the display case door and put it back on its stand.

His mother was still lying sprawled on the sofa so he gently woke her and helped her upstairs. Later, as he listened in the darkness to her deep breathing from the next room, he wondered idly whether he should be the one to buy the concert tickets for them next time.

He still hadn't made up his mind when he finally fell asleep.

The Investigator

Michiko Kichida was sure this time, there could no longer be any doubt about it; the small ratty-faced man in the brown windcheater jacket was following her. She looked around at the main entrance to her apartment block but saw no-one. He'd been there though, all the way back from the seven-eleven keeping to the shadows on the other side of the narrow street, twenty paces behind and sliding into shop doorways when she'd turned around suddenly to catch him out.

Michiko was scared of him because this wasn't the first instance of the little man's presence. She'd noticed him the other day tagging her movements. She'd seen his blue J-League baseball cap bobbing a few rows behind her in the bus on her way home from work.

Before that he'd been skulking around the park benches near the Social Services building where she ate her lunch; a scruffy loser in his late forties with constant cigarette fixed between fingers as he pretended to ogle the short summer skirts of the other office ladies whilst giving her the occasional glance.

At first she'd thought him a sex pest who'd somehow fixated on her. She wasn't bad looking, although nothing special compared to some of the brilliant creatures who paraded on Tokyo's dusty summer streets.

That wasn't it though; the sex thing was a front. He was after something else from her. Michiko would have gone to the police and pointed the little man out to them, but something in the back of her mind stopped her. Although her parents had never mentioned such things during her childhood she'd read about situations like this. There had been an article a few years ago in a glossy fashion magazine, unusual enough for the piece itself to make the national news. It still wasn't something most people liked to talk about in public. Could he be someone like that, a private investigator? And if he was, what should she do?

The wedding to Naoto was in a few weeks time. His family had seemed to welcome her into their midst with open arms, glad that their diffident son had finally decided to settle down. The fact that she had a difficult job as a social worker dealing with the rougher elements of the city didn't seem to faze them at all, in fact they gave Michiko the impression they were genuinely interested in her career at the Department.

"You won't be giving your job up once Naoto-chan and you are married will you Michiko dear, at least for a while?" That had been her fiancé's mother. And his dad: "We wouldn't want you to feel compromised, and two salaries are better than one if you want to live well in this city. Will you be selling your apartment and moving in, not that it's any business of ours. You young people know what's best for yourselves these days; everything's changed in that way."

It was a subtle pressure and she recognised it as such. No rush, but eventually we'd like you to conform to what we want you to be; the dutiful housewife behind your husband's burgeoning financial career in the city; the dedicated mother of our grandchildren; the daughter-in-law we were expecting to have and not somebody who mixes with wife-beaters and child-molesters for a living. All that would have to stop.

Michiko was just as adamant in her own mind that it wouldn't stop at all. She loved her job; even though she tended to the scatter-brained, when it came to the welfare and protection of the weak and powerless she was scrupulous and unbending in her efforts.

And Naoto's folks would have to get used to that about her; she could bend all they wanted, but she would never let herself be broken.

But this... this was completely different. Beneath their sheen of supposed modern-thinking they were still a traditional family, with a mindset to match. This might be a step too far for them.

Michiko entered her apartment and walked hurriedly across to the window. She pushed up one of the blinds and peered out down the street. A blur of brown crossed over the road further up, dodging a car which hooted. A few seconds later the intercom buzzer sounded.

She froze. He knew which apartment she lived in! But how could he... her mail! He must have checked it out, bribed the concierge downstairs for the key to her mailbox or maybe even prised it open himself. That meant he didn't care about the police; he'd tell them he was just doing his job. He probably had enough yen in his pocket to deal with that.

Oh God, this was really serious! She switched off the lights in the living room then quickly in the small galley kitchen. Michiko put her ear to the apartment's front door. There were footsteps coming up the stairs, not stealthily but with an arrogant clump. The old bitch had let him in!

The loud knock next to her head made her spring away. He knew she was in! Of course he did, hadn't he been following her?

What to do?

It came again, more persistent. This wasn't going to go away.

She put the chain on the door then opened it a sliver. He stood in the hallway's dim light slightly out of breath, a dew of perspiration on his face. The sharp little eyes stared at her unblinking.

"Michiko Suzuki?"

"Who wants to know?"

He cocked his head to one side, a quick animalistic gesture that enhanced his rodent qualities.

"Can I come in for a few minutes? I'd like for us to talk."

"These are private apartments. You're trespassing. Please go away."

He didn't seem put-off by this. In fact he actually smiled, showing her yellow-stained teeth. She caught a whiff of stale breath through the door gap and recoiled.

"It's in your best interests to let me in Suzuki-san. You're the subject of a survey I've been preparing on behalf of my client. I have most of the details but if I could check a few more err... personal ones that would complete my report satisfactorily. I could ask at your workplace of course, your boss; a Ms..." He took a battered notebook from the windcheater pocket and leafed through it. "Ah yes, Harada-san. I can ask her – in fact I've already booked an appointment with her for tomorrow. I can still cancel that of course..."

Michiko hesitated then unlatched the door.

"You can turn the lights back on now." She did, and the little man strode inside. "Ah, nice place; you must be doing very well. I admire your taste. Some of the people I have to deal with fill their homes with the most hideous shit, but this is most decorative."

"What is it you want?" Michiko asked. "Quickly or I'll call the police."

"No, you won't. You're getting married in two weeks aren't you? To Naoko Yamauchi."

"How do you know...?"

"Oh I know, Suzuki-san. May I call you Michiko, seeing as you'll be helping me with this?"

"With what...?"

He took off the baseball cap and scratched his head. Underneath it he was almost bald, with a few wisps of greasy hair combed across a flaky scalp. "You're not paying attention Michiko. I told you already you that you're the subject of my report. Please answer my questions and I'll leave you in peace. Ready?"

She said nothing.

"OK, number one. Your birthplace was Yoshikawa, is that accurate?"

Michiko continued to stare at him. Why should she have to do this? But he'd said he'd see her boss...

"Michiko...?"

She nodded.

"Excellent." He showed her something scrawled in the notebook. "This address right?"

She gave a sharp intake of breath then nodded again.

"And your father's occupation was this?" He pointed to a word circled in red.

"Yes."

"Now we're getting somewhere. Just a few more..."

The intercom buzzed. Michiko pushed it and a girl's excited voice grated mechanically in the apartment. "Hi Michiko-chan, it's me. Sorry, but I've got my results tomorrow. Is it OK if we go now, are you ready?"

"Who's that?" The little man asked, agitated.

She turned to him nervously. "It's my fiancé's kid sister. We were going to go shopping tonight, for the wedding.

She's early."

"Get rid of her. No, go down and see her and make some excuse. Say you've got a headache."

Michiko looked at him then around at the apartment.

"Don't worry, I won't steal anything."

A pretty girl in a pink dress and white cardigan stood in the lobby. She clasped a small pink Hello Kitty clutch bag to her with one hand while holding a mobile phone to her ear with the other which she gabbled into between breathless pauses. "Oh-my-god, yeah, I know... yeah, I'm soooo petrified... yeah OK, see you tomorrow..." She clicked it off. "Michiko! Hi, sorry, you must be knackered."

Michiko forced a smile. "Hi Haruma-chan." The two embraced. "Thanks for coming."

"Not too early? I can come back only I've got..."

"Your results, I know. How exciting for you. I'm sure you've done well."

"Yeah, but well enough... Michiko, what is it babe?"

"Nothing, it's nothing." She felt the tears creep into her eyes and tried to blink them away. "I'm a little tired that's all. Can we leave it tonight?"

"But we have to buy your Wataboshi and all that other stuff. It's only two weeks away. Naoko will kill me if I don't have you ready on time."

"Does he think me so useless that I can't organise myself?" The bitter words came out before she could stop herself.

"Michiko... I was only joking. Of course he doesn't think that. He thinks you're brilliant, so do I as a matter of fact."

"Really?"

"What's going on sister-in-law? You're not getting cold feet now? I'm joking, I'm joking for God's sake," as she saw Michiko's expression. "Something really is wrong isn't it?"

"It isn't you or Naoko. It's just... maybe it's not to be, you know. Your family, I mean they're never going to accept me are they? And now this...!"

"Now what...?" Haruma looked at her perplexed. "You're not making any sense. What's happened?"

"Maybe I just woke up to reality, Haruma."

Haruma's face darkened. "Have my parents said anything

to you?"

Michiko shook her head. The other girl put a hand up to her cheek to wipe the tears away.

"Listen to me. Naoko loves you very much, and so do I. We want you to be part of us."

"But if he knew..."

Haruma held Michiko's face in her hands to stare into her eyes. "Naoko knows a lot more about you than you think. He's not stupid you know. The shit you have to go through every day, the belief you have in others who can't help themselves. He knows why you do it and he loves you for it."

"But..."

"Michiko, he knows! He's proud of you! If he wasn't such an idiot he'd have told you so himself long ago, OK?"

"OK..."

"And we'll do this again tomorrow, yes?"

"Yes, but your results?"

"You can help me celebrate, or alternatively drown my sorrows. That's what sisters are for, right?"

"Right..." she replied and watched as Haruma gave her a cheery goodbye wave through the lobby's main door.

The little man was holding one of the porcelain figure's Naoko had bought for her on their trip to London, an eighteenth century shepherdess carrying a lamb in her arms. It was her favourite.

"You took your time, is she gone?"

"Put that down. I want you out of here – I don't have to answer any more of your questions."

"I thought we'd agreed you'd be sensible Michiko-san. I've only got a few more."

"I said put it down!"

He grinned at her then let the figure fall from his grasp. It smashed into pieces on the panelled flooring.

"Whoops, how careless of me. Sometimes we break the thing we love the most though don't we? Take Naoko's family for instance. Do you really want to break that?"

"You... get out of my home!"

"I just thought that with your background, your parents' background I mean..."

She crossed the floor in two strides as the broken shards cracked under her feet. The slap caught him full across the bridge of his nose, knocking the baseball cap flying. Shocked, he put a hand to his face then stared down at the blood on his fingers.

"You filthy little cow!"

She held up her hand to strike him again and he cringed back against the wall. "You're not fit to speak my parents' name you disgusting creep! I'm proud of whom I am, and you can tell your so-called clients that. If they've got a problem they can say it to my face. Now get the fuck out of my home before I report you to the police for molestation."

"But I haven't tried..." his voice had become a shaky whine.

She grabbed the collar of the brown windcheater and pulled him towards her so that his face was inches away from hers. "That would be your word against mine; and you're in my apartment..."

She could see panic in his eyes, the sweat from his forehead mingling with the blood. They flicked past her then he suddenly made a bolt for the door, grabbing up the baseball cap from the sofa as he went. Something fell from windcheater's pocket to slither under the dresser. In his flight he didn't notice.

Michiko listened to his feet pounding down the stairs then the sound of the lobby door being wrenched open. She bent down to pick up the battered note book then walked across to the window in time to see the little man running up the street.

Still watching him she began to tear the pages out, one by one.

Getting Rid of Aki

"I hate doing this!" Haruma Yamauchi said the words under her breath as she pushed the mop in angry stabs at the pale green linoleum floor. "We're not children anymore. It's so undignified!"

"Now, now!"

"But they've got no right to make us. We'll all be at university soon and we're still behaving like drudges. Other people's parents have written to the school about it. Their kids don't have to do all this shit so why didn't mine do the same? I told mum I hated it!"

"It's only for a few more days..."

"I can't wait, Aki! Will you come with me?"

"I think that maybe..."

"Please say you'll come. I know I'm going to fail. I need you there with me. Please..."

"Alright..."

"Haruma...? Are you OK?"

Satomi and Tomoko were staring at her. They wore the same regulation dark blue sailor-styled tops and skirts as Haruma, although Tomoko's skirt was a good deal shorter than the others.

In the evenings, after school, they were as different in appearance and character as friends could possibly be. Satomi was the shy one, her finely-honed little frame usually dressed in modest rather dull long skirts and ill-fitting jumpers. She even turned up in her tracksuit sometimes after one of her various never-ending sport sessions, much to Haruma and Tomoko's amusement and frustration.

"How we ever going to meet any good-looking boys with you dressed like that? You're not in the Olympics yet girl!"

But it was always said good-naturedly. Satomi was a natural athlete and you had to make allowances for that. She was the only one of the little group with real god-given talent, apart from Aki of course.

Tomoko was something else entirely. Tall for a Japanese girl, even by present day standards, she was all curves and legs, her body seemingly in a continual fight to free itself from the confines of the tight mini-skirts and even tighter daft-slogan t-shirts she loved. On their evenings out in the city's downtown clubs Tomoko sported giant bangle earrings, bows and fluorescent high heels, Satomi an Alice band and sneakers, and herself a strangely self-conscious hybrid of both.

And then there was Aki of course. Until now Haruma had always seen herself as the neutron these disparate electrons orbited around; the power that held their unlikely fellowship together. Not-sporty; not-glamour girl; not...Aki. No, she was the science geek. And like any self-respecting physicist she was reluctant to part with such a perfectly formulated equation. Not yet, anyway.

"Haruma...?" Tomoko spoke again. Satomi was looking at Haruma with a little knot of worry creasing her brow. She held her own mop with a light touch as if ready to throw it javelin-like into one of the classrooms or use it to pole-vault into the quad through an open window. Tomoko slouched against hers like it was her last dance partner for the evening.

Haruma looked over at them both and refocused. "Fine, I'm just dandy. Apart from this stupid mop in my hands and the fact I'm going to find out that I've failed my entrance exam tomorrow I feel brilliant."

"You're not going to fail." Tomoko's voice was a little too adamant to carry the conviction she'd obviously wished it to. "They'll take everything into consideration. And even if they don't you'll still walk it babe. You're our very own Albert Schweitzer."

"Einstein! Oh ha-ha, very funny!" Tomoko always managed to get her going. She sometimes felt that the girl actually spent time revising the subject just so she could take the piss.

"No, seriously though...?"

"It's nothing." A crowd of first year's raced down the corridor towards them, slaloming around the three girls as if any physical contact would lose them points. Tomoko kicked out a lazy foot at the last one. "I'll be OK when I get out of this damn place."

"Won't we all?"

"You'll make it, Haruma." Satomi's soft voice spoke up for the first time. "We've all had a rough time of it, especially you." She looked away from Haruma, down at the suds-covered lino. "I still cry sometimes when I'm trying to get to sleep. I try to think positive but it's not easy..." Tomoko moved to put an arm round her. Haruma noticed the tall girl's eyes were shiny but her words were as strong as ever.

"Haruma's going to do fine, we all are. We have to."

"Satomi's so sweet!" whispered Aki. Haruma nodded.

"Haruma...what is it?"

"I'm agreeing with you, Tomoko. You're right, Satomi. We all have to think positive from now on. Let's get on with this stupid floor. I want to go out clubbing tonight and forget about it all. To hell with Uni! If I don't get in I'll still always have you guys to annoy me. En garde!"

"Touché!" shouted Tomoko and Satomi in unison. The three of them danced around the corridor in a mop swordfight until the principle came out of his office down the hallway to tell them to stop acting like first years. And they all giggled at him.

"I don't think I've done it, Aki."

Haruma was making her way along the side of the quad beneath the peeling green tin-covered walkways. She was on her way to see Watanabe-san for the last time, to thank her old science teacher for his patience with her.

"I know that you have, Haruma."

"You don't know anything of the sort. You were useless at ordinary maths, never mind Advanced. You couldn't even work out your pool score without my help!"

"That's unkind. True, but unkind." Haruma heard Aki's sudden laughter in the overcast March air and just for a moment thought she might even see a trace of it curling around the edges of the walkway roof like a haze of sunbeams escaping back to the sky.

"Will you come with me this afternoon?" She tried not to make it sound like pleading.

"I said I would, didn't I?"

"Hmm, you did. But if you didn't want to..." Haruma paused. "I dreamt about you again last night," she said the words quietly. Nobody in the quad would hear her above the rat-a-tat of the rain, and most of the other school-leavers from her year had escaped the downpour to rush back into the cream-coloured buildings.

"I told you to stop doing that."

"I know, but we'd been out to that club in Shinjuku, the first one we all went to together; the old 'gang of four'. It just felt so weird... We talked about you all night. It was the first time we'd really done that you know, since..."

"Don't remind me..." She felt the other sigh. She stopped walking and waited for her to continue. Eventually, she couldn't resist.

"What was it like, Aki?"

"You've asked me that before." There was a warning note in Aki's voice.

"'Painful' isn't really an answer."

"Well it's the only one you're going to get. Why don't you try it yourself if you're so damn curious?"

"I'm sorry, I didn't mean..." But Aki was gone. Haruma could always tell straight away. She clutched the present she'd brought for Watanabe-san to her chest and ran across to the nearest doorway, skipping the puddles that created islands across the grey concrete.

She found the grey-haired old man in the main Chemistry classroom surrounded by a gaggle of school-leavers promising that 'cross their hearts' they'd keep in touch.

"Haruma!" He waved to her through the crowd and came over to where she stood hesitantly in the doorway. "How are you? Nervous...? It's this afternoon isn't it?"

She nodded. "I'm OK. I just wanted to give you this and say thank-you for everything."

He took the present but kept looking at her. "Thank-you, that's very kind. Are you really OK?"

"Not really." She felt tears prick her eyes and blinked them back self-consciously. Not now in front of Sensei. This was meant to be a fun day.

"I hope you don't still think about it. You must move on you know, Haruma."

"Yes, Sensei..."

But she saw Aki again in her mind: "I passed Haruma, I

passed, I got in!"

It was after Aki's scholarship exam for Tokyo College of Music, taken early as the winter began to fade and before all the others would have the chance of shaping their futures. Aki had always been different from them, special, talented, more than talented: exceptional. Like her name she sparkled, and it all seemed to come so easily for her. Only the others in the gang of four knew the hard work she put in. On that day, dancing in front of Haruma, joyful, blissfully unaware of her surroundings, she took a clumsy step backwards; perhaps the only clumsy thing Haruma had ever seen her do. Haruma remembered the famous American actor's giant face on the side of the bus. She would never be able to watch his films again; she knew that as a given, even as she was turning to run after the big silver bullet-shaped vehicle that was dragging Aki along the road then under its wheels. She hated him, even if his name always slipped her memory. Nothing else about that day ever did.

She was back in the classroom. "I'm sorry, I have to go check my results now. I really just wanted to say... y'know. Thanks... for helping me." She bowed to him, a hand to her mouth. "Arigato Sensei!"

She turned and fled.

The University of Tokyo was a big place. Haruma had got lost twice just trying to find the information desk. When she finally did, the woman in the neat grey suit left her not much the wiser.

"Back down the main corridor, turn right then left twice, I think, and up the stairs. The notice boards are on your right. No, left. You'll see the sign. The list will be along the far wall, next to the Department Head's office, or if not there, a little further down by the labs. Anyway, ask one of the administrative staff when you get there." She turned away from Haruma to confuse someone else.

"Silly cow...!" hissed Aki in her ear.

"Now, now."

"Now, now, silly cow!" Aki giggled. *'I must be more nervous than you.'*

"Impossible. I'm crapping myself!"

"What a charming image."

"You know what I mean. Oh Aki, If I screw this up my parents will kill me."

"No they won't."

"Well then *I'll* kill me!" There was silence in the high-ceilinged main hall as the other students wandered around her trying to find out where to go to receive their fate.

"Aki...?" she paused. "Let's go then, shall we?" Haruma started down the way she'd been pointed.

She found the lists where the woman had said they'd be, stuck to the wall-long notice board with bright colour-coded pins defining their various departments. The School of Science was brown, a crisp A4 sheet with about forty names making up two regimented columns. She traced it with an agitated finger before realising halfway down the first that it was in alphabetical order. She hadn't seen her name. Of course she hadn't: Yamauchi!

Haruma shut her eyes. Someone knocked her elbow but she refused to open them again. She could walk away now and never know, leave the country for some far off exotic place never to return. She would always wonder if she'd passed, never have to give up the delusion that she'd turned down The University of Tokyo for the life of a bohemian traveller; never have to... oh to hell with it!

Haruma screwed up her fists and opened her eyes. She focussed on the last two names in the second column:

JUICHI WAKAMI

HARUMA YAMAUCHI

Her, her name! It was there! She'd passed, been accepted... she was going to Tokyo University!

"I knew you'd make it."

"I'm in Aki!"

"I know."

"But I'm actually in!"

Silence; inside her head a silence. Not the thoughts about Uni and the next few years, they were whirring around her consciousness like angry dragonflies, each demanding her individual attention, each with its own set of doubts and problems and catastrophic scenarios. She shut the door on them and stepped outside.

Haruma was in a bright sunny field; in the distance the city's grey skyline hung suspended in the heat haze. There were no rain clouds here, no cold April winds to make her shiver. It was summertime, the summer she'd first met Aki. The day they went on that long bus ride out to the country, to explore, just for the hell of it.

"We're here again, Aki."

"Yes."

"Because. .?"

"Because I have to tell you something."

"And what if I don't want to hear?"

"You have to hear it, you have to listen. You've got to get rid of me Haruma, you've got to let me go. I've waited until now and now's the time; do it now or I'll stay forever. You don't want that."

"How do you know what I want?"

"I know you. You're going places Haruma, you always were. Don't let me hold you back anymore."

"Aki, don't..."

But she saw her friend now, ringed by sunlight, a young figure both Aki and not Aki anymore. She was walking slowly away from her through the fields and grasslands. The figure stopped for a moment at their edge, seemed to turn and wave once, then run with strides ever lengthening until the day swallowed it up.

And she was finally alone.

She found Satomi and Tomoko sitting on the steps outside the University waiting for her. Haruma wiped her face with her sleeve before walking down to them. She did so quietly and they only noticed her presence when she was almost on top of them.

"Haruma! Oh love, never mind." Tomoko's voice was soothing, her eyes full of sympathy. Satomi's face wore its worried expression. She reached out a hand to touch Haruma.

Haruma nodded at Tomoko.

"What?"

She nodded again.

"Yes? You passed? You passed! Bloody hell, you lucky cow!"

"I don't know if I'm ready for it yet, though," she told them. "Maybe I should do a gap year…"

And they both hit her at exactly the same time.

The Glass Wall

The bird flew over Akio Watanabe's head just as he bent to pick up the silver necklace bead from the concrete floor, a soft ruffle of air cut off by the hard dull thud of a body hitting the garage window.

He glanced up in time to see the knotted ball of feathers slide down the dirty glass and fall gracelessly to the ground. The thrush seemed at first motionless but as he bent to pick it up a long thin tongue began to ride up and down inside its beak as if searching for one last breath of air. For a moment it seemed to find it, then there was a barely perceptible rattle in its throat and the tongue stilled.

Watanabe carefully picked up the almost weightless body as the head flopped backwards. The creature's eyes had already dimmed, like shiny wet pebbles on a beach grown dull at the sea's retreat. Was he the last thing it had seen, some unknowable, unapproachable god from beyond its world dispassionately observing its last moments on Earth? He felt momentarily uncomfortable at being afforded such power. The late sun threw his shadow across the yard poised in silhouette, one hand at his side, the other holding out its pathetic burden as if in ritual sacrifice to the golden evening.

Was he responsible for the creature's death?

He had opened the garage door to show a fleeting glimpse of the yard beyond through the back window, had allowed it the masquerade of natural light framed by darkness as it swooped. There would have been no reflection on the window's glass wall, no hint of the bird's approaching nemesis; it was not the natural world's trusted landscape but man's own trickery of light and shade, clarity and density, unknowable limits the bird could have no intimation of even if it had lived a thousand years. Watanabe felt an irrational anger with the stupid creature but couldn't bring himself to throw it in the rubbish bin. He looked around for another vessel in which to place the lifeless body, settling at length for the plastic bucket his wife had used to move small plants from one ledge to another in the tidy little rock garden she'd always loved. He'd cleaned the bucket out, along with other pointless small tasks, the morning of the funeral. It had been raining hard but he'd barely noticed.

Now he placed the bird almost reverently inside the bucket's gleaming yellow plastic. He caught a sun-blasted image of himself in a pane of glass in the garage's window, the same one the bird had hit. It had a slight smudge on it now masking his face, framed by his wispy white hair.

He felt suddenly foolish and stood up too quickly, the blood rushing to his head. Stupid thing! Why couldn't it have used its nutshell brain to understand that buildings don't just have empty holes in them? But of course it couldn't have known that. It just didn't see what was coming.

Watanabe brushed the garage dust from his cardigan and trousers and went back inside the house. He came out again a few minutes later to pull shut the garage door.

Watanabe slept on the sofa, still in his rumpled gardening clothes. He'd meant to take a shower but sudden fatigue had got the better of him. His anger with the bird had dissipated as he slipped off into a shallow sleep full of half-formed images of the past.

Marie at the conference in Paris where he'd met her, their first 'date' when she'd offered to show him around the Louvre; he'd got lost and when they'd finally found each other again in the cafe she'd been crying. Later at the Institute after they'd married, sitting behind her desk arguing with him over some obscure data, an argument he'd finally stopped by kissing her. Marie leading him into the lab for the surprise birthday party that he'd known about for weeks. Marie sharing the celebrations with him and the team when the research was finally published, kicking over a chair in frustration when the funding was withdrawn, crying on his shoulder when they were told they had ten minutes to leave the Institute.

His head was full of Marie.

He was sitting high up in the giant wooden bowl of the lecture theatre, watching her as she spoke so passionately about the science she loved; watching as the bird filled the glass wall behind her; watching as it hit and died…

He awoke with a start. The door-bell was ringing, or maybe

the alarm clock. It was the door.

A young man he recognised only after groping for his glasses stood somewhat sheepishly outside in the little road as if uncommitted to any further action. Katashi Maruyama, his former research assistant.

"Katashi! What are you doing here? Its good to see you again, please, come in..."

His guest stepped forward after some hesitation and allowed himself to be shuffled into the living room.

"How are you? It's been nearly four years, hasn't it? I could be wrong, time seems to have a mind of its own once you near retirement you know. Well you will know, one day."

"I think its more like six, Professor Watanabe."

"Akio, please call me Akio. We're not work colleagues any longer. It's so nice to see you again, how's the old gang, do you see much of them?"

Maruyama looked uncomfortable. "I haven't really seen anyone since that last day."

"No, no of course you haven't. I'm being stupid aren't I? Everyone goes their own separate ways."

"I believe Atsuko got married."

"Did she? Did she... that's good..." Watanabe's voice tailed off. "And how about yourself...? You were a very promising young man, I'm sure you found a good position at the Institute after... after it all ended."

"I did some field work that didn't really get anywhere. I've been teaching at a crammers for the last three years but that's finished now. Actually, that's what I've come to see you about."

"A crammers...?" Watanabe looked puzzled, as if presented with an unfamiliar equation, "I don't understand Katashi, you are far better than that. What a waste of your time."

"We all have to live, Professor. I believe you're just a humble high school teacher these days. Quite a comedown but at least you still have work."

Watanabe's bewilderment must have shown in his face.

"I'm sorry for saying so," Mauryama continued, "but the rest of us would have kept our jobs if you and your wife had accepted the Institute's new policy agenda. It's good to have principles but they don't pay the rent. I have a young son now, and my wife can only work part-time…"

He seemed to suddenly catch himself and held up his hands in apology. "I'm sorry, my rudeness is unforgivable. I'm afraid the years of frustration have built up in me. It was difficult to find your house and I've not had much sleep lately. I must be tired, please forgive my outburst."

Watanabe studied the young man silently for a few moments as if bringing him into focus; a specimen on a glass slide beneath his eye. When he spoke again his voice had a guarded authority. "One shouldn't be tired at your age. I'm glad to hear you've started a family, Maruyama."

His guest bowed his head slightly at the first use of his surname. "Thank-you Professor. How is Mrs Watanabe, Marie? Is she in, I'd like to say hello?"

"My wife died a few years ago." The gaze did not falter.

"Oh. I'm terribly sorry to hear…"

"Cancer; most distressing as you might imagine, but all over now."

"I'm sorry…"

"Yes, so am I. Now, how can I be of help to you Mr Maruyama?" Watanabe asked.

"I've come to ask for your recommendation of me for a new post I'm applying for at the Institute. For a personal reference I mean." Maruyama's own voice was crisp and business-like now. Both men seemed to have silently accepted that formality would not be broken again.

"You've gone about it in a peculiar way, but I owe you that at least. What is it that you'd have me say?"

"Just the usual, I'm a hard worker and reliable, careful, you know, good at what I do."

"I don't have a problem with that. What exactly is it that you will be doing?"

"Research into Polyphonic Sleep patterns." Maruyama averted his eyes from the old man. "Actually I'd be a test subject, but it would be a chance to get onto their team. I would be monitoring myself and writing up my personal data afterwards. They told me that, anyway."

"A guinea pig?" Watanabe frowned. "I don't like the sound of that. Once you've crossed the line between researcher and subject its difficult going back. You'll lose respect and position, and your reputation."

"Reputation...?" Maruyama gave him a short mirthless laugh. "That's a word used by people like you, Professor. We can't eat my 'reputation'."

"Maybe not, but sleep pattern experimentation can be psychologically dangerous. That's why they use penniless students to do it, people who will vanish back into the crowd. I would seriously warn you against it."

"Thank-you for your concern, Sensei, but the Institute wish to keep this one in-house. It's going to be a big deal, and I'd be in at the start of it."

The old man tensed. He looked at the younger one for a long moment. "Don't do it, Katashi."

"I have to."

Watanabe dropped his shoulders and turned away from him. "Very well; I'll write something appropriate and send it to whoever you tell me to. Write it down for me before you go. Now, would you like some coffee or something?"

"Thank-you, but I really must be leaving. I've a lot to take care of." Maruyama scribbled some lines on a business card and placed it on the coffee table. "I'm very grateful to you."

"It seems the least I can do. I'm sorry Marie and my principles ruined your career." Watanabe held up a hand at the other's protest. "No, I'm not being facetious. When the Institute wanted to take our many years of work and use it for their Neuro-economics programme of course we protested. We started our project to help people with their behavioural problems, not to implant brand loyalty into their minds for commercial means. We thought that was a disgusting thing to do, irresponsible, even dangerous. We assumed you all did as well, but it seems we'd shut ourselves away from the real world for too long. It can't be helped now; it's all over. Please make the best of your life with my good wishes."

Maruyama seemed to be about to say something in reply then forced a hand to his mouth. He straightened and bowed deeply before Watanabe.

"Sensei!"

The old man somewhat stiffly returned the bow. "My good friend, Maruyama."

It was almost twilight when Watanabe remembered the bird. He'd been pottering around the house doing nothing in particular, re-filing old notes, reading last month's journal again, listlessly preparing a scrappy meal for himself. He brought the food into the living room on a tray and sat in his armchair but instead of eating, picked up the old photograph he'd found in the folder.

It was of the old team on the day of scientific publication, one he'd not remembered seeing before. He screwed up his eyes then put the tray down again and went to find the magnifying glass. Now he could see the happy faces quite sharply; Maruyama and Atsuko and the others, all a little the worse for wear, shouting at the camera and raising their little plastic cups so that champagne slopped down their white sleeves. Marie was there with her arms tightly clasped around his waist, the two of them grinning like school-kids as they stared bleary-eyed at the future out of the photograph's white shiny frame.

Watanabe found the little corpse where he'd left it. He'd half hoped, half been afraid that a neighbour's cat would have taken it as its plaything. But it was still there in the bucket, slight movements in its chest and feathers indicating that mites were already about their business. He put on his gardening gloves and lifted the dead bird out by its tail with the studied concentration of some miniature engineering project. Holding the bird at arm's length he took Marie's gardening trowel from the garage, returned to the rock garden and dug a shallow trench in an unused patch near its summit. He placed the bird inside, slowly despite its squirming carcass, then quickly covered it and flattened the loose earth with the trowel's blade.

Watanabe stood up panting with the air of a man caught in a guilty act. The sun's last rays caught the little mound as they climbed up the garden fence, casting its shadow against the slats. Atop its hill of cracked stone slabs in a momentary ring of sunbeams it had taken on the aspect of a fairy mausoleum. He took out the silver necklace bead from his pocket and pushed it down into the mound's centre. There – a monument to the blindness of fate.

Watanabe put his hands on his hips and gave the evening a

last tired smile.

Non-Sleeper

The serious young woman in the lab coat was talking over her shoulder again as he trailed behind her. "Seen enough?"

Katashi nodded. Her name was Aimi and she had a little plastic tag on her breast to prove it.

The courtesy tour was finally about to end. The glass doors of the reception area slid open and he followed her quick little steps up to the desk.

The place had changed quite a bit in five years. Like himself. The easy-going student on his first big research job, now a family man, nervous about making enough of an impact on his former employees at the Institute to regain a full-time position. He'd made big mistakes during his transition, bad choices forced on him to pay for the poky little flat he shared with Hiroko and the baby. He hadn't seen that coming, like a lot of the things that happened after Watanabe pulled the plug.

"You do know I used to work here?" he asked her.

"I believe it was mentioned in your files. The Professor doesn't remember you though."

"Does he remember my old boss, Professor Watanabe?"

The girl was busy talking to the pretty receptionist. "Ask him to come down, would you Jin?" She turned to face him with a slight tic of annoyance. "Perhaps you'd like to ask him yourself?"

Another set of glass doors slid open and Professor Oshiro walked in beaming at the two of them. He was a small nondescript man in his mid-forties with a bald patch. Katashi had seen his face in the journals and had somehow imagined him larger, to match his reputation.

"Hello Mr Maruyama, Katashi!" He offered Katashi an effusive handshake. "You've had the grand tour I see."

"The new labs in East Block look very impressive, Professor."

The little man looked momentarily confused then smote his head. "Of course, you used to work here didn't you. Something in Sensory Deprivation wasn't it?"

"Not quite." The guy was guessing. Had Oshiro even looked at the CV he'd sent him?

"Well you're a test subject now, not a scientist. Think you'll be able to cope with that?"

"I wouldn't be here if I didn't. And perhaps we can discuss that little matter regarding work?"

"Its cold out there in the real world, isn't it Mr Maruyama?" Oshiro raised his eyebrows at him playfully. "Don't worry; I'm sure we'll find something for you. After we get the test over with of course."

He led Katashi and the girl to a lift. They got out on the third floor and followed him down a wide corridor to a door at its far end.

"After you, Mr Maruyama..." Katashi stepped into a large area, part laboratory part living quarters. Lined up along one wall were various kitchen units, a cooker and a sink. In front of them were a table and chairs and even a couch with cushions facing a small TV. The lab with its various rows of equipment was on the other side, near the windows.

"Your own home from home for the next week." Oshiro told him brightly.

"It's bigger than my home." Katashi replied.

"Well...enjoy your time with us anyway. We've a couple of hours to go through some of the details a bit more comprehensively. You do fully understand what this experiment will involve?"

Of course he understood. Katashi had read the Professor's sleep deprivation paper until he knew it off by heart. He'd even completed a security check and signed a health waiver.

The subject, himself, would be given two recently-developed drugs, one of them highly controversial. The first, Pinealyn, would inhibit his pineal gland from creating melatonin, the chemical that causes drowsiness. That would allow his body to dispense with the first four stages of 'slow wave' sleep. The second, an untested drug the notes referred to only as a 'REM-booster', would modify the fifth stage, the 'Rapid Eye Movement' or REM sleep. This was the part of a normal sleep cycle where the EEG activity would be at its highest with heart-rate and blood-pressure levels similar to those during wakefulness. However, in this particular test the

REM-booster would flip this last section into full consciousness. He'd be continuously awake for a whole week.

"So remember, if you feel uncomfortable about anything tell us. At the end of the test we'll give you a shot to neutralise all the drugs and you'll be back to normal." He looked at the wall clock. "Let's get started then, shall we?"

A male technician entered the laboratory area through a side door and began to prepare two syringes of colourless liquid. He was younger than Katashi, good-looking in a boyish sort of way with quiffed, dyed blond hair and the hint of a well-developed sportsman's body under his lab coat.

Katashi saw the girl give him a quick intimate glance over her laptop.

"You're late, Hiro." Oshiro told him.

"Sorry, Professor." The young man didn't look up at him.

"That's alright, please see it doesn't happen again."

Oshiro turned his attention back to Katashi. "Ready?"

Katashi found his tongue was dry and nodded. He felt a moment of panic.

'Hiro' brought the two syringes over to them on a little steel tray.

The rest of that first day passed quickly. He watched some TV then read the newspapers for a few hours. The large window behind the laboratory showed the full nightscape of the Institute's rolling campus. Lights from adjacent buildings gradually extinguished themselves.

"I'm turning in." Aimi told him. "Hiro's on first shift, I'll take over at five." She went to the little camp bed in the storeroom where she and Hiro would take it in turns to sleep. Oshiro had left much earlier. Katashi knew nothing of his private life other than that he was married.

"My wife used to work to support me as well at first," he'd told Katashi. "And look at me now." It had seemed unnecessarily smug.

Katashi turned to the IQ tests laid out for him on the table. These or similar would be repeated each night to chart any decrease in his mental agility. They obviously hoped to find none.

The long night turned slowly into dawn. Aimi took over from Hiro, and Oshiro joined them at nine to begin his daily programme of health checks. It was as easy, and tedious, as that.

The next two days were exactly the same.

Now it was Thursday, four nights into the experiment. Hiro sat on the couch watching TV as Katashi once again worked through the tests. At four thirty he stretched and yawned.

"I'm making some coffee, Katashi. Want some?"

"OK, thanks."

"The REM booster should kick in pretty soon eh?"

"Don't I know it!" Katashi replied. The modified REM period was having a strange affect on him, as though his body somehow detached itself. The detachment was more powerful each night.

A short while later he felt a gradual stiffness overtake him. This hadn't happened before. He tried to stand but felt paralysed. Then the girl was in the room. He hadn't seen her enter but there she was, talking to Hiro right in front of him.

"You're a bit early tonight aren't you?" he told her. "Its not yet five..." Neither turned around. They seemed to be arguing, their voices strangely distant.

"I know what I'm doing." That was Aimi.

"But it's blackmail – it's dangerous!"

"What else can he do? He'd be ruined!"

The young man slammed the door as he left the lab. The girl sat down and stared at the TV.

"Hey, he's meant to stay, isn't he?" She ignored Katashi's question. He felt the stiffness begin to wear off. He walked over and waved a hand in her face. She sprang back in surprise.

"What are you doing?"

"Hiro's meant to stay here with us, isn't he?"

"He's sleeping!" She sounded annoyed.

"I just saw him leave."

She got up and stalked over to the storeroom, thrusting open the door. A muttered "What?" came from within. Katashi joined her and looked down at the figure of Hiro, lying there with his hand over his eyes.

"But..."

Aimi grabbed her laptop off the bench. "Excuse me, I've work to do."

As he shrugged and turned away the wall clock caught his eye; it was nearly six thirty. Somehow, he'd lost an hour and a half.

He told the Professor about the paralysis later that morning.

"It's nothing to worry about. The body becomes almost rigid during normal REM sleep when our brains and muscles are at their most active. It's a primitive safety device to prevent us from sleepwalking and suchlike. It's good; what this experiment is all about. Anything else...?'

Katashi hesitated. "I heard something strange." He shook his head. "Probably nothing, I may have been hallucinating."

Oshiro studied him more seriously. "Let me know if it happens again."

The long Friday night wore slowly into morning. The excitement of the experiment had long ago given way to tedium and the desire to get home to Hiroko and the baby. Even the possibility of a job offer at the Institute had palled. This time away from his problems had given him a new perspective; he'd find something else if he had to, something even better.

It was four thirty again and the inhibited REM cycle was beginning. He felt woolly-headed. His arms felt heavy and his legs paralysed. Hiro must have gone to the toilet for a moment.

Excited voices made him look up from the tests. Hiro was there with Aimi again, standing over by the lab speaking in hushed tones to each other. They both looked very intense. This was wrong, he told himself. From nowhere Professor Oshiro joined them. They started to argue then Oshiro pushed Aimi away shouting at her. "I won't stand for this! You're finished here, do you understand?!" The words were faint but edged in shock and anger. Oshiro walked away from them towards the storeroom. Katashi's eyes followed him until he slammed the door. When he glanced back to the others they'd disappeared and he was on his own in the room.

'Hiro, Aimi...is anyone there?" But there was only silence

and the static buzz of the TV. He stared out of the rain-lashed windows at the darkened campus then looked up at the wall clock. It had crept around to five twenty-seven, almost an hour on. A muffled sound came from the storeroom.

Slowly Katashi began to feel the blood return to his limbs. He pushed himself up from the table and crossed the room, swearing at the pins and needles in his legs. At the storeroom door he heard heavy breathing and gasps from inside. Something was thudding against a wall.

Katashi opened the door and light fell across the tensed naked back of Oshiro. There was a figure beneath him spread-eagled on the floor and for a moment Katashi thought the two men were fighting then he saw the matted blond hair and recognised the boy. A light came on from another area and he saw the tiny figure of Aimi, her face shadowed and hard. She put a delicate hand under the older man's chin then pulled his face back to look up at her. As Katashi saw Oshiro's shock of recognition, Aimi the pulled the knife around the Professor's throat in a spurting crescent of blood.

"Oh, God…! Fuck…!"

She turned at the sound of his voice, letting the body drop.

Hiro scrambled away from beneath the bloody corpse. "What? What is it?" The words were a hoarse whimper.

"I thought I heard someone. It's nothing. Help me get him into the bath then get the acid."

"I don't think I can do it, Aimi."

"You already have… what was that?"

Katashi's foot had banged against the door as he backed away. He saw Aimi's sharp little eyes focus on him, their jet-black pupils almost filling each iris. His hand worked for the door handle and pulled then he was twisting back into the laboratory. He pushed his legs to run to the main door but found it locked. He smashed at it with his fists then turned. At the far end of the long room two white blurs moved slowly towards him.

They formed themselves into the figures of Aimi and Hiro. As they got closer Katashi saw that they were both smiling.

"Can you hear me Katashi?" The pinprick of white light hurt his eyes. A balding head bobbed in his vision. Faces swam before him.

"Mr Maruyama, we gave you the neutraliser an hour ago. You were in a catatonic state and we ended the experiment. Can you focus on me?" It was Oshiro's voice, strained and worried.

Katashi looked up at him. "You're dead."

He heard the Professor's laughter, joined by Aimi and Hiro's. "What's that? Dead...?"

He sat up too rapidly, his head spinning. They sat grouped around him on the sofa, Aimi smiling pleasantly at him, Hiro patting his knee. "You'll be fine now Mr Maruyama. It's all over. The Professor thinks we've gained some very valuable data from the test. You were never in any danger but it's good to have you back with us."

Oshiro helped him to his feet. "We're all going out for a drink to celebrate, after we've completed your final checks of course. Won't you come along?"

Katashi looked around at the little group. "I really should be getting home to my wife..."

Oshiro smiled and nodded. "Yes, family always comes first. I'll let you know about that job."

Katashi sat in his car. In a few minutes time he'd drive out of the Institute's main gates and go home to Hiroko. He'd turn the key in the ignition and go. He really would. He stared out unseeing at the neatly cut lawns then pinched the flesh on his wrist, just to make sure he was really there.

The Room

The hotel corridor had a forest scene painted on its walls with miniature trees in sunken pots, their bases surrounded with little piles of carefully arranged stones like the ones in the Zen 'gardens' of Kyoto's temples. This place was a kind of temple as well, Jin Okamoto mused as she made her way to tonight's room. A temple dedicated to love. Well, not love, although in the more raunchy guidebooks such places were always listed under the coy pseudonym of 'love hotels'. This place, this modern complex of concrete and steel pushing in between the pachinko parlours and noodle shops of Shinjuku, was all about sex; sex by the hour.

Hiro, the 'manager' of Hotel Diana, had called her in for tonight's client with a peculiar premise. "You won't have done anything like this before Jin. This guy's different, had his own room made up to his own specifications. It's some kind of short-term thing, I don't know what exactly but I'm giving you another chance so screw him and don't screw-up."

That was because she'd hit the last guy back, a drunk Hiro should never have left her with. He'd threatened to take it out of her pay but then Hiro had never understood that about her; that it wasn't all about the money. Sure, that came in handy; for last year's trip to Bali and the brand new Nissan GTR that got admiring looks from the senior staff at the Institute. How could she afford it on a secretary's salary? They looked at her strangely when she brought them their post and showed their important visitors up to the pristine laboratories on the third floor. Did they guess she had this double life? Some of the younger ones must have done, but nothing was said.

She was reliable, good at her job, discreet to a fault about the inner workings of the Institute.

She had no friends, no family, no man; she knew all of that had been checked out before she was even offered the job.

And she knew how to keep her mouth shut about the secrets of the Institute.

Just as in her after-hours occupation she knew when to keep

it open.

Jin had been working as one of the 'helpers' at the Hotel Diana for the last two years. Hiro had personally given her a tour of the place on her first day and told her what was expected in each room.

"OK, let's start here. The Tube Room; as you can see it's the inside of a tube train." It was: black straps hanging down from metal poles, sliding doors, red plastic seats lining each side of the carriage. He'd smiled at her enquiring glance. "Touching up women on public transport is clamped down on now but some of our senior clients still yearn for the good old days. The office lady suit's in there." He pointed to a metal locker. "The dry cleaning bill will be yours of course."

Hiro took her through all the other rooms offering similar role briefings and wardrobe advice as they went: the traditional Samurai Room with its feudal wooden sex toys; the Manga Room, all round-eyed innocent baby dolls and sci-fi backdrops; the Playmates Room including its own bouncy castle and supply of over-sized nappies. By the end of it she was very clear what her part in each of the proceedings would be. That was fine as long as they played by the rules.

Luckily, most of the timid salarymen were too scared to do anything else. That meant she was in charge. Secretary no longer unless she chose to be in micro skirt and tightly bursting blouse, she would spend her nights corralling the same pathetic creatures she spent her days taking crap from. This time it would be Jin in skin-tight rubber cat-suit or schoolgirl uniform who did the dictating.

So when she entered room twenty-five that evening Jin mentally prepared herself for the evening's activities as she always did. What she wasn't prepared for however was the room itself.

There was nothing special about it and that's what made it so special, because in the middle of a building full of extraordinary rooms, someone had constructed a completely ordinary one. A living room in fact, a little more modern than most perhaps, but still a living room with a big leather sofa and thick shag pile carpet. There was a television and CD player, a microwave oven, a frosted glass table and two designer-styled chairs.

In one of the chairs sat a man in a business suit. He looked in his late forties, well-built but not heavy with severely-cut greying hair and a slightly loosened tie that he fiddled with nervously as he watched her approach.

"You're the girl?" He looked up at her with coldly vacant eyes.

"Yes."

He nodded. "There's a dress in there." He indicated a metal cupboard in the corner. "Put it on."

She took out the dress. It was a rather drab yellow, poorly cut and straight lined with a high neck. She thought it about as sexy as a shroud but unzipped her own and stepped into it, letting him see the full sweep of her breasts as she bent down. To her surprise he looked away.

"Come over here and sit down."

She took a seat opposite him, smoothing down the dress and rearranging her hair as she did so.

He took a sheaf of A4 paper from a slim briefcase and slid it across to her.

"Read this out loud, one line at a time. Don't say anything else." He nodded again. "Start now."

Jin looked at the neatly-typed sentences. This was weird and she didn't like it, didn't like him or the spooky room. For the first time at Hotel Diana she felt out of control of the situation. Hiro had promised her good money for this charade but hadn't gone into detail about the client's wishes or indeed the bizarre circumstances of the room. She'd thought that strange but now understood the little pimp's reluctance. The guy was odd, possibly violent, and this didn't promise to be fun. 'Do it and get out,' her mind told her.

"What are you waiting for?" his voice was flat as if addressing a shop girl.

"Sorry..." Jin flustered. She began. *"So you're home. Was everything OK at the office with the new account? Did it go the way you thought it would?"*

"It went well enough. What's for supper?" he answered, staring down at the table.

"Toncatsu, I'll warm it up, I was expecting you hours ago."

"I went to celebrate. You don't begrudge me that I hope."

"You could have phoned me though."

"You should have known."

"How could I? That's typical of you, thoughtless, arrogant and stupid. Sometimes I wish I'd never..."

The hand swept around in a blurred arc to stop an inch from Jin's face. He held it there for a second more then let it drop to the table. He clenched it into a fist and looked away from her.

"That's all for tonight," his voice sounded shaky.

She got to her feet and walked quickly to the door without a backward glance.

"Are you ready?" The man asked her.

It was two nights later. Hiro had tried another girl with the man in room twenty-five after Jin's refusal to go back but it had been an immediate failure. He'd complained after she'd rushed out in tears, and asked for Jin again. Hiro had offered her almost twice as much to return, stupid money but that wasn't why she did it. No-one treated her like that; she needed to regain control.

"Where's my script?"

He gave her the neatly-typed paper and they went through the first part again, Jin replying automatically to the litany of abuse as it intensified. She would get through it whatever happened, and then she would look down at this pathetic creep as she took his money. Sex would have been better, any kind of thing he'd wanted because she could have easily neutralised that. But she would finish this now, get to the end of it.

"You've had someone else here while I've been away. Haven't you?"

"No Riku..."

This time the hand made contact, even though he pulled the slap. She flinched and read on.

"*That's your answer to everything isn't it? You're a coward, a stupid selfish coward!*" The script told her to cry but Jin hadn't cried in years. She blinked hard trying to force the tears into her eyes. "*I hate you... I hate all this. I wish I'd never been born!*"

"Finally, something we both agree on!" he spat the words into her face. "Why don't you do something about it then?"

"You bastard!"

"Bitch!"

He slapped her again and this time the slap carried through. She stood up, reeling from the blow and staggered towards the door. The direction was in the script but she would have done so anyway. Jin was truly scared for her life now.

It had got out of control.

She got it half open but his fist slammed it shut again. She turned away from him but he grabbed her arm and spun her around then smacked her head back against the door with the flat of his hand. Her legs gave way and she slid to the floor. She put her hands up to protect her face expecting another blow but none came. There was silence in the room.

Then a low whimpering noise came, like an animal in pain. Slowly, her fingers parted. The man was on his knees in front of her as if praying.

He opened his mouth but no words came out. He was staring red-eyed, tears running down his cheeks. He reached out a shaking hand to her as she recoiled. The hand dropped away. "I'm sorry, I'm sorry Momoko. It's the drink, it's not me... please stay with me, please forgive me..."

Jin glanced down at the crumpled script lying next to her on the floor. It had blood on it: hers. She realised her nose was bleeding. There were spatters on the yellow dress. Only two more lines remained.

She swallowed, tasting blood on her lips. *"I. . I forgive you Riku..."* She felt like she might throw up but forced the feeling down. The back of her head ached. *"Everything...will be alright...from now on."*

"Do you promise Momoko? Promise me that it will."

"I...promise...my love."

And one last direction: Jin bent forward slowly, her whole body trembling. The man lowered his head to her as if in supplication. Her lips brushed his skin. *"I forgive you..."*

They were both quiet for a long moment, Jin's heart thumping wildly in her chest. Then the man rose quickly to his feet as if snapping out of a dream. He held out a hand to her. "That's it, we're finished. You were good."

Jin pushed the hand away and staggered up. She felt her nose but it seemed nothing was broken; at least the bleeding had almost stopped. She put a hand to the back of her throbbing head then stared down at the blood on her fingers.

Not so good.

He noticed her and held up a hand in apology. "Sorry for that, I meant to pull away; I'll pay extra of course."

"Damn right you will!" She tried to stop shaking and feel the control returning. It was going to take a while. "How many times have you done this?"

He looked away. "That's none of your business. Like I said, we're finished here. I gave that pimp enough cash to pay for my… carelessness. That's it."

"What happened to her?"

He shook his head. "That's it, we're done. Thank-you…"

"Tell me." He shook it again, refusing to meet her eyes. "Tell me or I'll call the police and say you tried to beat me up." He looked quickly at her. "I'll do it. We're not play-acting now."

The man took a deep breath then let it out slowly. "She went upstairs and hanged herself. I found her when I sobered up the next morning. No note, she must have done it straight away."

"And you never said that last stuff to her, all the begging?"

He snorted. "I was too pissed; I fell asleep." He pointed over at the sofa.

"And doing this makes it better?" Jin asked.

The man gave an odd little laugh. "For a while; I'm a rich man you know, run my own cleaning company; fifteen vans. I can buy any woman for this."

"Do you hit them as well?"

He shook his head. "I said I was sorry."

"My dad was a violent man." Jin told him. "My grandfather told me when I was thirteen that he'd killed my mum when I was little. He'd made up some crap about the gods wanting her to stay with them, then another lie when I grew out of that one. Finally he told me that the fucking bastard actually threw her down a mountain after an argument; they were on their honeymoon…" She shook herself then stared at him coldly. "You're just like him: your sort can't help it. It's in the blood."

He shrugged. "What about you? Why are you doing this

shit?"

"I can be whosoever I choose when I'm in here."

He gave her a dirty grin: "As long as you screw someone."

"I didn't screw you."

"In a way you kind of did," he sneered at her. "Congratulations on a fine performance my girl, you're a natural."

"What do you mean by that?" But the door had already closed behind him.

Jin flung it open and screamed down the corridor. "What the fuck did you mean by that?" Then: "I hope Momoko haunts you forever!"

She heard his laugh as he went down the stairs.

It was later now and the room was in semi-darkness. Jin had fallen asleep on the sofa but the coldness awoke her. There was a sticky stain of blood where her head had lain. Shivering, she pulled herself to her feet and wandered across to the window. Outside the Tokyo nightscape dazzled her eyes.

Then, as if a switch had been thrown somewhere, the lights began to go off: first in the distant high-rise apartments fringing the edges of the city, then the streetlights far off in the distance. It was like a tsunami of darkness rushing towards her, blotting out highways and thoroughfares, whole districts of department stores and towering office blocks until in a few moments it had reached the streets of Shinjuku itself. A power cut, when she wanted to get home!

Body still aching from the tension and with a thumping headache, Jin changed back into her own clothes, gathered up her jacket and handbag and stepped into the darkened corridor.

Instantly she knew something else was wrong; the trees were missing. Even with just the pale illumination of the moon in the corridor's far window she could see that someone had taken them down, removed the pots and stones as well for good measure. The walls were now bare as well, the forest scenes gone.

Why now, tonight? She'd heard nothing to wake her. She pushed the light on her watch. Only ten-thirty, she'd slept for just two hours, and yet everything had changed. She didn't like walking around the place in the dark, too many weirdos hanging around; it could get dangerous.

Suddenly Jin felt sick of it all. The bile welled up inside her stomach and she threw up an eruption of disgust that slapped against the wall and slid down to form a puddle on the carpet. She staggered and leant against the doorframe then wiped her mouth with the back of her hand. She brought a tissue out of her bag and wiped it again. This was it, enough! That man had finally got to her; she could take no more. She wanted to be someone else; anyone else but Jin, because he'd been right and she'd known it.

She *was* a natural – a natural victim, and all the control freak mind-games in the world could no longer hide that fact from her. She'd been born into self-loathing and deception; circumstances beyond her control had laid the course for her long ago. But she could change, couldn't she? Become a better person?

It's never too late to change...

Jin began to walk unsteadily down the corridor towards the stairwell at the far end but it seemed a long way now. The doors stretched out before her like coffins stacked in neat rows. What was happening? Had she been drugged? Or was it the bang on her head?

A noise came from one of the farthest doors; a child's whimpering. There were no children allowed in Hotel Diana. The waves of nausea gave way to anger at the little pimp. Then the whimpering stopped. Had she really heard it?

There was a click, then another. As she looked down the corridor one by one the doors began to open.

She stepped to the nearest one and peered inside: the room was even darker than the hallway. It seemed empty at first but then Jin heard groans from inside; another door opened somewhere and sharp white light outlined the back of a naked bald-headed man spread-eagled above another pinioned beneath him. He raised his head as a woman's figure crossed towards him. Jin saw something glitter in her hand then realised it was a knife; in one swift movement she wrenched the man's head backwards. As they both stared towards her, the door suddenly slammed shut before she could see anymore. With delayed shock Jin realised the bald-headed man had been Professor Oshiro from the Institute. And the girl had been Aimi...

Jin backed away to the far wall and stared at the shut door. Aimi had just murdered Professor Oshiro! But that couldn't be; she'd left them both back at the institute hours ago. What were they doing here, at Hotel Diana? Was it some kind of secret sex game gone hideously wrong? And who had been the powerfully built figure lying on the floor? It had looked like Hiro...

Gathering her shattered nerves she slowly crossed the corridor then pushed the door handle. The room was dark again and this time apparently empty.

A whining noise crept down the corridor towards her. As her mind struggled to identify it, the discordant sound grew until she was forced to hold her hands to her ears. The cacophony swelled to a climax then abruptly stopped. It had been coming from one of the other rooms. She looked in each one but all were dark. Then there came a quick tapping noise. It came again and this time Jin identified the sound; a conductor tapping their baton. And then she found the room.

Jin was standing in the wings of a large theatre. On stage a woman in a long black dress sat a grand piano. Beyond her rows of faces swept up into the darkness of the auditorium. The woman raised her arms as if to begin then turned her head to the audience. Jin followed her gaze and froze; propped up in a front row seat between the dinner jackets and gowns, the rotting corpse of a man raised its skull-like head. It nodded with a slack-jawed grin and the woman began to play.

Jin backed away, but as the piano's chords faded another sound replaced them: the whimpering child was back.

This room was white-walled and almost bare of furniture. Sitting on a plush white rug in the middle a small well-groomed woman in a sharp business suit was brushing the hair of a young girl sitting on her lap. The girl's hair was jet black, but her face was the whitest thing in the severe apartment. She stared up at the woman then pointed to Jin.

The woman slowly turned to face her then touching her fingers to her cheek whispered, "It's not just a one way street you know..." There was utter madness in her eyes.

Again, Jin backed away but couldn't run; her legs felt stiff and lifeless, as if she were trapped in a nightmare but lacked the will to awaken. There came a low murmuring from yet another room. Somehow she had to look.

This one was dark and moonlit from low window slits. In the middle a cracked and blackened wall ran across it behind a glass screen. A young man was kneeling down with his fingers splayed out on the glass, talking quietly to himself as if caught in the grip of an obsession. His eyes were tightly shut: body shaking so violently the screen itself began to vibrate.

Whatever he was going through she couldn't help him. She couldn't help any of them. Jin realised now that she was a mere observer of these tableaux: an unseen guest glancing at a random snapshot of their troubled worlds.

So why was she here, why was this happening to her?

There was one last room she'd not looked in yet; the first, right at the beginning of the darkened corridor. Jin listened: a distant buzz of voices leaked from its open doorway. Forcing her reluctant legs to obey her, she approached the room.

Inside it was small and box-like, surrounded by a steel frame. A tightly-packed crowd filled the area, swaying slightly where they stood. Apparently holiday-makers, they wore bright casual clothing; the women in blouses and slacks, the men in short sleeves and t-shirts. Some of the older guys wore thin windcheaters with light summer hats perched above sweating faces. A noisy group of long-haired boys in jeans and baggy t-shirts clustered together, children clung around their parents' legs or lined themselves along a set of steamed-up windows.

Jin had entered none of the other rooms but this last one seemed to want to pull her inside it, as if actually awaiting her presence. She felt the back of her head again and found more blood. The wooziness was still there but her brain was beginning to sharpen itself again, to think logically instead of cringing in fright. If she was indeed still lying on the sofa in that maniac's sordid attempt at redemption; if the power-cut and all these bizarre unsettling visions were merely by-products of her unconscious thought processes; if her own mind was trying to tell her something she needed to know...

Jin took a step forward.

The metal floor moved under her feet. Jin swayed uncertainly, trying to find a balance in the crowded cable car. The mountain scenery through the dusty glass was truly impressive. Steep boulder-strewn slopes swept away to either side beneath them as they began to climb. The lush caldera spread out towards a blue horizon like an undulating moss garden holding puddles of lakes and postage stamps of green rice paddies. A ribbon of road wound away through bumps and hollows until lost from view. She looked down to see the grey concrete block of the volcano museum growing ever smaller, as if being reduced to the status of a toy building on a model railway.

Jin knew where she was now. And looking around at her fellow passengers' general appearance: the subtle differences in their clothes, in what they carried, in what they said – she thought she knew when.

Someone nudged her arm. A man leant heavily against her for a few moments then pulled back into the press of people. "I'm sorry, someone pushed me..."

He was the same height as her so they were face to face in the cramped area, still just a few feet away from each other. Wearing a t-shirt, denim baseball cap and jeans he looked slightly younger than her; quite handsome in spite of the scruffily overlong hair. But his eyes were nervous, not settling on her but flicking around the crowd as if searching for someone.

"That's alright; it's very closely packed in here isn't it?"

"Yes, too much, the heat doesn't help either." He seemed to relax a little. She noticed his eyes glance quickly down her body.

Jin wore a thin black blouse, opened low enough to hint at the swell of her breasts. She had on a short tight red skirt that showed off her compact figure to its best advantage and black patent leather shoes. It was how she liked to dress for her evenings at Hotel Diana, a rebellion against her stuffily conservative work clothes. She sensed his appreciation, just as she did other men's whenever she sought their approval.

He paused then began to edge away, eyes again scanning those behind her. "Are you on holiday with someone?" she asked before he could retreat anymore. "Family; kids and stuff...?" Jin realised she wanted him to stay with her for a few moments longer; anything to maintain a semblance of normality in this world.

"Just my wife, and our daughter, it's a kind of delayed honeymoon I suppose." He looked embarrassed, somehow defensive. "We never had enough money when we first got married; expenses, bills..." his voice tailed away.

"How nice for both of you..." She tried a smile. "Have a good time then."

"Thank-you," he began backing away from her again, "excuse me..."

She nodded and turned to look out at the vista below her. She could smell the sulphur more powerfully now; it tingled in her nose, a sharp and pungent rotten eggs stink that began to make her eyes water. A young woman's sharp voice rose above the general hubbub in the car, making her look around.

"Who was she?"

"Who...?" It was the man speaking again. She saw his head across the car, earnestly bowed as if in deep conversation with another. There was a tiny child by his side with her hand in his.

"That woman you spoke to, the tarty one?"

"Just some woman..."

"What were you saying to her?" Jin couldn't see past his back to the woman's face. "Were you flirting with her while my back was turned?"

"Someone pushed me... I was just apologising. She asked why I was here, who I was with. We were just talking." Jin sensed a mounting panic in his words, as if he knew what was coming next. As if it always did.

"Did you try to touch her?"

"What...? Please darling, not here."

"I asked if you tried to touch her!" Others began to look around now at the raised voice. His own remained outwardly calm but Jin sensed it teetering on the brink.

"Of course I didn't touch her! I was looking for you, I couldn't see you anywhere; I thought maybe you hadn't got on."

"You mean hoped I hadn't, when you saw her!"

"Darling, please..." He tried to put an arm around her shoulder but she span away from him so that he was left standing in the middle of the car with the child. A few looked over to see what all the fuss was about; others stared pointedly away to the moving scenery outside. The man found a space at one of the windows and made a show of pointing out something to the child. He didn't look around again.

A short while later the car clanked into its berth and the doors slid noisily open. Jin threaded her way out with the others and onto the asphalt walkway leading to the volcano's rim. Up ahead in the crowd the arguing couple now walked silently side by side, the child between them. The man's head was lowered disconsolately, the woman's turned away to stare out at the hazy horizon. Then, as Jin continued to watch the young couple, she suddenly looked back and their eyes met. It was the first clear view Jin had managed to get of her.

Quite clear enough to see that it was her mother, Yuriko.

Jin had only seen a picture of her father once; when she was a child of thirteen she'd gone through her grandfather's wallet while he'd been out. He'd got rid of all photographs of his son-in-law from the house after his daughter's death, she'd found that out a few years before after constantly asking to see what he looked like. She'd thought at the time he might be lying about it but many fruitless searches had proved her wrong. Whenever she'd brought the subject up he'd feigned either deafness or, eventually, lost his temper: 'What do you want to see him for, why do you need to know? He's dead to us Jin, as dead as your poor mother!" At the time she'd understood this to mean that he actually was dead, but that day she found out the truth. And she saw his face; the coarse dots of the grainy newspaper photo on the scrap of paper showing a fuzzy image of a man in his mid twenties surrounded by policemen and crowds outside some big city building. She'd read the report as well of course; it was more or less what her grandfather had told her on her eighth birthday when the old lie about the God's wanting her mother to stay with them had been torn to pieces during the first of their many terrible arguments about what had really happened.

She hadn't recognised him in the cable car but now she could see the likeness more clearly; fill in the information missing from the photo's vague outlines. They were her parents from the time when her father killed her mother. And the little girl must be her; that meant her grandfather had lied because he'd always told her she'd stayed behind with him in Tokyo.

What else had he said that was wrong?

She shouldn't be here, shouldn't have to witness what inevitably was going to happen next. She should wake up, now. But she couldn't...

They'd all reached the crater by now, arranging themselves around its great lip as they stared into the steaming mouth. Slashes of fire tore open the black-sooted surface, belches of sulphur made the air thick and hard to breathe.

Her parents hung back from the rest of the onlookers crowding around the rickety wooden fence. Jin could see they were arguing again, at least Yuriko was. Her father seemed to be attempting to pacify her, the child wandering somewhere nearby. It was almost as if he were some kind of guardian trying to keep his charge under control. It wasn't at all like the way she'd been told. Toshiro seemed a very different kind of man from the one described to her by the grandfather who wouldn't even tell Jin his name; she'd had to get that from the newspaper.

He put his hands on her mother's shoulders; she shrugged and hung her head. The worst of the row seemed to be over. Then quite suddenly she ducked away from his reach and was running in the opposite direction to the cable car, knocking a child out of her way as if she hadn't even seen it. A woman remonstrated with her father but he barely shouted an apology as he picked up the little girl and dashed after Yuriko. There had been a look of panic twisting his features as if this kind of thing had happened before, maybe many times.

Jin followed them over a small bridge then onto a boarded pathway that stretched across a large area of black ash. She could see they were nearing a cleft in the tall rocks fringing the edges of the crater. Yuriko was already inside it, Toshiro just reaching its mouth when she'd got halfway across the pathway. She heard him shout for Yuriko to stop, the cry tinged with a terrible desperation as if he knew what was about to happen. Their footsteps echoed amongst the rocks as Jin lost sight of them for a few moments then she herself was scrambling along inside the narrow gully. The little girl was nowhere to be seen.

She stumbled as her foot caught in a cleft. As she picked herself up she saw them before her, their two silhouettes framed in a wedge of light at the gully's end. Like a shadow puppet show the two figures seemed to be frantically pulling and pushing each other: her to get away, him to hold onto her.

"Yuriko, please don't... please...!" He was panting for breath as she tore at his face but somehow still kept hold of the small twisting body. "You're not well darling, please, let's just..." She kicked out at his knee and Jin heard a crack. He cried out in pain then grabbed her again. "Come back to the hotel with us, please Yuriko..."

"No... No more! I can't take it anymore...!" she was screaming now, like a frightened child trying to escape an imagined monster. Jin wanted to go to her, comfort her, but was frozen to the spot. She could only watch. "No more...!" Yuriko twisted away from him again and flung herself at the gap. He made a desperate lunge to grab her back and for a moment they both teetered there: her flailing wildly, he somehow still holding on with his leg braced against the rock. Then his knee seemed to buckle beneath him and the two figures slid almost gently over the edge to disappear from sight.

She was alone.

In the silence she could hear the sound of the cicadas in the caldera below. A gust of oppressively hot air blew down the gully. The back of her head still hurt, she saw droplets of blood fleck the rock-face and realised they must be hers.

It had all happened again. She'd been too late to prevent it, too late by twenty-seven years.

But it had all been so different this time; her father had tried to save her mother, not kill her. He'd been gentle and loving, not the selfish jealous loser she'd been told about by her grandfather. The roles had been reversed; it had been Yuriko who was the clinging, unstable one, Toshiro the benign figure trying to give her his strength.

And there was one more thing she'd never dared to believe before, one very important detail left out of her life until now: Her father had loved her mother, so much so that he'd risked his own life to save her.

She'd been born from love; she knew that now.

And that meant everything.

Jin didn't know how long she remained standing in the gully but when she finally walked back to the sea of black ash she found it deserted. The child Jin wasn't there either. Perhaps she should ask someone what had happened to her? But there was no-one to ask; not one single sightseer remained on the wooden path or the little bridge. Even the lip of the giant crater and the concrete protection bunkers along its sides were deserted. And there were no staff anywhere either. It was starting to get dark, twilight edging deceptively into night. Lanterns had shone her way along the path and across the bridge but now the only light around the crater, apart from the last shreds of sunset, were the leaps of fire from below.

Had they left her up here to face the night alone? Then Jin laughed to herself suddenly remembering; this was a dream, a fantasy world inside a room. She'd let her mind get sucked in to its all too plausible reality but it was only the reality of distant memory. Where was 'up here'? On top of some mountain she'd never been to? But then again, presumably she had; how else could she experience this alternative version of the past?

She stopped on the asphalt path and coughed in the choking air. Again blood spattered on the walkway. She felt the wooziness returning. Was she actually dying then?

A clanking sound came from the bottom of the path as a cable car slowly climbed into view. With a shudder it came to a grinding halt at the station.

Jin breathed a sigh of relief and walked down towards it. The door slid back and she climbed inside gratefully.

The car's interior was in darkness. Perhaps they thought it empty down at the base station, were just bringing it back to its hanger for the night. They'd have quite a shock when she stepped out.

The dusky landscape swung past, a half moon rippling the ridges and ranges of the caldera with a dusting of silver. Blankets of mist hung around her. In the valley the stiflingly still air was now replaced by a warm breeze that rustled in the treetops below the gently swaying car.

Jin stared across the dark vista laid out beneath her, then turned in surprise as a light came on behind. A shadowy figure was sitting at a bulky-looking desk at the far end of the cabin. A desk light shone down on a large old-fashioned typewriter, gleaming off its black enamel sides. A sheet of paper sat up in the cartridge. The figure reached out a hand to pull it slowly from machine's grip then screw it almost fastidiously into a tight ball. It let the ball drop into a wicker wastepaper basket at the desk's side.

Then the figure leaned forward and Jin saw a man's face looking at her, the planes of its features exaggerated in the direct lighting. The lips moved and a deep, faintly amused voice spoke.

"What are you trying to do, Jin?"

For a long moment she was silent, mesmerised by the reproachful eyes that stared unblinkingly at her across the darkened cabin. Then she understood.

She tilted her chin defiantly. "I'm changing my story."

He sighed, as if disappointed in her. "I'm afraid it's not yours to change."

"I don't see it that way."

"Then perhaps you don't understand who I am."

She took a deep breath. "I understand exactly who you are, what you are. You've made my life horrible, degrading, you're cruel and manipulative and I've had enough of you; of all this."

"Then what do you propose to do about it?" She heard a sneer in the words.

"You'll see."

"Do you really think you can cross me, are you really so brave?"

She noticed that the cable car no longer moved. The two of them were hanging in mid-air, completely still. She glanced to her left then right; the dark valley had vanished, the mountainside disappeared. Wrapped around the windows now was a black void, a nothingness. Apart from him, Jin knew instinctively that she was completely alone in the world. She needed him if she were to return to her life of before, but that was the problem; she'd already rejected that life.

She could tell exactly the same thought had crossed his mind as he continued: "Jin, what am I do with you?"

Jin said nothing. There could be no going back now, no compromise. She'd seen too much, understood too many terrible things. She'd been redeemed.

She could never be the old Jin again; it would destroy her.

The man continued to stare at her but the amusement had vanished. The eyes were cold, calculating, as if already plotting the next move in some game.

"Do you trust me, Jin?"

Again she stood silent, unmoving.

"You have little choice…"

Slowly, Jin nodded her head.

With a metallic rumble the door to her right slid open.

"Then prove it. This is the only back for you. Trust my judgement in this or face oblivion. It's your choice, that's more than any of the others had."

But of course there *was* no choice: no game left for her to play. Glancing at him one last time, Jin took another deep breath then leapt into the darkness.

"Jin…its Jin Masayuki isn't it? Jin…!"

The distant voice came to her through the emptiness; she reached out for it the way a drowning person gropes for a lifeline. It doesn't matter who's holding on to the other end as long as they don't let go.

'Don't let me go,' she thought.

"Jin… I've called the ambulance. They say they're on their

way."

The words made no sense; 'Open your eyes,' she told herself, 'you need to open your eyes, to see.'

A thin lined face filled her vision; a woman's, old and wrinkled with straggly grey hair tucked into a plastic cap. Weak watery eyes concentrated on her. They had a natural kindness deep within them that Jin found immediately comforting; she could trust these eyes, the person behind them. That was the first coherent thought she had. The second was that she was in pain. She tried to locate the source and found it was her head, the back of it at the base of her skull. Something was pushing onto it, a phantom fist twisting its knuckles into a cavity she instinctively knew shouldn't be there; as if it was trying to burrow into her brain. The throbbing pain came again and she raised a stiff arm towards it. Her fingers touched a warm wetness. She pulled them away then tried to focus; there was a thin mess of blood on the tips running to a small puddle in the palm then on again in a single rivulet down her wrist. As she looked her mind identified these words: arm, fingers, blood, plastic; it continued to give names to other things as she tried to move: sofa, room, sticky, pool. Broken...

That was what had happened to her; something had been broken. Jin was not as she should be; she was wrong somehow. She must try to go back to the last thing she remembered before the emptiness:

On top of the mountain with her mother and father; how old had she been then, no more than four surely? She'd been carried by her father, jogged up and down as he ran across the sea of black ash, his feet pounding on the boards of the pathway. "Daddy...?" "It's alright sweetie," his voice had been breathless, "we just need to find Mummy..." He'd put her down. "Stay there Jin!" He was gone then she heard their muffled voices; Mummy's angry, like at home when things went bad, Daddy's panicky, the voice he used when Mummy was ill and he was worried about her. She didn't like those voices, something nasty always happened. She'd begun to cry, then got up and followed the sounds until she'd found the little pathway through the rocks. She'd been worried about the nasty thing happening again, but this time it was alright! They were both there at the end of the pathway; framed against a purple sky gripping each other tightly like they did when they thought her asleep and wanted to kiss. It was alright; Daddy loved Mummy, Mummy loved Daddy and they both loved her. With a whoop of joy she rushed to join them...

"... Jin, it's me: Ayano, the cleaner. What have those bastards done to you my girl? What have they done? Try to stay with me my love, they're nearly here; I heard the siren a few moments ago. We'll have you better. They'll put you back together again, I promise. Just try to hold on a little longer..."

Jin looked up into the old face. The years had not been kind but she could still see the faint tracery of her mother's beauty, the young woman in the photographs her grandfather had shown her with the brightly optimistic eyes and life-affirming grin; the Yuriko of her memory, the Yuriko who was fixed in time forever. The one she would always love.

She tasted the warm tang of blood in her mouth and spluttered. She managed to raise herself up on one elbow, feeling her senses swoon with the effort.

"I'm going to find him..."

"Don't try to talk now, Jin." She felt a frail hand placed on her forehead.

"I'm going to find Daddy. When I'm better I'm going to find him and then we'll all be together again. I'll fix it, you'll see..."

"Yes my love, of course you will."

And through her fading vision, Jin saw the red light flash across her mother's serene smile.

The End

Elsewhen Press
an independent publisher specialising in Speculative Fiction

Visit the Elsewhen Press website at elsewhen.co.uk for the latest information on all of our titles, authors and events, to read our blog; find out where to buy our books and ebooks; or to place an order.

Elsewhen Press
an independent publisher specialising in Speculative Fiction

Jacey's Kingdom
Dave Weaver

Jacey's Kingdom is an enthralling tale that revolves around a startlingly desperate reality: Jacey Jackson, a talented student destined for Cambridge, collapses with a brain tumour while sitting her final history exam at school. In her mind she struggles through a quasi-historical sixth century dreamscape whilst the surgeons fight to save her life.

Jacey is helped by a stranger called George, who finds himself trapped in her nightmare after a terrible car accident. There are quests, battles, and a love story ahead of them, before we find out if Jacey will awake from her coma or perish on the operating table. And who, or what, is George? In this book, Dave Weaver questions our perception of reality and the redemptive power of dreams; are our experiences of fear, conflict, friendship and love any less real or meaningful when they take place in the mind rather than the 'real' physical world?

Dave Weaver has been writing for ten years, with short stories published in anthologies, magazines and online in the UK and USA. Jacey's Kingdom is his first published novel. He cleverly weaves a tale that takes the almost unimaginable drama of an eighteen year-old girl whose life is in the balance, relying on modern surgery to bring her back from the brink, and conceives the world that she has constructed in her mind to deal with the trauma happening to her body. Developing the friendship between Jacey and George in a natural and witty style, despite their unlikely situation and the difference in their ages, Dave has produced a story that is both exciting and thought-provoking. This book will be a must-read story for adults and young adults alike.

ISBN: 9781908168313 (epub, kindle)
ISBN: 9781908168214 (272pp paperback)

Visit bit.ly/JaceysKingdom

Elsewhen Press
an independent publisher specialising in Speculative Fiction

THE RHYMER
an Heredyssey
DOUGLAS THOMPSON

The Rhymer, an Heredyssey defies classification in any one literary genre. A satire on contemporary society, particularly the art world, it is also a comic-poetic meditation on the nature of life, death and morality.

A mysterious tramp wanders from town to town, taking a new name and identity from whoever he encounters first. Apparently amnesiac or even brain-damaged, Nadith Learmot nonetheless has other means to access the past and perhaps even the future: upon his chest a dial, down his sleeves wires that he can connect to the walls of old buildings from which he believes he can read their ghosts like imprints on tape. Haunting him constantly is the resemblance he apparently bears to his supposed brother, a successful artist called Zenir. Setting out to pursue Zenir and denounce or blackmail him out of spite, in his travels around the satellite towns and suburbs surrounding a city called Urbis, Nadith finds he is always two steps behind a figure as enigmatic and polyfaceted as himself. But through second hand snippets of news he increasingly learns of how his brother's fortunes are waning, while his own, to his surprise, are on the rise. Along the way, he encounters unexpected clues to his own true identity how he came to lose his memory and acquire his strange 'contraption'. When Nadith finally catches up with Zenir, what will they make of each other?

Told entirely in the first person in a rhythmic stream of lyricism, Nadith's story reads like Shakespeare on acid, leaving the reader to guess at the truth that lies behind his madness. Is Nadith a mental health patient or a conman? ... Or as he himself comes to believe, the reincarnation of the thirteenth century Scottish seer True Thomas The Rhymer, a man who never lied nor died but disappeared one day to return to the realm of the faeries who had first given him his clairvoyant gifts?

Douglas Thompson's short stories have appeared in a wide range of magazines and anthologies. He won the Grolsch/Herald Question of Style Award in 1989 and second prize in the Neil Gunn Writing Competition in 2007. His first book, *Ultrameta*, published in 2009, was nominated for the Edge Hill Prize, and shortlisted for the BFS Best Newcomer Award. Since then he has published more novels, including *Entanglement* published by Elsewhen Press. *The Rhymer* is his eighth novel.

ISBN: 9781908168511 (epub, kindle)
ISBN: 9781908168412 (192pp paperback)
For more information visit bit.ly/TheRhymer-Heredyssey

Elsewhen Press
an independent publisher specialising in Speculative Fiction

Dandelion Trilogy
Mike French

Literary surrealism, contemporary fantasy, biting satire, dystopian science fiction. The Dandelion Trilogy by Mike French is all of these and more. Starting with *The Ascent of Isaac Steward*, this is literary surrealism at its most profound. A contemporary fantasy that follows one man's journey into his own mind as he struggles to come to terms with the trauma that has reshaped his life and starts to question his own existence. Moving forward to 2034 in *Blue Friday*, this biting satire warns of a Britain where overtime for married couples is banned, there is enforced viewing of family television (much of it repeats of old shows from the sixties and seventies), monitored family meal-times and a coming of age where twenty-five year-olds are automatically assigned a spouse by the state computer if they have failed to marry. Only the Overtime Underground network resists with the illicit Avodah drug to increase productivity. Finally *Convergence* delivers us into a truly dystopian future, where a covert military/governmental project uses prisoners on death row to explore what happens to people as they die, downloading the Convergence Point formed in the brain's memory at the point of death into clones. But when combined with Avodah they inadvertently trigger what may be the end of humanity – or a new beginning.

What does it have to do with dandelions? You'll have to read it to find out...

Mike French is the owner and senior editor of the prestigious literary magazine, *The View From Here*. Mike's debut novel, *The Ascent of Isaac Steward* was published in 2011 and nominated for The Galaxy National Book Awards. *Blue Friday* is his second novel. He currently lives in Luton with his wife, three children and a growing number of pets.

Book 1: The Ascent of Isaac Steward
ISBN: 9781908168351 (epub, kindle)
ISBN: 9781908168252 (224pp paperback)

Book 2: Blue Friday
ISBN: 9781908168177 (epub, kindle)
ISBN: 9781908168078 (192pp paperback)

Book 3: Convergence
ISBN: 9781908168368 (epub, kindle)
ISBN: 9781908168269 (256pp paperback)

Visit bit.ly/DandelionTrilogy

About the Author

Though born and raised in the distinctly un-exotic heartlands of Surrey, 'the land of the rising sun' has held a fascination for Dave since he first visited it with his Japanese wife. A fascination for the beautiful colours of its landscapes and the subtlety of its culture, for its contradictions and certainties, intelligence and passion, spirit and diversity. Yet beneath all these things lies another Japan; one of ghosts and shadows, unspoken secrets, demons from the past and uncertain visions of the future. It's what makes this intriguing country ultimately unknowable, unique, Nippon...